DRESSING
ETERNITY

Kimberly Carver and Candace Zangoei

ISBN: 1508555680
ISBN 13: 9781508555681

*__For__ all the sparkling souls who
have experienced
the ultimate bliss of finally
being understood*

TABLE OF CONTENTS

Lucille

There was nothing to be done but to acquiesce. Whatever nebulous feelings remained in her heart after forty odd years, when she hobbled out to the mailbox against the advice of Dr. Johnson (that old pooh-pooh) and pulled it out from beneath a colorful flier advertising the new dentist's office in town, her first instinct had been to laugh her head off. The postcard was a fair reproduction of a daguerreotyped Oscar Wilde leaning on his cane. She knew who the sender had to be just by the picture, but she greedily flipped it over, analyzing every scrap of information she could glean. There was an apparently foreign address at the top—she would have to look up what that arrangement meant—and the handwritten message, scrawled in an elderly hand but still dignified by a personal flourish, read: "My dear old friend—come for a long visit. Standing invitation, or sitting, if you prefer. Love, Luis."

Flustered and out of breath (she hoped it was from the Texas heat, but she had a troubling feeling her age was creeping up on her), she arrived inside. Once she had collected her wits, she called her older son and told him she was leaving immediately for a trip abroad (it wasn't really abroad... in the neighboring Caribbean, but it was exotic enough...now where was it? Turkish Cayman? Turks and Caicos, she read from the card) and she would certainly not be asking his permission. Of course not, Martin reassured her. She should go have a good time, take a load off. The old woman was relieved that her son was preoccupied with his client briefs and looming deadlines; she could hear the unmistakable dings and bleeps of his office gadgets in the background. The last thing she needed was his poking around in her personal affairs. She harrumphed anyway, making sure he knew her mind was made up just for future reference, and then slipped off the connection as quietly as she could so he wouldn't notice. After wrestling with the most horrible technological issues, she managed to book herself a flight for a couple days out (they seemed to make it as difficult as possible, never mind that her handheld computer was practically a dinosaur itself—imagine a physical computer anymore, her sons always laughed. *Mom, you're so old*). She was normally a light sleeper anyway, but she wondered how she ever managed to close her eyes that night.

The following day was frightfully busy and thrilling. She enlisted the help of her neighbor (she didn't know the woman very well, but she did know that the woman went to church so she'd probably never turn down the chance to help a sweet old lady in need, she cackled to herself) to drive her all over town collecting items she would need for her trip. She carefully packed and went over her to-do list, making sure she hadn't missed anything. Her passport was in her purse, and she had gone to the bank already (she still didn't trust the credit identity chip alone abroad... better to have paper for an emergency). But the most important thing--! And she'd almost forgotten! At the foot of her bed was an oaken hope chest. She had prayed for at least one granddaughter to bequeath it to, but alas, she'd had five grandsons. She couldn't complain—they were all as perfect as they could be but not one had an interest in the contents of an old woman's things. She pulled off the crocheted afghan that covered the chest, lifted the lid, resisted the impulse to linger over her past, and dove straight for the item she knew was placed carefully on the top. Holding it to her chest, she took it to the kitchen counter where the rest of her luggage was piled up together (she didn't want to risk forgetting anything, and she'd made a habit of checking the kitchen counter before she ever left the house). Checking her notes one last time, she nodded her approval and tucked the finished list into her billfold. She didn't sleep at all that night, except for a light after-dinner snooze; she was too worried about making sure to re-set the Electro-Grid to "Vacation" before she left the house.

When the scheduled day finally arrived, she ordered a DigiCab. With intense relief, she noticed that there was already a specific setting for the airport. She waved her hand under the scanner (still, that credit identity chip was a nice time-saver in most situations) and it thanked her by name. Martin had tried to get her to let him take her, but she'd told him she had it all arranged with a friend. No use in his taking a sudden interest on the way. When her husband had been alive, he had always wanted to know everything too, but, unlike Martin, he was always careful to respect her sense of independence. He had turned out to be a wonderful husband, she mused, and she had loved him very deeply even though he hadn't been the only love of her life. But he'd given her the boys, both of whom she couldn't be prouder. After having put her small amount of luggage in the trunk, she got in and leaned back against the plush leather seat, marveling at her good fortune in having outsmarted her shrewdest son, and then promptly settled in for a short victory nap on the way.

She only slept for a few minutes it seemed before a tender robotic voice was calling to her and announcing arrival at the curbside check-in for the elderly and reliant. She flagged an attendant who helped her fill out the tags and attach them to her bags. Though the IntraRail did make security and all that horrific flying stuff so much smoother and more efficient, she was still grateful that there were people you could ask about getting on the right line. Once you stepped onto an active line, you were whizzed to the gate so quickly there wasn't time to realize if you'd made an error. She made it through security and the boarding process relatively uneventfully (this time) except for when that horrid shuttle carrying a few smug passengers almost made her lose her traveling hat on her way to the gate (they really shouldn't be allowed to use those shuttles—the IntraRail was quick enough for any emergency). Her seat, she found, was quite to her satisfaction. She had plenty of leg room, and a handsome Auto Attendant had offered her his arm and helped her get seated. He showed her where her 4-D glasses were in case she wanted to catch a Short on the personal screen. She didn't want anything else, no thank you. She would keep her carry-on under her seat, she explained, because she had brought some light reading for the flight. She smiled at him, the residual facial expression relaxing into vacancy as she turned her head toward the window, and, reassured that it was finally permissible to do so, allowed the current of nostalgic retrospection to overwhelm her.

All the anxiety she had felt over using such advanced technology without help over the last few days reminded her of a comment Luis had made back when she first met him, in the early months of their friendship. He'd said that there was nothing magical or mystical but ignorance makes it so. The longer she had lived, the more that comment had impressed her as absolutely true. And then he'd added something about how the answer to a happy life lies not in willful ignorance but in a conscious and prolonged enjoyment of the things we like and a willful desire to expand our list of "things we like" through knowledge of ourselves and of the world around us. Something like that. How funny that she should remember words spoken to her so long ago. The mind was an interesting thing. But she suspected that it was the speaker of those words who lent them their power, or at least it seemed to her.

Luis's hilarity had been contagious. How he histrionically interjected his entire body into a conversation with a complete lack of restraint. His outrageous flare for the dramatic. Really, he'd seemed so caricatured, so endearing. She'd forgiven him long ago for his part in that horrific tragedy. But her present excitement was mingled with a faintly more sinister emotion that wasn't fear, exactly. It was wariness, the result of a lingering confusion over events that remained tangled in the underbrush of her subconscious for all these years. Still, she knew that her primary objective when she saw him again would be to at least delay his knowledge of the great joy their reunion would bring her. After all that had happened, it was the dignified thing to do.

She thought back to the first time she'd met him. He might have saved her life, that stranger at her beloved's funeral. She had felt ancient back then, weighted down by the reality of her tragedy. She remembered thinking that Diego had been like a timeless concerto tied to a mesquite tree. What had she meant by that? But then Luis had understood without another word; suddenly she could breathe because someone else had understood.

She had heard it said that perpetual desire was the hapless concession to being alive. There were no bounds to the swirling and fantastic aspirations of the conscious mind. But she never possessed more vitality than when she was in love; and their love had been unassuming, filling her deficiencies so completely that she had wanted nothing more than just to hold on to what she'd found. She could only begin to describe the perfection of her most personal moments with Diego through his music, a superior soundtrack evoking every emotional shade of the soul's elations. Being loved by him was like glimpsing a sliver of true immortality.

And then, too, when he died, she was never more conscious of that lingering mortality which is bereft of all desire. She first believed the emptiness inside her was all the more dangerous because she had swollen and stretched her capacity to love to accommodate Diego's romantic conjectures. Looking down upon the vacant corpse that had once housed the intense spring of all her joy, she quickly came to realize that the great void inside of her was not emptiness after all, but a black hole stuffed so full of memories and dead dreams that it threatened to collapse what remained of her into its gravitational field.

The notes had pealed from his flaming red guitar, forming watercolor panoramas of feeling and bearing its haunted listeners away over branches and thorns till they were torn and bleeding, delirious with raw emotion. Sadly, Diego's instrument would forever become as still and silent as its owner. Those frenzied hands that had once set the strings of passion ablaze were crossed carefully, impersonally, over the empty cavity where his heart had been. The breadth that had electrified her in his personality had finally been overborne by a more formidable depth, and he had wordlessly slipped into a hollow desolation from which he could not recover.

She had fainted at his funeral with something akin to these thoughts, which could only be sloppily expressed by an irascible sea of sensation. She was drunk, hiding behind sunglasses that dimmed the bright September afternoon into a slightly more tolerable darkness. Her eyes felt like two burning suns concealed by the heavy curtains of her eyelids. The early autumnal Texas breeze carried the smell of wood burning. Before she became totally insensate, she remembered thinking how a beautiful smattering of blue sage on the ground intensified her sadness.

Fall 2011—Diego's Funeral

Lucille found herself revitalized by soothing wafts of expensively scented air. Coming to, she realized she was in a cool executive limousine, and there was a man sitting next to her, calmly smoking a cigarette and staring at her. She was slightly ashamed of herself but more beyond caring about anything outside of her own pain. She began a half-hearted apology for her weakness, but he held up a hand.

"Ah, there she is. Lucille." He pronounced her name like he'd never said it before.

"*Do I know you?*" *she mumbled, sitting up.*

He continued to stare for a moment, took a long final drag of his cigarette, flicked it away, and gently smiled.

"*No.*" *He exhaled.* "*I'm afraid there wasn't time for that. I'm Luis.*"

A coldness ripped into her heart. "*Diego's Luis?*"

"*Yes.*" *He was respectfully silent.*

"*Why are you here?*" *she whispered.*

"*I've loved him since I was five years old,*" *he said. He waited for her reply.*

Sucking in a breath, she simply said, "*I know. He told me.*" *Her words were only slightly slurred.* "*You should be out there with everyone else. So should I,*" *she continued as she fumbled for the door.*

"*Lucille, I think you should let me take care of you for a little while longer.*" *His heart came out to her in the earnestness of his gaze as he removed her hand from the door with tender fingers. She gave in and lay back against the seat.*

His hands asked permission as he took off her dark sunglasses. "*They'll understand.*" *She nodded. Grabbing two small tumblers from the mini-bar, he poured her another drink from a silver flask in his jacket pocket and then one for himself. Holding hers out like a peace offering, he seemed relieved when she accepted it.*

"*I know it wasn't your fault,*" *she said. She looked into the glass.* "*It just seemed like a good idea to blame you. I don't know you. I'd only heard about you. And then you reappeared out of nowhere right before-- He came home so pensive after talking to you--I knew you had met with him those couple of times right before he—before he, uh—*" *Her eyes filled. Her lips trembled. She drank.* "*It must have been my fault.*" *She broke down. He set his tumbler down and comforted her until she was only quietly sobbing, the great racking spasms having passed.*

"*Lucille,*" *he began,* "*I want you to listen to me. Diego loved you more than anything in the world. He was my closest friend, the most talented and passionate man I've ever known. I hadn't seen him in years when I came here a few months ago for work, though--years--and you know what we stayed up all night talking about? Mostly you.*" *He took her hands into his own and leaned into her.* "*I must stress that this thing he did wasn't your fault either. Diego made the choice simply because it was his own to make. We may never know why. There was nothing you or I or anyone else could have done to prevent it."*

Leaning back, he said, "There were some other things, though. Other things we talked about those nights. Of course he brought his guitar. He touched the ceiling with his music, reached right into my heart and left a warm golden star inside of it." He smiled sadly.

"What other things did you talk about?" Lucille sniffed. "And how was he with you, those nights? Was he—sad?"

"There was always something sentimental about Diego, Lucille. Even when he was laughing, there was melancholy behind it, like a longing to get someplace he couldn't go back to."

She nodded. She knew exactly what Luis meant.

"Yes," she told him. "I asked him once how he made such beautiful, haunting music. He told me with a wicked smile on his face that one had to be damned by the angel of God and forsaken by everyone in order to do it. I thought he was teasing me, flirting, but now I wonder."

"He laughed a lot, though. He did," Luis reassured her. "Like I told you, he played guitar for me. We reminisced, caught up with one another, talked about you. We drank quite a bit, too. After all, we were both celebrating; I had just accepted a banking position here in Texas and looked him up as soon as I got settled in. And Diego got just a little bit more solemn when he drank. I thought it was just a passing comment when he asked me to be the executor of his will. He said it in an offhand way. I thought he was just drunk, just in a strange mood. I didn't think anything of it. I've got knowledge about these things, he's in his thirties, you know... I told him sure. I was taken completely by surprise when I got the phone call."

"I'm his fiancé. I...was." They both flinched at her correction. How could Diego be gone? The unasked and unanswered question rose up like vapor from her lips. Fresh tears welled up behind her eyes again.

Luis ran a ringed hand through thick waves of hair and sucked in a breath. "He told me that he knew I'd look out for his interests when the time came. I think he meant that I'd look out for you. And I will. I'm here, Lucille.

Close. I don't want to intrude upon your grief, but I'll take care of whatever you want me to. He mentioned that you didn't have much family left, and that the remaining members didn't live around here anymore. If you need to talk, if you need money, if you need a friend. I loved him, too. He was... well, he was Diego. And you were the most important person in his life. So you will have from me whatever I can give you, because he trusted me to and because I loved him. You aren't alone."

"Oh--were you his lover, too?" she snapped.

He looked pained. "No."

She was immediately sorry. "I didn't mean that. Look at me. I'm a mess. I don't even know what I'm saying." She wiped what she thought were sure to be mascara-laden tears from her cheek. "It wasn't your fault that he trusted you more than me." She looked at her hands, which were streaked with black.

"Oh—that." He took a handkerchief out of his pants pocket and gave it to her as he continued, "I call that look my average Sunday morning." He winked at her with a micro-expression of a grin and then resumed his earnest concern.

"He trusted me to take care of you in his absence. I'm sure you can take care of yourself, but it can't hurt to have others looking out for you too, right? At least until you get through all this. I'm going to help you through this if you'll let me. We can help each other."

She wiped her face with the handkerchief, her eyes remaining closed as she crumpled it up into her hands and lowered them shakily to her lap. She nodded her assent.

Shaking off some emotion, he began again, "I had heard from him that you two were very much in love. I'm so sorry. I'm sure we can talk later. Let me take you home. I think they're about finished out there."

"No. It helps to hear about him. Please. It's like he's still here. Please continue. How did you meet? Are you Brazilian too?" She compelled him to bequeath an unknown piece of her beloved to her, even as he was being lowered into the ground not more than thirty feet away. She had been placed on the side of the car facing away from it all during her collapse. She hadn't once tried to turn her head.

She continued, *"I mean he talked about you, told stories about you all the time. He smiled when he did. He said you were the grandest person he'd ever known. But he never said how you knew each other originally."*

"Grand?" Luis seemed pleased. *"What a funny word,"* he mused. *"We were neighbors. I shouldn't say merely neighbors, though. No, I shouldn't say that. I'm not Brazilian. We met in Arizona. His father was a poor but capable horse trainer when he wasn't drunk. He was a mean old bastard most of the time, though. Somehow he attracted the attention of some wealthy businessmen in Phoenix. My father was gifted with horses too. We'd been living in Phoenix for almost a year. One night, he and his father just wandered into one of our evening campfire gatherings. A lot of times, the vaqueros would blow off some steam with their alcoholic stories and banged-up guitars. All the families came to sit and listen. Diego must have been quite young then, though I was a couple of years younger than he was myself. Though he barely moved at all, standing outside the circle with his lips shut tightly over his teeth, his mind must have been whirring and his boyish heart set aflame, because the next time I saw him, he came to the campfire by himself. He walked right up to the group of men and asked one of the laughing cowboys to borrow his guitar. They offered him a nip from their dubious bottles, but he only shook his head with determination and reached for the guitar again. When he began to play, to perfectly mime what he had heard them play before, he earned their respect. I knew I loved him in that moment. Soon, Diego was a beloved son to them all, and he learned everything they could teach him. He eventually learned to play the guitar like he was rushing the stars with his notes, pleading with them for a solemn request. "* He trailed off.

"What was he like as a child?" she asked. *"I can't imagine him ever having been young."*

"In some ways, the same as he always was. He was serious, desperate. We grew close quickly. Once, early on, he came to me in the middle of the night and told me that his grandmother had visited his dreams. She had apparently been a local singer of some fame back in Brazil. She died right before his father moved him. I'm sure she was the only good thing in his poor little life because he never knew his mother, and his father abused him horribly. Anyway, he shook

all over and said that she had told him to find his salvation in music, that that's what she had done and it would honor her memory. I didn't know what to say, poor Diego—I could only tell him that I didn't think he needed a reason to play if he enjoyed it. I don't think he ever did, though. Enjoy it, I mean. He played because he had to. He played for her." He grimaced.

"Soon, he played because people begged him to. He played for pennies around the campfires, on the streets, and eventually at church services and hotel events. He was a prodigy on the guitar, but his music was inspired. I mean, technical knowledge alone could not create the enchantment he cast over his audience. Nothing brought me more pleasure than to hear him play. I never wanted him to stop. He had this beat-up old secondhand guitar one of the men gave him out of pity, and he played obsessively--"

"That sounds like him," Lucille affirmed.

Luis permitted himself to grin sentimentally. "Yes." His smile faded quickly. "But his obsession only increased once he bought that red guitar, some years later. He played it the last time I saw him. I went to all of his performances that I could, but we grew up, moved away... We always kept in touch, though, and I'd visit him sometimes. After one of his performances a few years ago, he was run down and sick-looking. I'd never seen him look so awful. He told me it was the music that did it to him, and he couldn't stop even if he wanted to. It was killing him, but he was trying to find something in it that wasn't there. It was there for the rest of us, but not for him." Luis's eyes shone with sadness.

"Why wasn't I enough?" For the first time, she gave voice to the real question, the solid question that had crushed her to the ground with its weight.

"You were loved by the greatest of men, Lucille. And his generosity was finite. It was nobody's fault." He paused.

Then he said, "The patient and the disciplined are those who have fathomed how swiftly time advances. Diego belonged to the order of people who cannot comprehend time because their existence is elevated to beauty admired, which is a deathless world. Dressing eternity with mortal skin must be the most torturous form of pain there ever was, Lucille, impossible to maintain."

Lucille grabbed his hand and squeezed it. "Thank you," she said softly.

⊷⊶

They arrived back at the downtown loft Diego and Lucille had shared, where Luis tucked her into bed, poured her a glass of water, and left her to her thoughts until she was finally borne away on a dark blast of senselessness into sleep.

When she awoke, she had two revelations. The first was that she would not be alone in her mourning—she had someone who understood. The second was that she could not bear to stay in the place where Diego and she had shared their lives together. From the moment she opened her eyes and reached out toward nothing for his sprawled-out form on the bed, she knew that she must begin preparations to leave immediately, for this their home had become a dangerous place for her indeed.

Coming to herself, she realized she had been daydreaming for longer than it had seemed. She pulled away from the window and leaned down with a grunt, retrieving her carry-on from underneath the seat. Opening a special compartment, she pulled out an old type-written manuscript: the same one that had been stowed away in her hope chest for this very day (she knew her boys would laugh at the fact that it had been printed out from a desktop computer). She had poured herself into the writing of it afterward—it had helped her process and helped her heal. Everything had happened exactly as she had written it. She couldn't try to publish it because it was too risky, too personal. But at least she'd had the foresight to change the names, just in case. She knew Luis would recognize himself immediately, and she hoped he would recognize what an impact he'd had on her decisions and her self-awareness, too. It was her gift to him.

She placed the manuscript on her lap, smoothed the pages, ran a hand over the title, and patiently waited to disembark.

GRIDLOCKED
By Lucille Vincent

"To a great mind, nothing is little." – Sir Arthur Conan Doyle

"It was the best of times, it was the worst of times, it was the age of wisdom, it was the age of foolishness, it was the epoch of belief, it was the epoch of incredulity, it was the season of light, it was the season of darkness, it was the spring of hope, it was the winter of despair, we had everything before us, we had nothing before us, we were all going direct to Heaven, we were all going direct the other way—in short, the period was so far like the present period, that some of its noisiest authorities insisted on its being received, for good or for evil, in the superlative degree of comparison only." – Charles Dickens

"If it's not paradoxical, it's not true." – Ancient Zen concept

PROLOGUE

A precious gem in a stud of our galaxy, the earth carousels through the coolness of space, gold schillers gleaming frenetically from the smooth lapis surface. Its neighbor, the ghostly red planet, looks shriveled and lifeless by comparison. This story takes place on one of the largest of these singular flashes where many of the greatest stories do: in the Lone Star State of Texas. And though I'm not certain my story will live up to some of those with the longest legacies, maybe ripples of dim recognition will wash over someone when they come to the part about banded cowboy hats or cypress trees or deviled eggs. Of course, in your mind, you can change the particulars to rose-scented perfume or beachfronts or an hourglass. The meaning remains the same: and our glittering souls, suspended in a fishbowl of time and space, can float contentedly together in the midst of our separate realities.

My own reality has often felt like our fishbowl, where I, like other fishes, have wanted to jump out just to see what could happen, but familiarity and a sense of maybe destiny or maybe just well-being have always kept me from it. Though I've never fully identified with all the swirling conceptions of the native Texan, I recognize in myself little symptoms of its indigenous peoples. Texans sing about not being able to stand fences, yet the first thing they do once they get their lots of land under starry skies is survey their bounds and pen themselves in. The truth is that Texans are overwhelmed by too much space; perhaps because of our unique history, we have to conquer entirely in order to feel that we truly possess anything. Vulnerability can look like a lone covered wagon on a plain or a man without a fence.

Davy Crockett famously said, "You may all go to Hell and I will go to Texas." When you see this quote on a T-Shirt, the wearer is evoking the hero from the tall tale—the hyperbolic Congressman who was so possessed by the revolutionary spirit of the land that he preached nothing but independence even before he got here. But the actual historical context of the famous quote somehow makes him seem shorter and more maniacal. He had been defeated one too many times in Tennessee politics and strutted into Texas because it still held enough space for him to grow a reputation as large in reality as it already was in his own mind. Our own Texas Napoleon succeeded: he's forever known as the King of the Wild Frontier. Lawless pioneers who settled the West, armed with guns, Bibles, and swinging saloon doors are often immortalized on the screen or through a legend. But if you're in the right place at the right time—the little bit of true frontier that still remains---you will see that the spirit of the Wild West is not impeded by society's progress. The adventurers, outlaws, and misfits that can't function in proper society are still thriving on its fringes here.

Of course you'll also find those who insist on defining "proper society" for everyone else. No one can claim they have more gracious and hospitable folks than we do. I love that about my home, but I also can't understand the logistics of it at the personal level. A feigned intimacy with every stranger one meets is like promising a closeness that cannot possibly be obtained with everyone. Sure, that southern hospitality poured out through an easygoing, unhurried drawl conveys our innocuous intentions toward newcomers and visitors, but it's presumptuous too; some of the biggest bastards I know are the sweetest people you'd ever hope to meet. So we perpetuate in our own hearts the same story we tell everyone else, even strangers, about ourselves. And deep in the heart of every Texan is a suspicion that only we are worthy of shouldering the burden of the master storyteller.

Unlike the tall tales told around campfires on the Texas prairies, this story is not about a larger-than-life hero or a villain who met his just ends. Much like how storms form over these same vast prairies, the convergence of many passionate natures can leave a person feeling like a weathered pebble that has lain in the creek bed so long that the current has entirely formed and reformed its surface. My story is about expeditions into the opacity of the collective human heart, a rhythmical sound-scape containing innumerable tributaries of dusky private impulses. And I believe that both solitude and suffering are vital to the navigation of this unknowable terrain.

Let's scoop up a handful of powdered eggshell from the hourglass, that chronological magic dust, will it upstream through the bottleneck, pack it back into a smooth hard oval, and polish it ever so carefully until—there she is!---my face—Stella's younger frantic face—productively tumultuous in her motionless white compact car one sticky Saturday evening last August...

SUMMER

CHAPTER ONE

"Once you are in Texas it seems to take forever to get out, and some people never make it." – John Steinbeck

August--

Looking down from the vantage point of an overpass at the Mixmaster, that precarious intersection of numerous highways, the sight of chaos gave me an unpleasant, anxious feeling. I turned on the radio and mindlessly sang along with the baffling but catchy primal sounds of the summer's biggest pop hit. I hummed under my breath as I gazed at three cars which seemed to be passing very quickly underneath me. I too was in a hurry, but there was a traffic pile-up around the stadium as cars honked and rudely elbowed their way into merging lanes. This crowd would be the largest I had attempted in a while, I thought to myself with slight trepidation.

Since my fiancé died, I'd had to give myself many pep talks to avoid total emotional paralysis. Santiago's funeral had been almost a year ago, and I had come through unendurable grief that sometimes still unexpectedly took my breath away. How did someone know when they had fully recovered, if it was even possible after genuine tragedy struck? I'd been granted a leave of absence for the remainder of the semester; the university had been generous since Santiago had been a music professor there and somewhat of a local celebrity. In fact, one of the members of the Board of Regents had invited me to the football game I was frantically trying not to be too late for, probably because she felt sorry for me, or maybe because her son was currently in my class. I'd made it through the spring semester back at work, and while my performance hadn't been award-winning, it was a small comfort to know they'd at least learned something about literature. But I still cried when I pulled out Santiago's special red guitar from the closet. He had taught me one song, and while I desperately wanted to recreate his magical sounds, I couldn't even hold it in my lap before I'd had to stow it back away into the unseen. I knew I wasn't yet recovered, but I had made progress. It had taken me months to build up to opening the closet door.

Of course I wouldn't have made it at all were it not for Orlando. We had only known each other for about a year, but since he'd materialized into my life, we had become best friends. It was easy for me to understand what Santiago had seen in him, what everybody seemed to see. We met at his funeral. Orlando had come to pay his respects to his old friend but instead had had to pluck me from the dusty cemetery soil where I had fainted and root me firmly back into the realm of the living. He cared for me with the conscientiousness he was capable of: seemingly haphazard but meticulous in its method. And I knew the love he had for me was grounded in the love we shared for Santiago.

I remembered very little those first few months after Santiago killed himself. I moved out of our home and into a modest apartment, which was both temporary and bare of any decoration that would designate it as a home. Though I was completely unattached to it, it quickly became familiar to me, and thus, I rarely left the comfort of the small protection it afforded me from the outside world. In December, however, I felt compelled to attend an awards ceremony in which all the scholarships for our department would be given out. Even in a fugue-like unconsciousness of the soul, I was still painfully aware of the politics involved with my job. I bumbled in and sat down, feeling small and paranoid. Orlando, who happened to be representing the bank he worked for at the same ceremony, came over to me and said something witty related to the Dean's wife, and whispered hilarious cynicisms into my ear all night. Somehow, I not only survived the evening but managed to almost enjoy myself in the process. He held me up through the worst of it with his entertaining visits and sensitivity to my every need. His deceptively sheepish grin, especially after a freshly delivered zinger, gave you the impression that he could absorb your personality into his with less energy than it took to raise an eyebrow. But he was only ever generous with me.

I pulled down the visor to wipe the remaining crumbs of the egg salad sandwich I had just finished eating off of the corners of my mouth. Traffic was at a standstill, but that didn't mean I had to be. I sang portions of the lyrics I could understand to myself... something about being good. But was I? I thought. Maybe not as generally good as Henry would prefer, but he would benefit from it that evening. He tended to think in black and white.

I'd been dating Henry for three months now, telling myself that I had to try to move on from the inertia of grief. Orlando had said so, too. After all, he pointed out, I was still relatively young and it would be a pity to waste too many years feeling sorry for myself. Henry was a safe choice for me, what others called a "nice" guy. I wasn't sure Orlando liked him personally, but he still encouraged me to go out on principle. I was just grateful for Henry's company and for the interest he'd shown in pursuing me.

I dug into my purse and fished out my lipstick. I bought it because I liked the name: Lady Wild. Luckily, the red tones turned out to be very complementary of my dark hair. I quickly applied a fresh layer to my lips. I could already smell the tailgaters' conglomerations of smoked meats-- hot dogs, brisket, and cheeseburgers--and I could hear the cadence of the drum line calling the fans to their places on each side of the battle line. Various fraternities and sororities advertised their Greek letters.

I rolled slowly along, shifting up as I finished putting my lipstick away, passing orange cones and oversized inflatables advertising everything from the best deals on used cars to the coldest beer. The added distractions of violent wind-whipped banners protruding from windows and excited fans forcing their way across the lanes were difficult to maneuver. I had my IPhone out because I was looking for the best way into the stadium given all of the recent construction, but it wasn't doing much good. I was on the verge of sliding it into my purse when it rang. A laughing couple crossed right in front of my car, he giving her a playful piggyback ride and she sporting pigtails and chatting excitedly. The shiny screen lit up; Orlando's vicious smirk heralded its owner.

He seemed to have an intuitive sense when I was somewhere he thought I shouldn't be. But if I didn't pick up, it would only double the length of his railing later. We were in that romantic stage of friendship where everything was still possible but the faint outline of solid familiarity was beginning to emerge. Intimacy had long removed the undertones of despair as foremost in our conversations. As time passed, he insisted less on hearing about my emotional state and more on what I was doing and what I'd be wearing while doing it. In other words, we were close. I turned down the radio and the freezing blast from the vents so I could hear, knowing that the conversation would be relatively short because I didn't want my hair to start curling up from the heat and the dampness behind my neck.

"Mmmyello?" I assumed what I hoped was a light, easy tone.

"Oh. My. God." Orlando began like we were already in the middle of a conversation. He snorted suggestively. I had the compulsion to laugh too, even though I merely guessed what he was calling about.

"It was that good, huh?" I affirmed. The night before, he had attended a gala he'd been talking up for weeks. Like a Greek Chorus, he would be calling to faithfully report what events had transpired, and he would assign to each event its significance, only hinting at what my appropriate emotional reaction should be.

"Estelle—" he used his more "fashionable because European" nickname for me—"it was exactly as I had hoped it would be: handshakes and smiles in the beginning, and hotel rooms and every kind of naughtiness and waking up next to people you don't know in the end. It was like watching a montage in a political box office hit. Bigwigs smiling over white tablecloths and posing for the cameras, donating big checks to charities and holding babies. Classical music playing, or something like that. Cut to heavy-metal scene of same faces in raunchy places in the dark doing cocaine or recruiting porn actresses for their 'little film.' Delightfully disgusting. But a fascinating study in psychology. How they manage it at all."

"It sounds exhausting to me," I said. While I found Orlando's stories entertaining, I was content to stop at living vicariously through him when it came to the seedier parts.

"No doubt it is. It is. I brought Doug with me, after all."

I remembered Orlando's agonizing confusion over whether or not to bring a date to the gala. He never cared what people thought; he just didn't do anything without calculating its effect.

"And how did that go?"

"We found out that there are more, uh, curious parties, shall we say, in this business than most want to admit. My CEO spent quite a bit of time chatting us up. And I don't think it was because he was interested in my personal history with the company."

"That'll make the next work party so much easier. And it can't be bad for business, if you know what I mean," I said. A horn honked at me to roll forward. I waved and mouthed "Sorry" and complied.

"Yeah. But Doug enjoyed himself so much he texted me first thing this morning. Like, four hours after I took him home."

"Well, that's kinda… eager, but sweet, isn't it?" I knew Orlando would balk at this sentiment.

"It's a reminder of your hangover. The last thing I want when I'm eating my oatmeal and trying to keep the food down is to remember the alcoholic smoke breath of the guy I made out with the night before. Ugh."

"Don't even try and pretend you were up before noon. Oatmeal. Yeah, right." I sniffed.

"Well, you know what I always say. There are only three times when you can tell people are being honest: when they're drunk, when they're angry, and when they say 'just kidding.' Oatmeal is a figure of speech."

My mind lingered on this supposed trinity of honesty. Only Orlando had the habit of speaking in ways which provoked both appreciative laughter and critical thought at the same time. His banter seemed so effortless, so debonair; either he was a prodigy of wit or he planned these quips out in advance and awaited any opportunity to spring them upon the unsuspecting victim. Either way, he was an impressive conversationalist who, while I had been thinking, had kept talking away about the horrors of mornings.

"So what happened last night?" I interjected. He had this habit of taking longer to set up the story than the actual telling of it, which was irritatingly endearing.

"—brilliant at breakfast." He got a little louder to emphasize that he wasn't finished yet.

"Wait a minute. Where are you?" he asked me with disdain. "I can hear it. You're at the football game. Stella, you're thirty-three. How long have you been dating? Football? How romantic. Surely Henry could do better than that."

It was hard for me to explain to Orlando exactly how I had felt when I had been placed into the same scenario over and over again in my life: within and without, caught between recognizing the frivolity of our modern Texas culture and wanting to be swept along in its comforting current of conformity and belonging. If language was a reflection of culture, my own vocabulary had been influenced by all the endangered or extinct cultures of the classic novels I'd read since I was a child. Infinite fabrics of words fashioned infinite worlds for me, and my physical existence in this one could seem an arbitrary reality in one moment and a pitifully restricting one in another. Having satisfied my curiosity by traveling to many exotic and colorful lands in college, these experiences only served to further my suspicion that I had a bigger imagination than was good for me: though I habitually thought outside the box, sometimes I had to fight to wedge my way back into it. Of course Orlando's understanding of this same feeling was one of the most solid foundations of our friendship, but he was still very judgmental of my casual participation, maybe because I was more able to blend in at will than he was.

I was chosen to be the high school mascot for our football team one year because I was rumored to have had the most school spirit. We were the Rattlesnakes, and we were deadly. Every time we scored a touchdown, I had to run the length of the field, shaking my tail as a warning to the other team. The only problem was that my tail was filled with coffee tins laden with pellets. It made a lot of noise and it was almost unbearably heavy. Coupled with the stifling heat of the costume itself, it made Friday nights bittersweet for me. When I went to any stadium, I always remembered the physical discomfort I felt during that long season. Living in Texas for me was like going to an exciting football game in that mascot's costume. I always enjoyed it, but sometimes I wished I could just take off the head and breathe a little—show everyone who I really was.

I was just about to defend Henry when Orlando cut me off. "Girl, if you don't need Spanx, there's nothing to look forward to." He sighed. "I know, I know. Your students. Did you ever find out about that kid?"

"Oh yeah. Richard. Big Dick."

Orlando erupted into laughter.

"You're kidding."

"No, I'm not. The whole team calls him that. He insists on it. You were right—his parents are really important. Mom's on the Board of

Regents, Dad is a war hero or something. Actually, she's the one who invited me to her suite tonight."

"Well, then, I feel much better about your date location. Henry's still an asshole, though. But it's okay. Some of my favorite people are, you know. The ones who are like characters in a novel."

"Ha. Yeah. Only because you're one of them." I pulled into an open parking spot I found at the back of the stadium. I was okay with stretching my legs a little, and besides, there was a gorgeous field of wildflowers across from my car, so I could use that as a landmark to help me find my car.

"Come to think of it—yes. That's right. Listen, I've got a plane to catch this evening so I'd better let you go. Family stuff. Time to break out the tequila and sombreros. If I'm lucky, I'll get down to the worm."

I was so busy chasing after the American Dream that I had to pencil in time to sit and do nothing. I once asked Orlando how he managed to paint the town red no matter where he was or who he was with. He shrugged and drunkenly spouted something about being a "maestro de diversión" and how having fun had become an elusive art form. Then he commenced singing a patriotic song about Mexico, a country to which, despite being Hispanic, he had only visited as a tourist: a fact which never deterred him from referencing the 'old country' no matter how often I reminded him. Every time I heard that phrase, I felt a compulsion to start humming *The Godfather* theme song. With maracas, maybe.

We said our quick goodbyes and hung up. I impulsively reached for my book bag in the backseat, and then realized I wasn't going to be reading or doing any work at the game. The heat hit me like viscous foam as I opened the car door. When I had made sure my face wasn't too melted, I scuttled into the archway, rather excited to see the handsome Henry. Instantly, I was overcome by the carnival atmosphere of heightened emotion, shows of allegiance, and bold personalities matching the bold colors of opposing teams. I had to excuse myself a few times as I bumped into fathers teaching their sons how to be dedicated to a cause, giggling women trailing after handsome boys who were more interested in discussing statistics of the game, and diverse groups of people forming roadblocks around the thousand stairwells that led into the stadium.

Henry would be annoyed that I was late. He was clean-shaven and imposing, and his mind was, too. He was confident and successful, and he couldn't forgive anyone who wasn't, though that person would never know they had committed a transgression. He often went on about the beauty of Emerson's transparent eyeball, that transcendental view of the entire world as one pulsing organism. But his own eagle eye breadth of vision cruelly rejected anything which he could not immediately grasp or which had the naughty capability of sticking in his craw. And yet, something inside me believed that once he figured out what it was about me that excited him, that enraged him—once he understood me—I would become an object without the least necessity for his consideration, like perhaps one of his own appendages. He radiated an attractive passion for the natural world and for social progress. He was thoughtful, well-educated, and respected by many who knew him. He struck me exactly like a good All-American football game did: while I wasn't certain if I loved him, his optimism and clean simplicity were seductively refreshing. I walked a little faster.

As an alarming number of people were herding themselves in, a little boy who was too young to enjoy the clamor of a sporting event threw down a toy his mother had brought him. His hair was clinging to his head in sweaty patches. He screamed, "I don't want that!" She picked him up, cooing in a soothing voice, and then they evaporated into the crowd. I bent down out of curiosity to see what the little boy had thrown down, nearly got bowled over by three chattering preteens, and quickly straightened myself up and moved with the current. In my hand, I held a Rubik's cube. Now there was a flashback to my childhood, I thought, and, still walking briskly, I put it in my purse. It might have been fun to see if my problem-solving skills had improved any over the decades, and at any rate, I was always looking for something quick and fun to do in the short lulls of my day rather than ruminate.

Coming through the tunnel and glimpsing the inside of the oval stadium, I felt my emotions swell and surge. Atop the field were two equally gigantic flags, an American flag and a Texas flag, both almost entirely motionless. The huge Jumbo Tron in the center of the arena showed gladiator-like men wrestling in protective helmets and zeroed in on one fit and capable running-back sprinting only a few feet toward the goal line before being forced onto the sideline. The football looked fifty feet tall and the football players like giants. I tried to buck the contagion of the opening guitar riffs and bass drum beat of "Black Betty" playing over the speakers as the first down of the game was made. In spite of myself, my body swayed with the music as I walked.

I looked up, trying to locate the alumni's box seats, where Henry and Mrs. Bludworth, Richard's mother, were probably making uncomfortable small talk. My eyes roamed first over the lower sections of the stadium, filled with eager-faced season-ticket holders peering at the blue screen displaying the rosters and the team's statistics; up to the higher sections, bulging with families of ticket holders who bought their low-priced tickets at the gate and spent their weekly paychecks on the overpriced food of the stadium, scarfing down chili dogs, brisket sandwiches, and nachos; and finally to the box seats of the privileged and suites of the corporate sponsors, where whiskies, vodkas, and beer were poured out like forgiveness would be the next morning. There the airy smell of buttered popcorn was replaced by more substantial, savory scents. Platters of smoked brisket and chicken were sure to be laid out next to mounds of potato salad, pickle spears, and meringue pies. In one of these suites, Henry was smiling and talking to people with a large plate of food in his hand. At the top, the stadium lights were already twinkling clusters of stars.

I showed my ticket to the attendant in an orange jacket who pointed the way to the suite entrances. The closer I got to the suites, the more printed names in varying fonts and sizes I recognized on the walls. As I came into the box, I was greeted by currents of frigid air which blew my hair back. A little jarred by the sudden change in temperature, I was still immediately relieved that I was no longer breathing in what seemed like steam vapors. Henry saw me and waved me to him with a boyish grin. I came over to him, nodding hello to all the attractive, well-to-do alumni in their school colors and Board of Regents members scattered around the room. They were telling stories and drinking beer and responding with emotion to the events on the field. Some seemed like they might be making business deals. One burly man kept clapping at short intervals without anyone else knowing why.

Henry and I exchanged a pleasant greeting and he motioned toward the two very glamorous looking older women with whom he had been talking. They both seemed to have been conjured from someone's idea of a contemporary southern woman. One was more beautiful than the other, and though she was around fifty, I guessed, she projected vitality and warmth. Her thick and perfectly straight hair shone like a golden pat of butter melting under a hot sky. The other resembled an armadillo wearing a wig, but both emanated an impression of what would be accepted as general respectability.

"Stella, I've had the honor of meeting these two beautiful ladies while I was waiting for you." Henry said the last three words intimately, his eyebrow ever-so-slightly raised in hidden exasperation. He introduced them with pompous hands.

"This is Mrs. Jada Bludworth and Mrs. Lorena Stern."

Mrs. Bludworth, the beautiful one, softly said, "I'm so glad you came. It's nice to meet you in person," while simultaneously a much louder Mrs. Stern asserted, "Oh, hon, bless your heart for teaching these students. That must require the patience of Job. Lord knows I love a good read, but I'd be praying every day for the help of Jesus in a classroom! You know what? I'll put you on my prayer list at church!" Her laugh hit me over the head like an anvil covered in maple syrup.

I liked Jada instantly. Her e-mail left much to the imagination. She had simply invited me to the game and added that my name would be on a list. She was moderately tall, with slender arms but a very curvaceous lower half that probably still figured into some suggestive conversations. There was an understated elegance about her that transcended the fact that she was expensively dressed. She struck me as the type of woman who undertook everything with infinite care. Lorena wasn't doing herself any favors by choosing Jada as the backdrop for the cheap picture of herself she presented to me.

It was hard to believe that Richard—Big Dick-- was Jada's son. I had invited Henry to act as a buffer between me and Richard's Mother. I could tell from his first writing assignment that Richard thought in generalities; he was careless and sneering. His body was large and tan and he always looked like he had just come from a workout. He wore a large gold chain around his neck which glistened like chest sweat. I had taught many of his type before. Girls wanted to reform him; his teammates feared him but didn't respect him. He possessed a brute sexuality that was about as subtle as a hammer. I was willing to bet that the only time he would probably pay attention in my class would be when we studied Hemingway, the man's man whose idea of heaven was having lots of mistresses. One time I ran into him and a couple buddies on campus and he whispered something about me being a cougar loud enough for me to hear. No, this gentle, polished woman could not be Richard's Mother.

Lorena adjusted her bosom, which she had put on display for god knows who.

"Heather is down there. That's my daughter." She dragged me two steps closer to the window, linking her arm through mine.

"See the blonde with the ribbons in her ponytail?"

"Which one?"

Impatiently, she pointed. "That one! On the left."

"Oh yes." I tried to be accommodating, but I didn't see.

"She's going to cheer for the Dallas Cowboys. She's the best one on that field."

"Is that so?"

Jada looked over the top of imaginary sunglasses at Lorena. "She'll try out. She really is good enough to make it. We came to watch our talented children. There's Richard. He's number 56."

Her face was guarded. She must have known about him.

"Yes." I couldn't think of anything to add, so I mumbled somewhat apologetically, "He's one of our outstanding players, isn't he?"

"*I* think so. You have to have a good defense to win, don't you?" she said.

Just then the door opened and an oversized arrangement of cotton candy came through the door on an aluminum tray, followed by the lady holding it and a couple of others.

"Cotton candy?" Henry asked, a hopeful gleam in his eye.

"The booster club brings up stuff like that every once in a while," Jada explained. She took two packets of it, thanked the woman, and passed one over to Henry.

"And ribbons!" Lorena ran over to grab a few from another woman who was passing them out.

Jada rolled her eyes ever so slightly and touched a red fingernail to a teardrop earring. She deftly plucked a tuft off of the cotton candy spindle she had been holding, her fingers dissolving the web of sugar the moment they separated from the whorl. She rose up in excitement and yelled when the team scored a touchdown, raising her hands in triumph. The random clapper pressed on with his one-man mission to aid the team. Victorious fireworks were set off, and the game was off to a propitious beginning.

It was as though the small fluffy piece had never been, the thick pink cloud, whole as ever, creating a contrast against Jada's smiling, empty mouth.

Lorena dutifully distributed ribbons to us, already pinning a yellow one onto her shirt with pride. Her rhinestone cross earrings swung like dowsing rods.

"Is the yellow one to support the troops?" I asked. I couldn't remember.

Lorena frowned. "Of course it is. Jada's husband served for years. Thank God he's back home, right Jada?"

"They have ribbons for everything nowadays, don't they?" Jada warmly laughed. Henry took up this subject happily. He raised his beer.

"Yes-- we support cancer survivors and our troops of course--" he nodded at Jada charitably-- "and abuse survivors-- in fact, anyone who can make it out alive, I suppose." He chuckled.

Jada held out the ribbon in her hand and looked at it blankly. Then she began to fiddle with it as she pinned it uncomfortably to herself.

There was a short silence between us all as we turned our attention back to the field. I heard a few older men talking behind me as they watched. One was saying, "They nicknamed the whole area Wall Street because the land was good and a bunch of rich farmers lived in those parts. You don't have to be a yuppie to have good business sense. In fact, I haven't met many of 'em who had any kind of sense at all! " Three men sitting around him snickered.

Around the room, other groups of people were talking about historical football games they had had the good fortune to attend. There was a pervasive air of youthful hope and general goodwill. Music oscillated between the college band and the manufactured drum beats of the latest pop hits. When the band crescendoed into an epic note and held it-- like the final chord of a brassy masterpiece—adding suspense to an already suspenseful moment in the game, I shivered with ecstasy. Our team didn't get the first down and possession of the ball went to the other team. Everyone let out a collective groan. After heaving a large sigh, Jada turned to us and asked us politely, "So. Do you have any plans for the holiday weekend?"

Holidays. I loved the colors and food and music and games of all the holidays when I was a child—Easter eggs, magic, storytelling, dinner tables, summer dresses and church steeples--but I dreaded the inevitable anticipation. Waiting in traffic, parents telling you it wasn't time, don't open that, don't start yet. That's what had stuck with me most: the desperation, the panic I felt because it was always possible that the light wouldn't ever turn green. Or maybe I panicked because I wouldn't hear someone telling me it *was* time and then I would miss all the best parts because I hadn't been paying attention.

"Is it Labor Day coming up?" I asked. She nodded.

I always mixed up which was Labor Day and which was Memorial Day. Both were holidays which gave us superficial excuses to go to the lake, but I supposed both gave us reasons to raise our glasses—here's to a day we didn't have to work—here's to a day we remembered all the work we'd done and all we'd left to do—and which obliterated the free space in our calendars like it was manna from Heaven (no rest for the weary). On one day, we were hopeful; on the other, we were somber; for both, I was grateful. Season after season, circle cycle sickle.

"I'm working on my cabin this weekend," Henry replied.

"Your cabin? That sounds interesting," Jada turned her attention from the field to Henry.

"Well, I love being outside so much. I have a landscaping business—"

"Do you? Now I am always looking for a good landscaping consultant." Her teeth were perfectly white and even as she finally showed personal interest in him.

"Most of my customers are corporate. But maybe I could give you some tips off the clock."

"I'm somewhat of a gardener myself," Jada said. "I've got a lot of experience with flowers, but every now and then I've got a question about presentation."

"You?" Lorena butted in. "You have the most style of anyone I've ever known. And your yard is breathtaking, too. Hey—let's get a picture!" She pulled out her phone, which was encased by sparkly gold sequins.

"Say cheese!" We leaned into each other and smiled obediently. There was a flash, and we quickly separated.

"But my cabin—"

Henry tried to finish but another touchdown was scored and the whole box erupted into cheers and yells. I looked out at the crowd to see people making mascot gestures with their hands, high-fiving each other, and stomping their approval with their feet on the bleachers. The clapper broke into a short burst of riotous applause and then switched to deafening whistles. His hands were probably raw.

I couldn't help grinning. Henry gave me a questioning look, and I gestured to the guy. Jada caught the interaction and leaned in as we were re-seating ourselves.

"He's probably got a nice little sum riding on this one. It's been known to happen." She winked and put a finger to her lips.

"You were saying?" Jada encouraged Henry to continue once the excitement had died down. She seemed genuinely interested in his project.

"It'll be finished soon. I like to go out and commune with God in a natural setting—kind of like Thoreau, you know." She nodded appreciatively. Henry, pleased that she seemed to understand the reference, continued.

"But mine is going to have a little more of a modern touch. It'll be less rustic. Even Stella could come out and enjoy it. It'll have a bathtub." He gave me an exaggerated wink that was more for everyone else than for me.

I shrugged my shoulders. "What can I say? I like flowers, too. I'm just a city girl, I guess, although all this traffic on the way to the stadium made me want to rethink that." I was reminded of my tardiness and felt glad I had inserted this excuse into the conversation.

Jada was sympathetic.

"This intersection right outside is always tricky. TxDOT has this area permanently under construction because of the burgeoning population. It's since become a labyrinth of orange cones and detour signs and DO NOT ENTERs. We've tried to get something done about it, but you know how these things go. Slowly, if at all." She laughed apologetically and then excused herself to go talk to a frumpy but executive-looking older woman who had been trying to get her attention. Lorena used the interlude to get a second helping of brisket and potato salad.

Henry looked so much like part of a commercial magazine shoot that I decided to forgive him for making me feel self-conscious. He was wearing a short-sleeved linen print shirt in the college's colors, medium wash jeans that were tailored to his body, and a pair of extremely intricate cowboy boots. Everything about him could have been described as "crisp," which was hard to achieve in that sweaty summer month. Sometimes I wondered what he saw in me. I often felt rumpled and clumsy by comparison.

He gave me a quick peck on the lips and squeezed my hand.

I said, "Thanks for coming. I'm having a ball. You can't beat box seats! Free food, a great view, and really a fun group, don't you think?"

"Thanks for inviting me. You're making a splash with these ladies. You never know when that might come in handy. Everyone in this box is a VIP. They're almost all either on the Board of Regents or the City Council. And we are definitely watching in style."

Behind me a man began cursing the referees. When a yellow penalty flag was thrown out on the field, he only got louder. "What took you so long? My God, we could see that right away from up here!"

When Henry and I turned to see who the voice belonged to, a couple of ladies who were sitting with him snickered at him. The man was unfazed.

"You can change your seats, you know. We don't mind. He always does this." At the same time, they flashed him teasing indulgent smiles. I smiled back at them and told them not to worry.

When we were turned back around, Henry muttered, "Everyone thinks they're offensive coordinators or referees. It's obnoxious."

Jada and Lorena returned after a few minutes and we continued to cheer and yell and boo and make small talk in between until right before halftime, when Lorena asked me to come to the bathroom with her. I didn't know her well enough to decline, but I thought a woman her age should be shod of the habit of needing a partner to help powder her nose. Sighing, I asked Henry if he needed anything. He didn't. He and Jada were laughing and talking like old friends as I glanced back toward them on the way out. I felt glad that Henry was so likeable. I hoped that it would keep Jada on my side should any problems arise with her son.

Lorena's orange-red hair was blown out. Half of it was piled on top of her head in a high bouffant, and the other half fell perfectly straight onto her shoulders. She was wearing a low-cut V-neck collegiate T-shirt with tight jeans and outrageous high heels. I could see freckles on her cheeks, which were not entirely covered by a thick layer of powder just a shade too light for her skin tone. When someone else was speaking, her tongue ran over her teeth, which were too large and peg-like not to be veneers, in impatience. She grabbed me by the arm and began commandeering me through the crowd.

"We've got to hurry. I don't want to miss Heather's performance! I never miss it unless I'm sick. My whole family has bad health, but Heather's counselor told me that she shouldn't miss any more practices. He said missing too much was bad for her self-esteem and sense of duty. But if she's sick, she's sick! She has never missed an actual performance. Well, except for her eighth grade tap recital. She had swine flu."

"I remember that whole panic. Wow."

Lorena scrambled up and down a dissonant scale of common subjects, performing her ossified speeches about education, her new hairdresser, Jada's gardening skills, and men like Henry (who wore designer boots); like a novice recitalist, she took flying leaps over the half- steps with a confident smile until we made it to the bathroom. She eagerly hobbled over to a stall, her high heels clacking against the cement floor and puncturing a discarded hot dog carton.

While I waited, I pulled out my phone. Orlando had sent me a text. He often interrupted my day with funny little messages that led me to ponder and imagine. As a result, I felt like he was right in front of me even when he wasn't. He rode atop ghostly radio waves, rippling out whispers of his spirit through the air until the completed incarnation stood before me again. This one read, "People who don't accept change in the moral compass should not ride in airplanes but in trains." I envisioned Orlando finishing up his third martini at the airport and saying this to a disapproving elderly couple as he flounced by them. It made me smile to think of it. He never wanted to assert himself so much as interrupt others, he said. Some people just had too much power, or thought they did. I texted a smart retort back to him and slipped my phone back into my purse with a tight smile at Lorena as she began prattling again while she washed and dried her hands.

The bathroom was loud. Above the sounds of running water and flushing, women were giggling and talking above each other about various aspects of their lives, the intimate content of which depended on their perceived emotional proximity to their listeners. Most were talking about how hot it was outside and how the skies this afternoon were dimming a little too early for this time of year. Groups of women were having variations of the same conversation:

"I'll bet we have storms tonight. Everything is too still."

"I guess we'll see. The weather app says we'll have some rain, at least."

"It sure is hot, though, isn't it? We could always use some rain."

"You got that right." Lots of obligatory giggles and chatter as the next rotation of women replaced these.

Lorena and I joined in on one of these conversations and smiled to each other as I hit the door open with my elbow for her and we made our way back to the suite for halftime. The atmosphere had darkened considerably just since we had left the suite.

We joined Jada and Henry in our seats. The band played loud music and made clever designs with marching bodies; the announcers rallied the crowd with advertisements and statistics and name drops; the cheerleaders performed a suggestive dance, after which the stadium erupted into catcalls and appreciative whoops and applause. All in all, it was an entertaining half hour. A few minutes into the third quarter, the Jumbo Tron changed to a Smile Cam. An advertisement of a local dentist framed the few lucky crowd participants who were chosen to smile for the camera. For a moment, the stadium was presided over by numerous benignant rows of teeth.

Somehow the conversation got turned to politics—Henry must've been responsible for that one—and I squirmed in my chair a little. One thing I disliked about local culture was that people wanted to pigeonhole you right away. What church did you go to? Who did you vote for? Henry and Jada seemed at their ease, but I was uncomfortable. Used to, people were taught not to talk about religion or politics because it wasn't polite unless you were with your most intimate friends. Nowadays, though we were still taught not to flaunt our opinions on weighty subjects, we weren't so formal with our social proprieties—we wore jeans to work and called our elders by their first names—and we assumed that if we liked somebody after five minutes of small talk, they were our best friends and any topic was fair game. It was almost serendipitous if you agreed with the opinion of the speaker, but nothing made people hate you more than ac-knowledgement of dissent, which is why we were taught not to corner people into those intimate conversations in the first place. It was too bad that this black-and-white kind of thinking was all too common. I would have loved to have seen a prism of perspectives represented and appreciated, both in our national and personal lives, but when you were presenting the gift of progress to a conservative group, you had to make the wrapping paper shiny enough not to arouse their inherent suspicions.

Ironically, as I was thinking this, Henry was slamming the Tea Party for the government shutdown. I winced, wondering how I would have to pay for this social blunder. Jada was only a few shades lighter than Sarah Palin, after all. Her sweet smile was frozen onto her face as Henry worked himself into an eventual full-fledged politi-cal pontification.

Lorena inserted herself into Henry's oratory. Her mouth was an angry faucet which released a torrent of mildewed platitudes loosely connected by leaky logic and rusty rhetoric. Jada kept silent. In be-tween first downs and field goals, Henry and Lorena sparred, if you could call it that. I was afraid for a moment that they would be like two black holes hurtling towards each other, spinning recklessly to-ward either cannibalistic absorption or a cosmic collision. At first I feigned intense interest in the lull on the field, but then I noticed how the lights in the suite seemed much brighter, like electric lights did when it rained outside. But it wasn't raining. The sky had changed colors more than once already. Something—an act of God-- was go-ing to happen.

More tornadoes were reported in Texas than any other state, but I'd never actually seen one in person. I remembered being at Mawmaw and Pawpaw's house one afternoon as a kid when the wind started blowing erratically and everything went still outside. My Aunt (pronounced Aint) Loribeth was over there, too. She was a nervous type anyway, but she was fit to be tied when the sirens started going off and hail battered against the windows. She made us all get in the bathtub and cower under mattresses with flashlights and an old weather radio with intermittent functionality. Pawpaw said he would come in as soon as he finished shooting the scurrying squirrels out of the trees with his BB gun. He was a card-carrying member of the NRA, and he hadn't had this many live targets maybe ever. That the weather looked like a chapter from Revelation outside was a matter which, far from causing him concern, only amped up his action hero-ics, as it served to provide an epic backdrop for them. We all tried to get him to come inside, but he kept yelling out, "hold your horses" and "just a couple more." He was having a hell of a time. I guessed I had a little bit of both him and Aint Loribeth in me. She scolded him to death when he finally did come inside, and he just laughed and said he always knew God had a plan for him, and He wasn't finished with him yet.

I wondered if I should express my concern out loud, but no one else seemed troubled, not inside or even on the field. Light rain be-gan to sprinkle down on us, but the game continued. In our suite, the mist only caused a couple of grumbling comments about visibil-ity. Jada seemed perfectly poised and even entertained by Henry and Lorena's heated exchange. She turned now to Henry, now to Lorena, watching them with amused curiosity. Once Lorena had run out of things to say, Henry smugly let up. He couldn't help, however, throw-ing in a few last comments, one of which had to do with values voting and how ridiculous it was that some people still insisted on mixing up religion with their political affiliations.

Jada blushed at this. Obviously miffed, she retained her gracious demeanor.

"How can a Christian just leave God at the door, especially when it comes to something as important as the mouthpiece of our na-tion?" She was soft-spoken and matter-of-fact.

"How can a Christian silence all the other voices just because they disagree with the loudest voice coming out of that mouthpiece?" In his intensity, Henry didn't seem to recognize that he had raised his own voice until he was almost yelling.

"God will not bless a nation who disobeys him." Jada's eyes flashed.

"God will not bless a nation who twists His will for their own ends." He licked his lips.

We all got quiet.

I couldn't stand it. Finally, I said, "And this is why we are grid-locked. Because there's someone in front of us who won't budge an inch and someone behind us who yells at us to go faster."

Jada swiveled toward me. She narrowed her eyes, cocked her head, and opened her lips. I expected her to either redirect her passion from Henry to me or icily retort something obviously meant to put me in my place. But she only asked me to have coffee with her the following morning as though she'd planned to ask all along. Too shocked to say anything but yes, I quickly assented. Henry gaped at us with surprise, and then, once he had recovered, winked at me. I knew that meant that he was proud of me. Probably he would take all the credit for it later, though if Jada had been offended, he'd have lectured me all the way home. Lorena, who was no longer the center of attention, excused herself. Running a hand through her hair, she visibly sucked in her stomach and paraded off, shoulders back, hips swinging. Right after she left, the picture she took of us flashed onto the Jumbo Tron. She had Tweeted it with the message: Enjoying the game with old friends and new! #blessed #BTHOOU. I had to lean over and ask Henry what the second hash tag meant. He rolled his eyes and whispered, "Beat the hell out of OU" like he should've expected I'd ask. We were all flattered and enjoyed our few seconds of fame. It also gave us a chance to gracefully change the subject.

"It's a pity Lorena missed that. She won't be happy to hear it." Jada's smug tone made it clear that she, however, was quite amused.

The remainder of the game was uneventful in the box. We made some more small talk, mainly about the increasingly overcast skies and the divine quality of the food. Before I knew it, our team had claimed the victory. Everyone around us was in high spirits. Henry kissed me sweetly. I asked him if it would be alright if I just headed home, given that there was a storm coming and I was going to have to get up early to meet Jada. My smile muscles were overexerted.

"I'm a little scared of this weather. What if it turns into a tornado?" I asked him.

"Well, just go on home. That's okay with me. No matter what happens, you'll be fine," he reassured me.

"Henry—" I paused, trying to collect my thoughts. "I can't help shaking the feeling that this storm is a bad omen."

"You sound just like Lorena," he hissed. "What, now you're going to believe that God sends tornadoes to smite sinners? It's scientifically proven that tornadoes form from warm moist air colliding with cool, dry air, which creates an unstable atmosphere. Given that we live in Tornado Alley, it makes sense that we might have to live through a few of them. Come on, Stella," he said. Realizing that he might have offended me, he softened his voice.

"Don't give it a thought," he whispered in my ear as we walked out of the box after extended goodbyes and thanks to everyone. "You scored big tonight. Those women might be misled, but whatever their beliefs, they are good for your career and a good influence over you. I think you could learn a lot from Jada. She's an amazing woman, I can see that."

I was annoyed by Henry's valuation of her. While I completely agreed that there was something powerful and alluring about her, I knew that what he wanted me to "learn" from Jada was how to make a man feel important and interesting, or maybe how to be a rich housewife, neither of which I felt was for my own benefit. Texas men—even those as successful and progressive as Henry—seemed to feel that a woman who wasn't willing to be broken in like a good filly wasn't worth the trouble it took to tame her. And they wanted a return on their investment: a second mother to tell them they were the most handsome and to do their laundry for them and raise their children.

I didn't think I'd mind being that for someone someday. But I knew one thing about myself: I didn't like being told what to do. I figured that was just what made me a real Texas woman.

Henry had parked on the opposite side of the stadium, so we kissed again and parted for the night. People were scattering like animals driven by instinct. Around me, I overheard multiple breathless comments spoken into the wind about tornadoes and the metallic smell in the air. I stopped one man who had grabbed his family and was scurrying away as quickly as his stubby legs could take him. Testily, he told me that there were tornadoes spotted all around, and that if I knew what was good for me, I should get home as quickly as I could. I thanked him and picked up my pace, adrenaline surging through my body as I jogged to my car.

I kept looking up, feeling overlapping elements of terror and wonder at the murky skies which seemed so incongruous with the liquefying August heat. As I drove home, the music on the radio was interrupted by a severe weather alert. A cacophonous shrill blared three times, and then a man's voice came on: "This is a tornado warning. Please seek shelter immediately. Three separate vortices have been spotted in Cooke County and surrounding areas. Our local meteorologists have confirmed that they expect more to form this evening. I repeat-- this is a tornado warning. Please seek shelter immediately."

My apartment was only a few miles away. Surely I could make it there, I thought. But the traffic kept getting thicker, and people seemed more finicky the stranger the weather acted, turning their cars sharply, honking, and tapping their feet nervously on and off their brakes. Also, my car began feeling like it was bending with the strong winds, so I decided to go ahead and pull over. In the ominous greenish blackness, a neon orange sign over a gas station flashed like a beacon. I steered into the lot and parked under the cover. This was what I had felt, I thought, when Santiago died. This darkness, this chaos. Only this wasn't a feeling. It was outside of me, and everyone else was also afraid.

Imagining that I was going to be stolen from the earth by a scribble of dark concentric circles, I ducked inside with my purse and my book bag, joining some other people who had come in off the road, dirt and dust stinging my legs as I ran headlong into the wind. Small debris—empty fast food cups and napkins, bits of paper or leaves--alighted on the ground and fluttered up again like insects. I heard the city's warning sirens blaring from miles away.

We all watched out the window of the store front for a glimpse of a funnel. A couple of curious young men had their phones out so they could film it, should they be witness to anything tangible, but everyone moved in agile jerks and twitches, ready to sprint back to safety. The rain had begun to pour down in earnest. When torrential hail began to batter down on the roof, most of us ran to the safety of the storage room, relying on the reports hollered back to us from the bravest, who were still recording from the front lines. I stood outside of it, watching the backs of a few heads pressed up against the glass.

"There's lightning. I've never seen anything like this. Look at this lightning," one guy said to his friend. "Does that look like a funnel?" The sirens were still blaring. I could only hear them because their voices were raised in anticipation and fear.

"No, I don't—"

"Yeah, man. Yeah it is." He pointed to a dark blur. The friend looked more closely.

"No, that's just some scary-ass clouds, dude," he pronounced.

"Oh yeah. Okay. This is some freaky shit, for real." I silently agreed with him. For a moment, the entire store was illuminated by the flash of a nearby lightning storm, the brightness of which made the sickly yellow light put off by the fluorescent bulbs of the store's interior seem insufficient by comparison. Instinctively, everyone turned away from the spectacle with whoops of terror and surprise, scrambling toward the center of the room.

A woman crouching just inside the storage room door with her young son looked up at me and said, "We'll be okay, right?"

"Sure we will," I tried to say with conviction. She went back to comforting her son, smoothing his hair, telling him that his father was safe at home, she had just talked to him a few minutes before. Suddenly, I could still see her mouth moving but I couldn't hear her voice anymore. A turbulent roar like the angry din of the deadliest childhood monster sniffing out our hiding place replaced all sounds. We all dove into the storage room and held the door fast.

In almost complete darkness, we waited to be devoured. Time stopped. I saw Santiago, watched him in slow motion as he gave an intimate performance for me like he had done before, saw myself gazing spellbound at the beauty of the man, the beauty of the spirit. Then I heard the notes of our song. I knew if I watched long enough, I could see him laugh humbly afterward and call me to him by the setting down of his instrument. I could see myself once again in his arms. But I stayed with the song; it was there that I knew I could encounter the indestructible Santiago for eternity. I yearned to join myself to him again, to flow into the ageless rhythm so that I would no longer suffer fear or despair or uncertainty. But my magic was one-sided; I could conjure him and demand that he play for me, and like the girl with the red shoes, he would have no choice but to acquiesce, again and again; but he would never again play of his own volition. So the once-spellbound girl was left with no trace of the elemental magic that had bewitched her, just its empty form without its power.

The roaring subsided almost as quickly as it had come. After huddling in the same place for long after we were pretty sure we were safe, we trickled out with trembling limbs, some sobbing, some cursing, and some struck dumb. And we found that the store had suffered only one broken window, probably from a hail stone. The lights were still functioning and everything was in its place.

Nobody ended up seeing anything substantial, really; later we heard that we had lain almost directly in the path of a smaller but particularly destructive tornado.

CHAPTER TWO

"They lacked a sense of proportion." – Mrs. Dalloway, Virginia Woolf

*S*he was reminded of polished brass and plastic. Military uniforms and cosmetics. Discarded coffee cup with a smudge of true red lip stain on the edge. A smooth oblong egg packaged as an on-the-go protein laid in a glass case. The sun wreathed in a cumulus cloud laid in a reflective sky. "The service industry is the backbone of our economy," someone said.

It was true that the morning after a storm was bright and the sky was lighter. It was like a seismic vacuum had come and sucked away all the dust out of the atmosphere. I was awakened by diamonds of yellow daylight glinting off of some unknown object in my room. I felt unusually optimistic. Waking up naturally to a blissful summer morning was one of my favorite sensations, even when I had only beaten my alarm by a few minutes. I spent my few remaining moments in bed scrolling through the latest articles in my news apps, as was my custom. When the alarm began to blare, I turned it off and spent ten more minutes wrapped in a cocoon of blankets, feeling both oddly soothed and self-disciplined by this ritual. A few years ago I would have been solely interested in the social media posts of my small group of intimate friends; having expanded my horizons, however, I learned that I enjoyed knowing about what was going on outside my local sphere. And sometimes you could read about things in national media that directly impacted you, no doubt about it.

Right before I slid out of the covers to hop in the shower, a head-line caught my eye. BEST EMPLOYERS IN AMERICA. Last one be-fore I really had to get out of bed, I told myself. Apparently Lone Star's Finest, a Texas-based national coffee chain, was on the list. I was supposed to meet Jada at one of their many locations. I was heart-ened to see such a successful company recognizing that they could make billions of dollars and still take care of their employees. I knew of a few companies around here who could take a lesson from Lone Star's corporate magnanimity. I closed the app, firmly telling myself that I couldn't be late, and with a sigh, I planted my feet onto the soft carpet and prepared to make up my face for the occasion.

As usual LSF's parking lot was full, cars crowded like so many coffee cups in a cupboard. The drive thru was seven cars deep. Fortunately, right when I was cursing the lack of spaces, a lady in a pink jogging suit blew through the doors and got into her car to leave. On the back of her GMC Yukon her bumper sticker read: "I wasn't born in Texas, but I got here as fast as I could." I was sure she did, considering the comparatively low gas prices around here. Her Texas was quite a contrast from my Grandma Lucille's; that old Texas she often sentimentalized became symbolized for me by the painting she hung in her hallway. It depicted a solitary windmill blowing soothing white noise upon a wild yellow rosebush which brushed up against the side of a barn. There were no people or ani-mals in the scene: just a barnyard with a fecund garden that didn't seem to give a thought to who would tend to it the next day or the day after that.

Right before she died, Grandma Lucille, after whom I had been named, gave me her wedding ring. I wore it every day until the gold eventually became too thin to survive my busy lifestyle. Since she'd been gone, our family had drifted now close, now away, like an accordion, because most of the time there were explosions of emotion which repelled us from each other for a short time. The matriarchs were often the most vivid memory-makers we had from our childhoods, and once they were gone, the memories we had to make for ourselves never seemed to hold us together so much as those from earlier times.

I happily took the lady's parking spot near an oak tree and made my way up the wrought-iron steps to the front door. A couple of russet squirrels were spiraling up and down the trunk of the stately old tree. There were daisies and sunflowers planted all around, and though it was a bright Indian summer day, the hot flood lights were still on from before sunrise, beaming down an assurance that this establishment was definitely open and had been for hours. The speakers were unobtrusively murmuring "Vanilla Sky." I passed what seemed to be either college students or aspiring writers wearing expensive headphones and typing away, and various types sitting in groups, talking and laughing in circles with their mouths full and their hands flying. I found Jada inside sitting in a corner by the window. Her light hair hung loose around her shoulders, and the thick choppy side-swept bangs that were part of her hairstyle gave her a trendy youngish air. While it was obvious she was wearing a fair amount of make-up, it was the expensive stuff, and her bronzed face was right out of a magazine ad. She had an oversized bag next to her sandaled feet, and her Dolce and Gabbana sunglasses were folded up in front of her on the table. She was wearing a black blazer and a white designer shirt underneath. Her red lips were pursed together. Funky gold accessories completed Jada's classic look. Making my way over to her, I could see she was typing on her phone, rather adeptly for her acrylic nails, and hadn't noticed me yet. I took a deep breath and walked up to the table.

"Hey, Jada. I hope you haven't been waiting long."

Slightly startled, she put her phone down and brushed an imaginary strand of hair away from her eyes. "Stella! Not at all! I was just texting a friend." She flushed slightly but smiled warmly at me. Her dark eyes were shining.

She continued, "I had been intending for some time to make your acquaintance and was finally happy to last night. Being on the board has given me a chance to hear so many good things about you from different faculty members." I noticed she didn't mention Richard at all.

It was my turn to blush at this kind but unexpected compliment. "Oh, well thank you. I really love my job at the university. I hope it shows."

"I'm sure it does, hon. I'm sure it does. Listen—why don't you go ahead and order yourself something? I've gone ahead and ordered my soy Big'Un sized Cinnamon Cowgirl with an extra shot of espresso. It sounds so silly when you say it out loud. But when you're drinking it, it's worth the mouthful it takes to order it."

"Sure. I'll be back in a minute."

People were rushing up to the counter ordering specialty coffees and pastries with such precision that from far away, it sounded like they were reading the backs of shampoo bottles or pharmaceutical labels. And why not? The effects were similar: temporary and expensive. Students and businessmen alike sat in their own well-lit corners on the free Wi-Fi, linked together solely through this trendy coffee shop and the World Wide Web. I took my place in line and placed my order—a Teensy Vanilla Bean Cattle Roper—and looked back at Jada. She was looking down at her phone again and frowning.

While I was waiting for my coffee, I returned to her table. "Is everything okay?"

"Hmm? Oh, yes. It's just..." She sighed. "...this lady at church. We're trying to come to an agreement. See, we're on this committee together and—I don't know – I-I-It's just so much harder to work with some people—to serve with them—than it is to serve the Lord. That in itself is the simplest thing in the world." Something about her body language suggested to me that she wasn't talking to any church lady. Shoulders hunched over and one crossed leg bouncing over the other, she looked guilty.

"But we are called to do what we must, and not everything we must do is pleasant-or-or-or *easy*, now, is it?" She put her phone away in frustration and went digging through her handbag for something else. But she was interrupted by the sound of her name at the counter.

Though I know she didn't mean it like that, Jada's pronouncement that she served the Lord in this particular setting had me envisioning her drawing a smiley face on a cup that said God on the side and calling out his name expectantly. The truth was that watching Jada in this environment was uncomfortable. When the barista called her name, her face arranged itself into two hastily scribbled dots and a sagging line, indicating a forced gaiety which she had convinced herself she genuinely felt. But I wasn't convinced. As soon as she turned toward me, drink in hand, while the college kid behind the counter went back to replenishing his whipped cream or rinsing out a container, an expression of melancholy sophistication punctured the illusion. By contrast, I was reminded of an earlier shopping trip to the grocery store. The cashier, a droopy middle-aged woman, was mindlessly smiling and audibly bopping to the song in her head as she rang up my groceries. By the time she got to the part in the song where Eminem starts rapping about killing someone by setting their house on fire, I could barely hold in the laughter. It was eight o'clock on a Saturday morning and this girl-- for that's how she struck me in spite of the greying mouse-colored hair and the deep lines around her mouth-- this poor oblivious girl was happily rapping about homicide as she put my hair products and produce into plastic bags with their own smiley faces on them.

When Jada came back, she seated herself and sipped her coffee, and we talked about the storm last night for a few minutes, swapping anecdotes and gossip about the damage it had caused. I didn't tell her how shaken up I had really been about it. It seemed so remote from our little table.

Suddenly, she looked at me and her eyes softened.

"I asked you here today because I wanted to make sure you were alright. In a way, I cannot imagine what you have endured. Losing a loved one, especially like you did." She glossed over the last phrase like she was uncomfortable with even the words she had carefully chosen.

"But in a way, I can imagine it. I've had to. Now I don't pretend to know Santiago so well. But having watched his performances around town, and having heard so many personal stories about him from the alumni, and having had a few conversations with him myself, I have begun to form a picture in my head of what he was like. And that picture is a familiar one." Sensing that she was confusing my emotions, she lowered her voice and placed her hand over mine.

"My husband is a genius, gifted with many talents through which to display it. I fell in love with him because of his passion, his raw ability to see bigger pictures and strategize accordingly. I knew I could trust him. I could stand behind him without any doubt that he would always protect me. You know he was in the Navy for most of his career, and what a career it was! And he was the most handsome man I'd ever laid eyes on. But the bedrock from which his entire personality had sprung was cracked, or so he says all the time. I try to keep mum about my personal life most of the time, Stella. But you remind me of myself, and I think it might do us both some good to talk about it. Then you will know that what I feel for you isn't just pity for your loss. It's identification to some degree." She removed her hand from mine to take a drink and exhaled heavily.

"His parents were strict military people who had no sense of humor and no time for the mundane. They bred Heath—my husband—to save the world. Every morning he had to wake before dawn to study for a few hours before school. Every evening, they set him to

work until he dropped. They sent him to military camps every summer, assuming they would raise a super soldier. Each time he met
their mythological expectations of him, they only raised their expectations higher. They were never proud of him, then; they were only
proud of their fulfilled demands. As a result, my husband became
both immensely powerful and yet also unbearably vulnerable. In his
career, he was the most capable; but between us, I've always had to be
the strong one. You can understand that, can't you, I mean, in your
experience?"

I nodded. Between Santiago and myself, I was not the genius, but
I'd had to learn quickly how to hold it together for both of us on
more than one occasion, until it became too much for me, beyond
my ability to sustain.

"At first, it felt good to be needed, especially by such a powerful
man. But then, the more power he acquired at work, the more broken
he would come home, the more needy and desperate. It happens so
often, you know, that someone's strength is also their weakness. And
this is how it is. His brilliance has split him down the middle. And I
have to try to love the dark, depressive wreck that he is, increasingly
unstable, along with the genius and the talent and the passion."

A recurrent image of Santiago, haggard, wan, in the early hours
of the morning shot through my consciousness. He would close himself up for days in a room, playing, composing, seeking. But then,
when he performed, the beauty of his sacrifice would permeate the
room in an awed hush from the crowd. And he was as enslaved to this
cycle of self-sacrifice as his audience was to the result of it.

"It's not beyond reason to consider my husband suicidal. He has
been in mental agony for years. Probably some form of post-traumatic
stress from his experiences. I pray to God every day to help him not
do anything rash. And, I'm ashamed to say it, but I also pray for Him
to help me not want him to. Sometimes I do. I can't help it."

I was caught between feelings of empathy and distress by Jada's
admission. I could definitely relate to the difficulties of living with a

broken man, but was it really necessary for her to admit something so private, so terrible? What did she want from me? As she continued to draw me in, I chided myself for being so cynical of her. She was beautiful, kind, and successful; she had made a strong impression upon Henry; and besides, I couldn't see any way she would benefit from closeness to me, except that I taught her son. But he seemed capable of passing without her help, overall smarminess aside. And she hadn't so much as mentioned him. I decided to consciously reserve my judgment. I told her that her feeling was understandable.

"I admire your generosity, Stella. You must have the capacity to forgive much in people."

"Thank you. You must also." I thought of Lorena's freckled condescension and swinging earrings.

She didn't seem to hear this comment. She continued, "Do you believe that God will hear my prayers? I do, but it couldn't hurt to hear it from someone else too, right? I couldn't possibly reveal this shameful feeling to anyone else. They wouldn't understand. And I would feel so much better knowing that someone is praying on my behalf. Will you pray for me? Of course I've prayed for you, too, every day since I heard, even though I didn't know you. I just felt led to do so, from the very moment I found out."

Open-mouthed, I tried to form a response. What could I say to her that wouldn't upset her? I didn't believe in anything remotely supernatural, but the last thing I wanted to do was offend such a powerful woman, especially one who was trying in her own way, it seemed, to reach out to me. I didn't even know how to pray. But I nodded helplessly.

Sensing my hesitation, she said, "I don't even know if you're a Christian. I'm sure He will hear your prayer even if you aren't. Just... for me, please." She paused, leaning ever so slightly forward in her search for an answer to her unspoken question in my face. Having received confirmation of her suspicion, she sat back, then sprang forward again, brows creased in genuine confusion. "But how did you get through everything then? And what do you make of it all?

I could never make it a day without Him. If you don't surrender to God, you're missing out on the *wonder,* the *essence...*of real, everlasting life." She said this factually, like a parent might explain to their child the importance of flossing to healthy gums.

I didn't know what I was going to say, but primal fragments of feeling and thought were already floating around in my mind. I silently compelled them to join themselves together into a coherent whole that would be representative of what I wanted to communicate, with the added desire that they should do so at the speed of sound.

"Jada---" I began.

But she cut me off. "Dear. I don't mean to preach at you. Let's talk about Henry. What's he like, other than passionately devoted to you?" She leaned in, again placing her hand over mine and shaking it playfully.

"Is he?" I was surprised. It was humorous to think of Henry as a swooning lover. He wasn't the type to lose his head over something as impractical as love.

"Oh, he seemed it. Is he not?"

"I know he's very fond of me. Come to think of it, when I met him, I felt just like Cinderella. For the first time in my life, I was courted rather than blindly pursued. He's very tame, you know, for all his wild notions. Henry wasn't sex; he was romance."

"Aw, that's a beautiful sentiment," Jada purred. "But the past tense? Am I sensing a little friction?"

"Not really," I said quickly.

Jada smiled coyly as she looked down at her drink. Inexplicably, I felt a need to explain myself.

"It's just that with men like Henry, women have to be delicate. He thinks they should be flower-like," I said, trying to put my thought into words that would resonate with her.

"Mmm," she empathized. "I see what you mean. But I love flowers! They are so necessary."

I didn't have time to answer before she scowled. "You're not into that bra-burning, man-hating stuff, are you?" She shuddered. "Look. Having been married for over twenty years, I can tell you that marriage is hard. But women who are truly captivating have just as much power as their partners do, if not more. Heathenism has got to be stamped out, and that means keeping troublemakers from causing too much of a ruckus. Don't let them steal your destiny from you."

I set my teeth together. Probably our private estimations of what constituted heathenism would be at odds with each other, and besides, I didn't want to stamp anyone out. But then the image that occurred to me of Jada as the Queen of Hearts screaming "Off with his head!" seemed so incongruous with the murmuring intimate woman in front of me that it raised a smile to my lips. Apparently Jada interpreted this as encouragement.

"I don't want to overstep my bounds, Stella. But I feel that I've known you forever. Can I suggest something to you?"

"Sure," I said.

"I wonder if you didn't choose Henry because he's the exact opposite of Santiago."

Instantly, I knew she was right. It was the truth.

She continued, "You think you probably won't fall in love with him. But if you do, he's not going to give you the same experience as you've had, you think. You won't care nearly so much for him as you did for Santiago. So you'll be safe. But maybe you don't always have sheer gratefulness for the safety that Henry provides; it might come and go, depending on how strong you feel. Maybe you're not always sure that trading powerful but dangerous possibilities for a safe bet is what you really want long-term. Am I hitting home?"

I admitted that she was, but I added that I still cared very much for Henry and that it was still possible to have something good with him.

"Well, it's all perfectly understandable. But if you're serious about Henry, don't give him too hard of a time. Someone's liable to come along and snatch him up, as devoted as he may seem."

I rolled my eyes. "I'll keep that in mind. Trust me, though, Henry has it easier than you think. He didn't complain when he got suite access to the game last night, did he?" I winked. "Thanks again. It was good of you to invite us."

"You're welcome. And I didn't say he didn't have it made. You're beautiful, successful, and smart. I didn't mean to insinuate that I don't think the world of you. I simply adore you. Of course he does, too." She grinned mischievously.

Suddenly, an enormous beast of a man came over to our table. He had his maroon LSF apron draped over his arm and his cologne smelled deliciously like cedar wood. If he had been older, he would have looked like Santa Claus in summer. His dark beard served to emphasize the merry light in his eyes. He greeted Jada by name and asked her if we needed anything.

"I've had a short break and couldn't help but say hello to one of my favorite gals! And who's this lovely lady?" He positively twinkled as he awaited my reply.

"I'm Stella. Pleased to meet you."

"Ditto. Hey. Have a pastry on me, ladies."

"Oh that's so sweet of you, Bruce, but I couldn't possibly. I've got to stay low-carb if I can," Jada said.

"Of course," he said. "What can I get for you?" He looked at me expectantly.

"Um…" I didn't really know what my options were.

" Blueberry crumble? Cranberry loaf? Chocolate chunk muffin?" he offered.

"The cranberry loaf. MMM," Jada suggested.

"Sure. I'll take that. So kind of you," I said.

"Hey, sweet pea, it's my pleasure. And I hope to see you in here again." He brought my pastry back on a napkin and a Darn Healthy pack for Jada, and patted my hand.

I raised my eyebrows when he had gone.

"That was so kind of him! So you're a regular, huh?"

"Well, Bruce is just a fantastic businessman. This is only one of his franchises. I come in here on occasion because he works with me on fundraising for some of my charities. He's on the Board of Deacons at our church. Plus, the coffee is wonderful, and I like the music, too."

She started opening her pack. It was filled with fruits and cheeses and a large boiled egg. She only opted to eat a few grapes and the egg. The rest she pushed away with long spindly fingers.

"I see—"

She cut me off.

"The Lord has really blessed him. His wife died when they were young. In a tragic way, too. Cancer or something unexpected. He was really searching. Then he came to our church and found Jesus and worked there full-time for a few years before branching out and spreading the love of Christ through his life's work. That's another reason I come here so often. Many of our church members congregate here because we want to show our support for Bruce."

I could just envision what Orlando would say to that: "So Jesus saved more than just Bruce's soul." Aloud, I told her that I'd definitely be coming here again.

We covered a few other miscellaneous topics and then, tossing her coffee cup into the recycling bin, Jada slipped on her sunglasses and motioned to the door. I had finished my own drink long ago, so we gathered our belongings and headed out.

"I remember what it was like to be thirty-three. So long ago, and yet, it was like yesterday. Richard was young. I was in love." She smiled wistfully.

"What's Richard up to these days?" I asked.

How had we gotten through the last hour together without any mention of her son? I tried to think back but couldn't see how it hadn't come up. Maybe I had just been monopolizing the conversation. I resolved to be more considerate next time I saw her. We were at Jada's sleek new Cadillac. She opened the door, got behind the wheel, and started the soft motor. The radio began to blast mid-song. I thought I recognized the melody but couldn't quite recall where I'd heard it before. She snapped it off.

"He's at the gym a lot," she said hurriedly. "You know, getting ready to beat the hell out of somebody." She sneered, shut the car door, waved goodbye, and sped off. As she drove away, I noticed her personalized license plate: THNKGOD. After a moment, I realized what the song had been: "I Dreamed a Dream" from the new *Les Miserables* soundtrack. And nobody had ever sounded more heartbroken in the history of the world.

FALL

CHAPTER THREE

"Truly the universe is full of ghosts, not sheeted churchyard spectres but the inextinguishable and immortal elements of life, which, having once been, can never die, though they blend and change and change again forever." – H. Rider Haggard

October--

A *much-loved children's book with talking animals. Amid the comfort of the homey flowers, a kindly rabbit with glasses addressed his brothers and sisters. Remember the greatest story ever told, he admonished them with his hand solemnly placed over his heart. And beware of the sly old fox who will tell you it isn't true.*

In the distance perched the great rock building on a hill like a fat matriarch ready to welcome her children by the armfuls. But I was stuck in a roadblock, orange cones lining the streets and police directing traffic on foot, the red and blue lights of their nearby cars lending them authority. Those not entering the church were still forced to take a detour and inch their way through the gridlock created by the 9:30 service. The House of God was open, and I was crawling slowly toward possible redemption and definite parking troubles.

In the short time that Jada and I had known each other, we had held a fascination for each other. We understood each other, up to a point; each of us gave the other fresh insight when it came to jumbled matters of our own hearts. But I wasn't really as anxious to emulate her as she wanted me to be. It seemed to me that Jada used her wealth as a self-evident morality: she was obviously successful, and therefore, her decisions had been the right ones. Yet her overt desire to act as a mentor to someone, to create something in her own image, didn't so much suggest evidence of her feelings of superiority as a pitiable desire to be validated. I found her effrontery quite charming. She was always inviting me places, suggesting new hairstyles, bestowing little "gifts" upon me that would brighten up my living room or alter my views on the importance of hand towels. Mostly, I had enjoyed our increasingly frequent visits and appreciated the new experiences she introduced to me. I had finally shown my gratitude to her through acceptance of one of her relentless invitations to church.

I was in many ways a Texan, but too often I sensed a general reluctance to change here that could cause bent shoulders from the burdens of shame or self-sacrifice or embittered natures bent on vigilantism. I knew I was fundamentally different from people around here in that way. Santiago had been, too. I was still prone to unexpected bouts of depression since he had gone. They were admittedly shorter and less frequent, but when they hit I experienced a complete loss of control. I felt helpless to prevent them, and finally it seemed to me that the best thing for it was to become proactive in my battle against these debilitating waves. In my opinion, self-awareness was one of the must undervalued traits a person could possess. It was probably because of my own self-awareness that I was also so painfully self-conscious. As difficult as change could be to accept, my first instinct was to search for a solution, or at least a tool that would help me shed my fear of reverting permanently back to the crippled state I had so often slipped into. In the back of my mind, I was aware that part of me harbored plans to begin again in a far-off place. Another part of me, perhaps identified as the most indigenous part, was terrified by that knowledge, and so I found myself, one cool unremarkable Sunday morning, experimenting with the less traumatic option of full-fledged conversion.

After twenty minutes of parking woes, I finally made it to the entrance of the building, which definitely qualified as a "megachurch," one of the true flavors of any suburban Texas landscape. Of course I had seen many of these imposing superstructures from the interstate—you couldn't go very far without passing one or ten around here—but I'd never seen one up close. Though I knew it wasn't really true, all too often, the general implication seemed to be that if you were decent, you went to church, no matter your own personal beliefs about God. More often than not, just by sheer probability, any person you met on the sidewalk belonged to one of these mega-church congregations. Santiago had joked, or so I thought, that he might have to become a member himself if he ever fell out of favor with the Board.

I had expected a grander entrance from the limited experience I'd had of smaller rural churches in my youth, but to my surprise, there were two innocuous glass doors with the church name stenciled on them like a dentist's office. All along the walls were orderly flower beds of white mums. Tidy, I thought, and quite unlike those intimidating wooden arches and pronounced steeples which were meant to reprimand the sinner into inspired reverence upon encountering the sacred threshold. Perhaps religion really did evolve over time—softening, mellowing, like the change one saw so often in harsher personalities once old age settled in. Jada had recently brought me some beautiful mums in a modern-looking vase just like those lining the entrance. She was crazy about flowers, she had said, and her husband was always making pots and vases for them as a hobby since retirement. I was nervous about watering them correctly, but Jada assured me they were hearty.

People of all ages were filing in, wide smiles and handshakes abounding. Naturally an introvert, I felt a little awkward but determined that I would be friendly and receptive. As soon as I cleared the foyer, I saw the coffee shop where I was supposed to meet Jada. It was another Lone Star's Finest. I remembered Jada's twinkling business friend and wondered if he'd had a hand in running this location as well. I glimpsed her sitting at a round table near a wall engaged in conversation with a gray-haired couple standing near her who looked to be in their sixties. Jada was stunning in a yolk-colored linen pantsuit. I bought a latte and greeted them.

"Stella. I'm so glad you made it. I was just talking to the Williamsons here about our plans for a mission trip for the adults over fifty this spring. Bill and Karen, this is Stella. She's an English professor at the university." She looked triumphant.

I was used to people being mildly surprised at first at my relatively young age in my profession. These people were not the exception. They shook my hand, the woman first with a clammy limp grip, and then the man, more energetically. They were both wearing flag pins.

"Got any good book recommendations?" he asked.

"I've got some great books in my book bag out in my car, actually. If you want..."

I trailed off because he started shaking my hand again and said quickly, "We hope you enjoy our service today. We always welcome visitors with open arms and hope you decide to return. Jada, we need to get our seats but-- so good to visit with you. We'll get back to you on the details for the trip."

She gave them tight hugs and then, with a short burst, released them in succession.

I wondered about this mission trip for people over fifty, since most in my experience were geared toward teens looking for a way to travel to exotic places with friends and a few chaperones. I had gone on a mission trip like that myself to Germany. It had been life-changing. Even our chaperones were shocked to see German parents and their teens casually drinking beer with their meals and seeing nudity on television commercials like it was nothing. That had been my first culture shock. After that I was never sure that Truth with a capital T had ever really existed. I sipped on my latte, smiling quietly.

The absence of any Mr. Bludworth was noticeable. I had been expecting to meet him and had conjured up all sorts of images of him based on Jada's descriptions. I asked her if he ever came with her to church. Jada looked defensive and responded that he hadn't come. He didn't come to church when he could help it. He didn't get out at all, she reminded me. I knew that he was rather anti-social, but I thought that Jada would have insisted upon his presence beside her on Sundays. It seemed that Heath Bludworth was more adamant than she was on this point. Trying to be kind, I told her I could empathize with his feelings, being a bookworm-y sort who enjoyed quiet afternoons inside. Jada didn't respond to me, changing the topic instead.

She took in a breath and beamed at me with her best lipsticked smile. "I am just thrilled you could make it today. We at Faith Community Church pride ourselves on being more than just a place to come and worship on Sundays. We are more of a way-of-life church. We have received God's grace and want to extend social grace to all. Do you have a church home?"

She had to know I didn't. I shrugged my shoulders and grinned. She sounded like she'd already given this speech a few dozen times before on behalf of the church and hadn't the inclination to amend it for a good friend.

"Well, I hope we can change that. Quite frankly, I can't imagine my life without the support of this community of believers. The more I've plugged in, the better it's gotten for me. We've got to get our seats soon, but I think we have time for a quick tour." She led me down one of the many corridors, pointing out various departments and amenities, talking all the while.

"You know, the church has seven service times, but the 9:30 Sunday morning service is still the most crowded. This one is the most anointed, if you ask me. Saturday night church just gets me all off schedule, and I feel like I need to get up and do it over again. But the young people like having options. Lorena usually goes to that service with her daughter, I think. "

The wide hall was painted in tones of goldenrod and wheat with murals of action heroes, cartoon characters, and bible stories. It was visually pleasing and must have required many hours of work. I assumed some artistic member had donated their time and imagination to the project. Each side of the corridor was lined with various classrooms and color schemes. Every child there must have looked forward to coming to Sunday school. I knew the classrooms I had frequented in my youth were never so appealing. I remarked as much to Jada and she said that the church wanted the children to associate good, positive feelings with the experience. That and some good snacks made them so much more amenable to hearing the gospel. It made sense to me. Thinking of the coffee shop we had just left with its steaming coffees and delectable pastries, I thought to myself that creating a magical, stimulating environment worked wonders with every age group.

After stopping to introduce me to a few other members on the way, we entered the auditorium. Many people were seated and others were buzzing about, talking and laughing in groups. The ceiling of the worship center looked much like the inside of a concert hall. The lighting and sound systems were a steel web of intricate cords and rows of technology. Three huge televisions hung above the seating sections and in front of the stage. Clips about upcoming church events, worship times, employment opportunities at the church, and reminders to silence all cell phones played on a loop with soft, recognizable background music. Behind the stage and to the side of it were bars of neon blue and green lighting. Folding cushioned chairs filled the three sections of seating. We chose the middle section. Behind each chair was a pocket filled with guest cards, church bulletins, tithing envelopes, and hardcover bibles. I flipped through the bible at the back of the chair in front of me. Jesus' words were in red. I had forgotten that. It had been years since I had read the bible all the way through, and I felt a renewal of interest. I decided to pull out my old bible and begin the New Testament again when I got home. Jada and I talked pleasantly and every now and then she would nod and wave to people she knew all around us. In spite of the actual expectations I held for a church service, I felt a naked excitement welling up in me.

"I don't want to seem irreverent," I whispered to Jada, "but I feel exactly the same as before a football game!"

She nodded knowingly, as though she had expected that response.

"That's the Spirit of the Lord. Watch and see if He doesn't move you," she said.

The blue glow gradually turned red as the drums started in the background and the Jumbo Tron televisions announced the worship band emerging from behind the stage. There was a collective gasp as the praise music started and arms went up in the air all over the auditorium. Jada was beaming beside me as she swayed and sang to the catchy rhythms of a modern church song. One woman a few rows up and over was beating a tambourine with red streamers flying from it, her tattooed arms jiggling as she arced it up over her head and down again. We were sitting next to a well-dressed black family, and I was touched by the passion with which they all sang together. Their rich voices, amplified by the acoustics of the large room, gave me goose bumps. I tried to be an active participant, but the most I could manage was to stand, clap, and appreciate the music. All around me members were either grinning from ear to ear or crying.

Suddenly, the familiar notes of a song began. I recognized U2's, "I Still Haven't Found What I'm Looking For." It seemed the song could have been about me. I sang away, enjoying the opportunity to join in with a melody I knew by heart. Jada rubbed my shoulder reassuringly and gave me the knowing look again. I didn't know if it was the "Spirit of the Lord" or the amazing sound system combined with the united purpose of so many happy people that moved me, but I had to admit that I was amazed at the immediacy of the reactive cathartic properties I felt swirling inside me. The best way to describe how I was feeling was this: when I was younger, my mother told me I couldn't drink until I was legally allowed to. She wasn't worried about me getting pregnant or making her look bad out in public. It was just that having something to look forward to in life was the key, she said, and this was her gift to me. More time to enjoy what I couldn't have. I'd understand when I was older, she said. And somehow, singing along about a God who loved me and glorious streets of gold, I got it.

As the band moved on to a song called "Cornerstone," I could see that Jada was completely lost in the lyrics. She sang every word with her eyes tightly closed.

"My hope is built on nothing less than Jesus' blood and righteousness

I dare not trust the sweetest frame but wholly trust in Jesus' name

My anchor holds within the veil...weak made strong in savior's love..."

I was beginning to see that Jada was fragile in places that were invisible to the naked eye. That shouldn't have surprised me, but it did deepen the sense of mystery about her that I had felt since I had received her first e-mail. I was reminded that quite often nothing was as it seemed.

As the band wound down and the last notes died away, Jada opened her eyes. They were dewy and full of calm wonder. We were told that we could be seated. Pastor Sam came up to the pulpit dragging a stool and a bottle of water.

"He's got his mind right, set on things above, like the Bible says. He's focused on the Kingdom, aiming for the finish line," Jada leaned over and whispered to me.

Pastor Sam's far-sightedness had apparently been a blessing indeed, for his glasses, which had burrowed into his face, lent his words an authority which he never abused, resulting in the definitive confidence with which his herd regarded those words, despite the timidity with which he pronounced them. He was a harmless looking man in his thirties who carried his bible at his waist and wore clothing that was casual but pressed and starched, and thus conveyed freshness. He wore a familiar, ingratiating smile. He began by leading the flock in a prayer.

While all the heads were bowed, I looked down at the program, noting that "The Greatest Story Ever Told" was the name of the sermon. I thought about how effective storytelling was. Maybe one of the oldest traditions in itself, stories kept history and memories alive. They connected us to each other and all our pasts, just like our matriarchs did when we were young. But I remembered my own grandmother sitting me down for a serious talk at the table, reproaching me for "telling stories," which was her idiomatic way of telling me that lies were bad. When did "stories" become lies, and how could one tell the difference between them, I asked myself. And could a story be a valid way to get at the truth?

"You do not move, nor shake, nor waver. You are the rock," the pastor was saying into the microphone with eyes closed.

Jada mouthed "Amen" with the rest of the congregation at the end of the prayer and primly awaited the Word of God, looking over at me with an expectant smile. Not knowing what else to do, I smiled, sat back, and prepared to open myself to that unassuming young man with the microphone.

His sermon's focus was the act of communion and consisted of a lot of stories about his wife, kids, and parents. They were modern day parables like those in the scriptures. As he spoke, bible verses and numbered points would show up on the screens, or clips from movies that illustrated those points visually. He gesticulated often with the microphone and paced the stage as he spoke softly. His charm came directly from the fact that his message was not filled with fire and brimstone. He seemed a rather normal guy who was in the habit of proscribing sensible ways to live. Everyone else, having grown accustomed to these ways themselves over the past two thousand years and recognizing what he was identifying as righteousness in themselves, was inclined to approve of this pillar of the community as a result. Quite often congregants would laugh aloud and interject loud signs of encouragement and agreement. I was listening but also trying to process everything he said and the way people were reacting to it, looking around me with interest.

"Communion is when you invite Jesus back into your story," he was saying. "God loves to tell stories, but He wants His people to tell His stories about Him so they don't forget. He tells the Israelites in Deuteronomy 6—verses 6-8: 'These commandments I give you today are to be upon your hearts. Impress them on your children. Talk about them when you sit at home and when you walk along the road, when you lie down and when you get up. Tie them as symbols on your hands and bind them on your foreheads.' I don't know about you, but I had an old uncle who, growing up, would come to dinner and tell us stories all about himself so us young'uns wouldn't forget about him." His nose twitched in good humor. "We sure never did, and Mom and Dad didn't either. They'd always groan when he called to tell us he was coming." Appreciative laughter rang out across the auditorium.

"But Jesus is the author and perfector of faith. The feasts and festivals we have are visual reminders of communion-- which is a way to remember Him and remind ourselves of His story. Why do we take pictures? So we can remember certain stories about our lives and about ourselves. God wants us to remember who we are through Him. Communion is supposed to be a story we tell ourselves. Communion is an incredibly powerful and profound thing."

I thought to myself that it surely was. The power of people coming together over food was undeniable. And weren't the components of communion really just stories and food? Of course, both of these were just major components of culture itself. But all the southern fried comfort foods in the world couldn't have compared to the comfort of believing that one was saved, that one's sins had been erased by the power of love.

The word "communion" reminded me of the New England Transcendentalists of which Henry was so fond. Their attempt at communal living at Brook Farm hadn't been much of a success in the end, but I did appreciate their philosophies regarding nature. That was one quality that attracted me to Henry. I wondered what they would think of this indoor setting bringing them closer to the Oversoul. Maybe our idea of God had changed with technology. The contemporary spiritual or religious experience was obviously more uniformly achieved via special effects indoors. It seemed these people with their eyes closed and arms outstretched were not reaching for anything beyond an emotional sensation to permeate the body so strongly that it guided the mind. Ironic as it seemed, since the avid church-goers I had known talked about how imperative it was to connect to God through the weekly services, as I had looked around me, they had all seemed desperate to connect with thin air. I could not deny that I had felt the charged energy of the moment in the form of the goose bumps that covered my skin as I participated in the confederation of an entire auditorium of people with music and light. Perhaps the experience itself hadn't changed: just the means to the end.

After showing us a clip from a recent movie that had everyone in the room laughing and bumping elbows into ribs, Pastor Sam was listing yet another reason that communion was important.

"We also take communion to receive grace. Ephesians 1:7. See, we have been trained to feel guilty." He told a touching anecdote about his daughter's old boyfriend refusing to take communion one Sunday because he didn't feel worthy.

"He said he knew his heart wasn't in the right place. I don't know what sin weighed heavy on his heart, but *he* knew it. He didn't want to blaspheme. So he passed the plate. My daughter thought that sounded pretty good. Pretty religious of him, right? Pretty humble? So she emulated him. When it got back to me that she had been doing this,

I pulled her into a family meeting and we just talked about it. I told her, 'Sweetie, the last place you should ever feel guilty is during communion. We have the *forgiveness of sin and redemption*. Taking communion means we accept that grace, and we are in turn accepted.' See, her boyfriend made a common error in logic. We prayed for him, spoke to him, and I'm proud to announce he's since become a summer counselor for Mercy Point's No Child Left Behind youth program. And he takes communion every chance he gets."

"Jesus paid it all, folks. Sin had left a crimson stain, but He—" here he pointed upwards, "--*He* washed it white as snow. It's not about us being good or worthy of grace; it is about *God* being good. That's the revelation of grace. And communion should be a celebration-- do this in remembrance of *me*, not yourselves." Here he told a story about his parents handing down recipes and celebrating traditions around the table, hoping that their children would carry on the tradition, would do it in remembrance of them. "There should be no guilt-- it's not about what I do but what He has already done." He took a sip of water.

"Submitting to his lordship is another reason to perform communion. Obedience. I no longer belong to myself but to Jesus. He is supreme master and sits on the throne of my heart. 'Why do you call me Lord and not do what I say?'"

I thought about the specific words he was using. Submission. Obedience. Surrender. Master. Service. Jada's word. And I started to see her in a different light. Jada was a strong woman. She truly believed that united we stood and divided we fell. The church was her strength, and it was a formidable support system for her. She served and surrendered in obedience to her master, which was this room and these people and the lights and sound systems and the traditions that were passed down to her to help her remember her roots.

The pastor was saying, "Communion is a mirror that reflects our hearts back to us—'Jesus, what's inside of me that I cannot see?' It is a way to declare our identity, one of the biggest root issues we struggle with as individuals and as a church. 'Who Am I?' we ask ourselves. Now we know people are going to be quick to define you, to try to tell you who you are and who you aren't, but nobody else *can* truly define you. Even the view we hold of ourselves is false. We don't have omnipotence; we don't know what the future holds. But I know someone who does. Only He has the power to tell us who we are. Communion is an opportunity to declare our true identity in Christ, then. Sin is gone! Because HE is, I am. You know the phrase 'You are what you eat?' Well, Jesus gave us his body and his blood in order that we may become as blameless as he is! We receive this provision in communion, health, abundance, joy, and freedom. Like the woman who touched the hem of Jesus' garment, our faith can heal us too. Since Jesus suffered, we don't have to. Jesus has already written the end of the story. It might look like we're losing the battle but we have already won the war. Jesus drank the cup of sorrow so we could drink the cup of life. Remember the greatest story ever told, Jesus says to his disciples. The story of God sending His son as a savior for all mankind."

At this, there were whoops and standing ovations and even cat-calls. The outburst lasted well over a full minute, and the pastor just received it, pointing upward and himself participating in the clapping. The praise band re-entered the stage and they stood behind the pastor, ready to receive his cue.

I was not convinced that God existed. But I was still very much moved by the words of the pastor, by the thoroughness with which he had researched his sermon, and by the certainty with which he pronounced his ideas. Perhaps that was how faith was born: by being so certain of something that you could even get someone else to bet their lives on it.

At the end of the sermon, Pastor Sam led us in the act he had been symbolizing. The band played a slow version of "The Old Rugged

Cross" as the lights dimmed to an afterglow of red. He leaned into the microphone and softly reminded us that Jesus was waiting to be invited into the hearts of each and every one of us if He did not already reside there. Tithing plates and servings of juice and crackers were passed down each aisle by well-dressed deacons in cowboy boots. Pastor Sam prayed over the blood of Christ and laced his prayer with quoted verses. As one, the auditorium sipped from thimblefuls of juice. Solemnly, he prayed over the body of Christ, and we slipped the wafer into our mouths. After a few parting comments, he exited the stage. The house lights came on as the praise band struck up a strident cheerful chorus as a soundtrack for the emptying of rows. I saw many people wiping away tears as they left, hugging other people, whispering soberly to each other.

As we filed out, a group of teenagers walking ahead of me were talking about where they were going to meet for lunch. One woman had just discovered that her son had taken two grape juices and was loudly chastising him. I felt a sort of sensory overload. No wonder people came to church every week. A person felt like they had been witness to an ancient supernatural spectacle.

Jada asked me if I would come back sometime on the way out.

"I have certainly been given a lot to consider," I said non-committally. "I thoroughly enjoyed myself, if that's what you want to know."

We discussed our feelings about the service and other pleasantries. I asked her to lunch but she demurred.

"Oh, that would be lovely, but I've got somewhere else to be. Next time," she promised.

As we passed out of the church, I commented upon the rows of beautiful flowers I had noticed earlier. Her pleased laugh tinkled away into the crisp noon air.

"I'm glad you like them. I suggested them, you know. Mums are one of my favorites, especially in this season when not much else grows very easily."

She headed toward her car and then, as though she had remembered something, turned back to address me. "Let's make plans soon. I so enjoy your company."

"Great! I'm in." I watched her walk away, wondering why I suddenly felt so empty.

CHAPTER FOUR

"The life which men praise and regard as successful is but one kind. Why should we exaggerate any one kind at the expense of the others?"—Henry David Thoreau

*F*leets *of cotton dipped in shoe polish were reflected by yellow rain boots. Grey tweed and cherry pipe tobacco in the mind of a university student shattered like a thin glass pane pounded by a pendulum. Caramel apple and pumpkin spice candles wreathed the atmosphere. I read old books with new eyes. I tried to align the coffee mug with the antecedent ring on my desk. Look to me, look to me, for I'm talking to you up there.*

I sensed a covenanted renewal amidst the crackling departure of summer's fanfare. Red and gold leaves fluttered down to litter sides of roads. The juxtaposition of the transitory and the eternal roused within me a consummate sense of self which had often infused itself into the literature of my autumn courses. I pondered how awareness of the cyclical nature of the weather amplified the experience of each singular season, brought with it a brisk acuteness. In Whitman's "Song of Myself," the poetic language of the temporal man stretched out its arms toward the divine and became timeless. His palpable exhilaration at being alive must have sprung from his success in the art of transgressing boundaries. Perhaps it taught him that every moment and every man were, when you really looked at them, just self-contained slivers of forever and everyone.

Like Whitman, Santiago had possessed artistic genius, either an agonizing burden in itself or otherwise actually wrought from his pain, a coping mechanism that sprung from his need to digest it, to expel it. His music had also become timeless, and yet he had been driven to commit suicide because he couldn't bear whatever it was that haunted him. What had Whitman discovered that Santiago had not? In pondering these things to myself on the way to work one morning, I thought back to the first time I'd been told that where there was passion, there was also suffering.

I had a professor in college who wore a bow tie to work every day. One of the students had carefully leaked the phrase "friends with benefits" in a circle discussion about a short story we had been assigned for that class. His face froze in genuine disbelief and then that bowtie began to smolder when we told him what it meant. It led to a discussion about changing beliefs about sex and love over generations. Though he wasn't up on even the stalest slang words, that day Dr. Lewis eternally impressed upon us the etymology of the word "passion." The Latin root of the word meant "to suffer." Someone whispered "The Passion of the Christ" with the reverence any mention of that Mel Gibson movie deserved while simultaneously a girl started cracking jokes about her passionate ex-boyfriends. But that knowledge was something I'd been churning in my mind ever since, fascinated by the conundrum of caring.

When I became an English professor myself, I recognized how that lesson colored my own approach to teaching. I tried to profess it with the passion it deserved. My lessons were part of a curriculum, of course, but I strove to make each renewed connection between myself, the text, and the students as personal as I could. It wasn't that I wanted my students to suffer as I had through the years because of my passions; it was that I wanted them to feel that there were sometimes more important things in life than mere happiness. So often society placed an undue importance upon being joyful or cheerful, I thought; where was the meaning in it? I tried to convey in my lessons that the pilgrim seeking truth and beauty—in other words, he who is searching for the meaning of life-- could possibly find himself walking a much more treacherous path than the pleasure seeker. I pictured Santiago's face as it was, the worry lines imprinted there making him seem far older than he really was.

I had always assumed these were two different paths. But maybe the champion of lasting comfort and happiness, *meaningful* comfort and happiness, must have first confronted the sorrows along that road where truth and beauty were sought, and learned how to manage his suffering by those sorrows, not by shrinking away from them or diminishing himself but by opening himself up until he became the entire world. Maybe that was the difference between the two men—these two composers of the soul. My lost lover had tried to contain a universe consisting of only himself inside of himself. Whitman had had his share of suffering, but he had used it to climb to an elevated understanding and acceptance of the natural workings of all life. In his poetry, there was evidence of not just wisdom but also contentment.

All four seasons bore their own seeds, I said to myself, and one should experience them equally. Consider people who deliberately circumvented one season by escaping to Florida or insisted on remaining pent up year-long on a mountain top because it was conducive to their own misery. A miscarriage of balance had occurred in these cases—an unwillingness that had hardened their personalities against the fading outlines of possibilities. What might cause someone pain in one season could become a genuine source of delight for them at a different time, if they'd just keep themselves open to it, I thought. That was a big "if" for some people.

I hopped out of my car, slinging my book bag and my purse over my shoulder, anticipating the leisurely stroll to my building. It wasn't very far from where I had parked, only about a ten-minute walk, but I had gotten to work early enough so that I didn't have to rush. There had been a chill in the air on consecutive days so people could justify switching out their seasonal wardrobes, though Texas weather was often capricious enough that you could never be entirely sure whether it was just waiting for you to turn your back before blasting you with hundred degree temperatures again or whether it was genuinely cooling down. On campus, I had recently noticed shorts and flip-flops being traded for jeans, leggings, and boots; t-shirts for button-downs, sweaters, or cardigans; and with the addition of scarves, hats, and jackets, even the most outrageous fashions were tempered by a seeming collegiate sophistication. And the deepening palettes characteristic of this season—the charcoals, plums, chocolates, and cranberries-- contrasted for a time with the still bright, colorful hues of nature. Yes, I thought, fall lent itself to inner contemplation and philosophical moods.

My thoughts were interrupted when, amid a pile of decaying leaves, a tall man in a black shirt ambled into view, blocking the entrance to my building. Though there was something familiar about him, as I closed the distance between us, I realized I didn't know him at all. He was handsome, with the only slightly faded good looks of a movie star. He had a body that had maintained its natural athletic shape with the years, though he was a little thinner than he might've been. There was a collision of dusk and twilight at the hairline, which was grown out a little more than was stylish for the clean cut he had chosen. The light spray of stubble on his square-shaped jaw only added to the impression I received of a man taken unawares. In my opinion, it only made him the more attractive.

He looked dazed, but his bearing suggested it wasn't a common expression for him, as though the muscles in his face weren't used to that particular contraction or arrangement. He held a piece of paper in his hand and kept looking up from it to his surroundings. He was clutching it tightly enough so that the sinews in his arm were accentuated. When he saw me approaching, he folded it up and slipped it into his pocket.

"Can I help you?" I asked.

"Yes, um…" He pursed his lips, looking around and over me as though he didn't have faith that I could. "I'm, uh… not quite sure," he said distractedly, turning himself around in a slow circle, surveying the campus, until he faced me again.

I was torn between feelings of impatience and curiosity. If he would just tell me what he wanted, I could send him on his way. But the sweeping in of this handsome stranger with the autumn wind appealed to my sense of adventure and romance. His brow knit as his passionate, glittering eyes concentrated themselves into an intense periwinkle glare which fell squarely upon my face. Instantly, I felt the need to suck in a deep breath. My ambivalence melted away, and I was left feeling a little light-headed by his undivided attention.

"I'm so sorry. I don't quite know what I'm doing here, to be honest. I received a message. I'm…." Realizing he was rambling, he collected himself and then, with more self-assurance, said calmly, "I'm looking for my wife. I heard she'd be around here." He didn't say anything else.

"What's her name?" I asked, wondering if he could guess the effect he was producing upon me. I cursed myself for behaving like a teenager. He was married, for God's sakes. And I had a boyfriend.

"Jada."

I could feel my eyes widening in shock and recognition. Immediately he backed away from me. "You know what? I've just realized I'm in the wrong place. I'll give her a call. Thanks." He began to walk away hurriedly.

"Wait," I called after him. "I know her." He walked faster.

"Heath?" I called again. He stopped and whirled around to face me as I caught up to him. I almost smashed into him.

"You know me?" The question was uttered like an accusation, two inches from my face.

"I know your wife. She's a good friend of mine." I righted my uncomfortable mistake and stepped back from him.

He eyed me with suspicion. "Is that so?" He stayed where he was.

"Yes. I'm Stella Wellborn. Jada has been very kind to me. In fact, we've spent a lot of time together lately. She hasn't mentioned me?"

It was his turn to be surprised. "My wife talks about you incessantly. I thought you were a guise. Maybe it's just a new charity, then. She's the kind of woman who isn't happy unless she's up to something, you see." He half-smiled, relaxing his entire demeanor as he did so.

"Oh yes," I said, not sure if he meant to disparage his wife or if he was teasing in an effort to be charming. "I can see that. Hey, if you want to show me that message, maybe I can help you get to where you need to go. I'm not sure where Jada would be if she's on campus."

"It's fine. Don't worry about that. I'm sure it was just some sort of misunderstanding. I haven't been myself lately," he said quickly, and then, "Well, now, and aren't you Richard's English professor?"

"Yes, I am." I could have led with that. That would have made more sense. It hadn't occurred to me.

We both stood there, waiting for the other to speak.

"He's never been very good at English," Heath declared.

"We all have our talents," I said stupidly.

He looked around and spotted a bench next to an adjacent building which was under a large tree. With a wicked gleam, he pulled from his pocket a crumpling packet of cigarettes and offered me one. He motioned to the bench, and I acquiesced. It was far enough away that we wouldn't be watched, and I still had plenty of time before class began.

We sat. He lit my cigarette and then his own with a red plastic lighter. As he lifted his shirt slightly to replace it, I caught the gleam of a small revolver sticking up from his pants. I tried to look away in time, but he knew I saw it.

"I have a permit, you know. You can't be too careful these days. I take it everywhere I go," he said.

I changed the subject. "I don't usually smoke. It's been a long time since I've had a cigarette. It's really the only vice I was drawn to, which was why I was scared into quitting. But how I do enjoy them!" I exaggerated the next drag to prove my point.

With a smirk, he said, "Yes, well, I have so many vices I figured what's the point in worrying about this one?" We both laughed.

Still laughing, he continued, "No, I'm just kidding. I quit back at the Naval Academy when I was... God, I must've been 19 or so." His face fell. "Things have gotten pretty stressful for me lately. Enough that I said to hell with it and bought a pack a few weeks ago."

"I'm sorry to hear that," I said with genuine concern. I remembered everything Jada had told me about him. She hadn't done him justice, though. In spite of her complaints that he was falling apart, completely dependent upon her, he exuded power and easy confidence. He seemed to be controlling that power, suppressing it, even when he was just sitting there. I watched the silky movements he made with his arm as he lifted the cigarette to his lips and back down again. And he was polite enough without overdoing it; I could see how his manner might put others at their ease. I was anything but at my ease, a breathless exhilaration pulsing through my body, producing the effect of intense alertness.

"Jada doesn't know, though. You know how she'd be." He inserted this fact into the conversation purposefully. He winked at me.

"Puritanical?" I asked.

He roared with laughter and shook his head. "Worried," he said. Then he conceded, "Well, maybe both. Either way, let's keep it between us," he added conspiratorially.

"Let's do," I affirmed.

"Listen," he said. "I want to tell you about Richard. Richard...." He paused as he sucked in a drag, "...is a little bit of a bastard." The phrase was exhaled along with a lungful of smoke.

I tried to protest because I thought politeness demanded it but he wouldn't hear of it. He raised a hand and continued.

"I blame myself for it. I was away for most of his formative years, and Jada went too soft on him. He doesn't respect authority, especially women, and I came back into the picture too late to change it. We don't really understand each other—that's also my fault. You will find that he's a little rough around the edges. On the field, though, I can be proud of him because he's in his element there. The meaner he is, the more everyone likes it."

"He's fine," I said unconvincingly.

"Mmm," he responded, and that was that.

We watched a light wind tickle the tree branches, the rustling leaves sounding like waves breaking on a shore. We shared a comfortable silence before Heath said, "Jada told me what happened to your husband. I'm really sorry to hear it. To say the world lost some of its magic is an understatement. I used to listen to his music all the time. Actually, I still do. He was brilliant. His music..." He looked into my eyes again.

"Thanks." At the sudden mention of Santiago, I averted his gaze and focused my attention on the cigarette I held carefully between my two fingers. My husband, he said. He almost was. I watched the trails of smoke making mystical designs as they rose from the glowing butt before dissipating into the atmosphere.

Noticing the change in my mood right away, he winced and put his hand over both temples, shading his face. "Listen to me. I should have known better. Stella, I only meant to pay you a compliment."

I could tell he was in earnest. It was well over a year ago that Santiago had died. To show him I hadn't taken offense, I told him I was dating someone else now, that it was okay, that though I still suffered, I was beginning to move forward with my life. I didn't know if what I said was totally true, though. I *had* been able to pull out the red guitar from its closet once or twice and play the one song Santiago had taught me. The spirit in which I had forced myself to do it was anything but healing, though. It felt more like a form of self-flagellation. My emotions were every bit as concentrated, as powerful, as they had ever been. Still, my ability to acknowledge the enormity of my loss showed I had progressed incrementally. At least I was confronting my pain.

"It's good that you're moving on," he said in a tone that contradicted his words. "One thing, though: make sure he's someone who'll understand what you've been through. When you've gone through something unimaginable—so painful that your essential composition is "--he searched for the words—"permanently transformed from the shake-up, the only way to bear it is to find someone who has gone through something tremendous like that themselves. They'll never get it otherwise. You, I mean. They won't love you. Or maybe it's you who won't be able to love them. Just—from one of us to another." He took a last puff and then stubbed out his cigarette on the concrete, rising to leave.

One of us? Did he mean cigarette smokers? Imperfect people who had occasional lapses in self-control? Or could he recognize in me one of those people who had suffered "tremendously?" Maybe his meaning encompassed all of it. I knew we shared more than just a common vice. I was sure of that, and I was certain he felt it too. I wondered if his advice was more than a subtle hint that his marriage was lonely. Jada herself had been forthright enough on that point.

All of a sudden, I felt sorry for him. He was mysterious, handsome, powerful, it was true; nevertheless, there was something else about him, something familiar, that spoke to me in a wordless language. My overwhelming instinct was to throw him up against the side of the building, to assert my willingness to be placed into whichever Members Only club he assigned us to, just so he wouldn't be alone. Instead, I snuffed my own cigarette out after one last delicious, desperate drag, forcing myself to break away from such unworthy musings. At that moment, Richard and his minions came around the corner. He had been laughing, but upon seeing (me? his father? us together? or maybe the cigarettes?), he stopped abruptly. He looked ready to tackle someone, his body slipping naturally into the well-rehearsed defensive position. Heath waved to his son but made no attempt to speak with him. Richard stalked into the building, leaving his unobservant friends behind, who, unaware that he was no longer interested, were still laughing and cracking jokes. After they realized he was gone, they followed him inside with timid, questioning glances.

Heath walked me to the building entrance and then stopped at the large double doors. "It was lovely to meet you, Stella. I'm glad you and my wife are so close. And how fortunate that you're my son's professor, too. Almost like it was fate," he said softly.

"Yes, it is strange, isn't it? I hope you take it as a good sign?" I asked.

"The best," he said intimately. He touched his palms together like he was praying and held them out toward me in a plea, then swung his arms down to his sides, pivoted around, and walked away. When I looked back to try to catch a last glimpse of him, he was rifling through his pocket, unfolding the piece of paper he found there, and resuming his previous confusion, almost as though our meeting had never happened.

When I came into the classroom, however, Richard didn't even acknowledge my presence. My father was friends with a guy who used to raise cattle and he told me once that a non-aggressive animal would raise his head and then go back to eating if you entered his pen, but the really dangerous ones wouldn't even look up. In Richard's mind, it seemed, there was simply him and then almost everyone else. I had come to regard him as one of the most non-discriminatory people I had ever known, only because he couldn't see past the initial enraging quality with which everyone tantalized him: the waving red cape of another player in the ring.

I mentally chastised myself for comparing him to an animal, but he was so primitive in his behavior and appearance that it was hard not to, especially when compared to the sleek, purposeful movements of his own father. He had deep-set eyes with an overhanging forehead and carried himself with an almost comical consciousness of his physical body. I thought with a blush of how consciously the veins popped from his bulk in contrast to his father's lean, sinewy forearms. He often flaunted his preoccupation with fitness and sex. He brushed up against people too closely and was almost never seen without a smorgasbord of protein bars, smoothies, or snacks with which to sate his outrageous appetite. He was really just a common specimen around here, but for some reason, all the traits that I found unappealing about some native Texas boys were magnified in him: his good old boy mentality, his natural skepticism of people who admitted to thinking too much, and a hard shell which protected his fragile ego. In other words, he was a bully. Maybe with some self-control and maturity he would become more like his father, but I couldn't imagine Heath having ever been anything like Richard was in his youth.

I had read widely enough to become familiar with not only the physical process of evolution but also the psychological evolution of individuals, groups, and cultures. And just like with the evolution of a species, the environment played a big role in how entire cultures evolved. Since Texas was so much land and sky, many Texans felt a more entitled sense of free reign. Freer to carry weapons, take larger portions for themselves, and give the middle finger to anyone who questioned their rights. On the other hand, because of this vast frontier and open horizon, Texans were friendly folks who loved to spin yarns and open their homes. Texans needed free space like all animals did-- to roam, to explore, to laze and graze and mark as their own. When you took that space away, they were liable to bristle and react with a primal rage, and then you didn't know what the results might be.

Looking over at Richard, however, I thought that some animals maybe should be penned into their own large spaces for the protection of others. Though fences made people feel less vulnerable to all that openness, complete geographical freedom inspired a boundless imagination without the learned reserve of the citizen in deference to his neighbor's comfort. The limitless skies and undeveloped ranges of Texas influenced a man to believe in his inherent right to a rugged individualism, which was a natural consequence of gazing up at the moon until one lost one's senses. I didn't really think it was Richard's own fault that he was the way he was. But it still didn't change the fact that I was on my guard around him.

I wondered how many of my other students were from around here. I would have guessed most of them, but carrying the title Native Texan wasn't as commonplace as it once was because of the global economy. McMansions or cookie cutter housing additions dotted the landscape leaving little farming or ranch land available for agriculture. Most ranches or farms in Texas were operated by the rich, consisting of thousands of acres, rather than the paltry fifty or so of my forefathers. Most of what remained of the Texas State of Mind was just that: a state of mind, no longer grounded in physical reality but nebulously floating amid whitewashed conceptions of the past.

Some of my other students acknowledged me with a nod as they came in and set down their bags. I set down my own book bag, pulling out notebooks on which I had carefully inscribed many personal reminders, lesson plans, and well-worn books. As I logged on to the computer and pulled up all of my materials, I made small talk with a couple in the front by my desk. They were good-humored and relaxed. This undergraduate course was relatively small—under thirty-five students.

I felt especially prepared to teach Whitman's poetry that day, not just because of my mental preparations on the way in, but also because a re-reading of *Leaves of Grass* had strengthened my emotional connection to the text, possibly because of my frequent encounters with Jada and Henry. My recent church experiences with Jada awakened a sensibility in me which made the spiritual and the sublime seem more tangible, though no less magnificent for that.

And Henry and I had discussed Whitman in great depth on one of our early dates, which had impressed me. I thought maybe he used it as a screening device, some sort of compatibility test. To my chagrin, I'd recently discovered that outside of a couple of his favorite high school authors (all Transcendentalists), he himself really didn't read much else, though I noticed that he would often superficially allude to books he had read about in order to seem intellectually imposing to others.

"Let's talk about *Breaking Bad.*" The students who looked ready to mutiny were unprepared for this olive branch. They had steeled themselves for a long boring lecture on Whitman and Transcendentalism. I walked over to an unoccupied desk and sat down and looked at them. They shrank away at first, but then the temptation to discuss a real interest of theirs broke through their defenses.

"This isn't a trick. What do you think about it? Why is it so interesting?"

A few of my more sincere students began explaining in detail the appeal of the show. A pimpled guy in a black hoodie listed its good qualities: the cinematography, the acting, the script, the story arc, and its literary qualities. A girl with curly red hair and a pink IPad case delved into those literary qualities thoroughly and impressively. I jokingly told her she got an A and we all laughed as she reddened, pleased as punch. Others slowly began to chime in when the discussion led to the moral gray areas that made it the most popular show on television. Some were quick to pass judgment on all of the characters which triggered rebuttals from all over the room. I had successfully piqued their interest. We talked about what it meant to "break bad" and how "bad" and "good" were such relative terms.

I asked them if they thought "Bad Walter" (aka Heisenberg, as he christened himself) had existed inside the meek chemistry teacher from the beginning. Their answers were varied. I then asked them if the Walter from the beginning of the show was still present in Heisenberg. Again, there was no unity in their conclusions. Some thought both were present all the time, like a sort of Jekyll and Hyde, and others thought that Walter mutated, one comprehensible poor decision at a time. One hipster student with a long beard told me he thought Walter hadn't "mutated," exactly, but evolved, survival-of-the-fittest style.

"I mean, what we would call the 'fittest' are those who adapt to their situation. The problem lies with our society, not Walter. He was just able to see that the people who live in fear and thus are deemed 'good' because they don't cause anyone else problems never get rewarded. Fortune favors the bold, you know, man. And I guess Walter proved that the bold favor fortune."

I asked them which one was the real Walter. This time, they unanimously agreed that both of them were really Walter White. They showed his range and his capabilities.

"Aha. That's interesting, isn't it? That one is so divergent from the other, but they both exist inside the same person? Contrast. Opposition. Tension. Dualities are present in everyone and everything. Walter White is full of paradoxes. So was Walt Whitman. Why do you think they alluded to Whitman so often in the show, even going so far as to name their main character after him?" Some students offered their opinions, some of which were insightful, others off-topic.

"How about if I direct your attention to Whitman's famous lines: 'Do I contradict myself? Very well then, I contradict myself. (I am large; I contain multitudes.)' Does this enlighten you at all? Did Walter, in fact, contain multitudes within himself? And hadn't he always, even before the producers made that very Whitman-esque point clearly by having Walter take on the characteristics of everyone he killed?"

"Wait—" the student with the black hoodie responded. "After reading this poem, I don't understand how you can say that it's Whitman-esque to kill people at all."

"Oh, I wouldn't say it was and I wouldn't say it wasn't. Whitman accepted killers as part of reality. He could sympathize with them as easily as he could with the victims. It's hard to agree to, but he says as much. However, what I meant was that Walter could be seen as a microcosm for American society at large. He is one of us, and he is all of us. In fact, the show could even be called *Breaking Barriers*, right? Whitman is still called the Father of American Poetry. He wrote in free verse because he could not be constrained. He accepted all definitions of 'American.' Do you recall in your reading his ambitious listings of all kinds of lifestyles and perspectives and points of view? He truly promotes democracy because he promotes *all* the peoples and landscapes and ideas that make this nation great," I suggested.

Right away, the student said, "But I have to insist that Whitman is calling us to love everyone through the breaking down of barriers, not to absorb their characteristics through the slaying of them—even figuratively. It's like the show *Heroes*, where the villain's superpower is the ability to absorb everyone else's superpowers but only after their deaths. It's too—I don't know. Selfish. I don't think Whitman is being selfish or self-centered at all. Yes, the poem is a celebration of himself, but 'himself' includes everyone, so he really isn't a narcissist or anything. I think Walter's biggest fault is his superiority complex, and that's the opposite of what Whitman is. So maybe the producers used the allusion ironically."

Out loud I said, "I would accept that argument absolutely. You got it." Internally, however, my wheels started turning. This kid had something. I shelved my thoughts in order to continue my lesson.

"So let me ask you then. If the moral dilemma of the show is a big appeal, let's revisit this idea of right and wrong. The title of the show alludes to an idea of good and bad as separate places on a linear path. The further away you get from one, the closer you get to the other. And it sure makes it sound like it's almost a finite decision, right? Is there a point of no return when someone 'breaks bad,' or can you always come back?"

A girl with long mousy-colored hair and an air of efficiency about her timidly raised her hand. So did some others. The guy with the black hoodie raised his eyebrows and arduously leaned forward as he raised his. I let the girl speak first.

"I think there is always a chance for someone to redeem themselves. They may not actually be able to go back to life as it was. I mean, if Walter had stopped before he got too carried away, he may or may not have been able to go back to his normal life. Probably not. But he still could have made better choices that kept him from going downhill so fast."

Another girl responded, "But some people just give up and in that case, it's the same as there actually not being a point of return because they can't recognize it exists as a possibility."

I called on Black Hoodie. "I think there is a point of no return. Walt couldn't stop himself once he let Heisenberg out. He was having too much fun. Could he have restrained himself a little from going to the extreme? Yes. But could he ever go back to the chemistry teacher he was? Never. It changed him into a new person. He didn't have to stay Heisenberg, but he couldn't go backward."

I thought we could have spent hours talking about the show itself, but I really wanted a more philosophical angle to surface for this conversation. I redirected my questioning.

"Okay. Bearing everything we have talked about in mind, I want to ask you to come up with a metaphor that describes what you think about good and bad existing inside the same person. Do you see it as linear?"

"What do you mean by linear?" I heard from the back.

"Well, two separate places. For instance, if you break bad at a water line, let's say, each time you do more evil, you get deeper in the water until you look around and realize you're completely submerged. Or think about it like Heaven and Hell. A vertical line. The more bad you do, the lower you go on the spectrum."

Hands shot up all over the room. They had been ruminating on this question throughout the entire discussion without knowing it. I called on students in succession.

"I think good and bad are like two sides of the same coin. It completely depends on your angle what you think is good or bad, but they are the same thing. And since everyone has good and bad in them, it's a toss-up which one will come out for any decision."

"Well I think it's kind of like a scale. We all have this scale inside of us, and the amount of choices you make will pile up on one side or the other. If one side's too heavy, just go the other way for a while."

A third opinion was voiced. "I agree with the balance idea. It's like fire. If all fire was outlawed because of the damage it could do, it would have destroyed our civilization. But if we don't restrict it, a large fire could easily ruin whole ecosystems." The speaker paused. "I guess what I'm trying to say is that if good and bad are actually linear, then good is the middle and bad is both extremes."

"Evil is a seed that, once planted, can take over."

Richard said, "It's like that story about two wolves warring inside every one—good and bad. And the wolf that wins is the one you feed." I chuckled to myself that he had probably heard that from his mother. I thought I remembered her using that parable in one of our conversations.

Another student said, "I think good and bad are like a canvas. Once you start painting, you're kind of committed. You can choose what colors you will use—light or dark. But once you've painted colors that are too dark, it takes an immense amount of time and light paint to lighten it back. And even then, the dark colors would still show underneath the lighter paint."

The very Americanized Indian student said, "I haven't seen the show, but I can tell you what I think. It's like drilling a hole in wood. If you don't do it right, you can really mess up the hole. But you can always take it out and start a new hole."

"Yeah, but there'd always be that old hole there as a blight on the board. I'd want a new board," someone pointed out.

"No—I like that," a blond girl with a headband said. "Because eventually if you keep drilling that hole the wrong way, you're going to split the board. That's a good one."

A long-haired boy wearing a grunge band t-shirt underneath a flannel shirt asked, "Isn't time the same question? I mean, like, is it linear or is it a circle? Because in one of my philosophy classes, we talked about how Westerners think time is linear but Easterners think of time as a circle."

"I think many things depend on perspective and the metaphor you use to make sense of what you're thinking about," I said.

"Well, ye-es," he said slowly, absorbing the impact of what I had said. "But it's kinda cool because with the question of morality, maybe there's linear and circular too."

"What do you mean?" I asked.

"Well, what you were talking about with bad and good being separate places on a road and you can find yourself in Bad city limits if you go far enough from Good Land. But if you think about it as a coin, or as yin and yang, then it's really all the same all the time. And those are circular, self-contained things."

We kept the conversation going for a few more minutes before I realized we were really going to run out of time. I had to come back to Whitman. We discussed dualities in conjunction with morality and I began to tie it back to "Song of Myself."

"Let's look at some of the tensions Whitman deliberately represents in his poetry. Let's brainstorm together some of the dualities in 'Song of Myself.' Get out your books. You don't have to have examples with page numbers right now. This is just an exercise in thought." I walked over to the whiteboard and picked up a purple marker. The students were flipping through pages, some with moving lips and others shifting their weight in concentration.

"I'll go first. How about parts and the whole? Remember that synecdoche is a figure of speech that relates the whole to the part or the part to the whole. For example, "You've got nice wheels" is synecdoche because I am really complimenting your entire car by addressing only one part of it. Whitman uses synecdoche to show how everyone is connected to everyone else through the Transcendental Oversoul.

Over and again he alludes to this belief throughout the stanzas. We
are all parts of a giant whole. "

After a moment, I asked if anyone else noticed any other dualities
present, reminding them of what dualities were again.

My red-headed girl raised her hand immediately. "I can think of
three off of the top of my head: wickedness and goodness, life and
death, and people and animals."

"Great. Those are all good examples of what I'm after."

Others raised their hands after having a moment to peruse the
text.

"Science and spirituality."

"Individual and society."

"Order and chaos."

After a few minutes, I had a nice list on the whiteboard. Besides
those mentioned, we had added:

past and future

physical and spiritual

love and war

mortal and immortal

people and ideas

youth and age

innocence and experience

progressive and historical

technological and natural

elitist and egalitarian

"These certainly aren't all. Any more before we move on?"

Richard raised his hand. Surprised, I called on him. His eyes
danced as he smirked.

"Queer sexual stuff and straight sexual stuff."

"Okay," I accepted his comment and even ran with it. "Yes, there's a
lot of sensual and sexual content in this poem. For his time, Whitman
was considered pornographic, certainly. But could he really ignore

this aspect of American life and be all-encompassing? As a matter of fact—"

As I launched into an explanation of the sexual nature of the poem, Richard leaned over to a couple of his friends and whispered something to them. They all looked up at me and grinned. He made a lewd gesture at me and I averted my eyes.

"Notice that he embraces these dualities and doesn't force us to draw lines in the sand. Do these dualities still exist in America today? In the world?"

The bearded hipster raised his braceleted hand and asked for a little more clarification. I had an example prepared for them already. I had picked out two sections of stanzas which I felt represented tensions between the sexes that were still relevant to modern discussions about gender.

11: The young men float on their backs, their white bellies bulge to the sun, they do not ask who seizes fast to them,
They do not know who puffs and declines with pendant and bending arch,
They do not think whom they souse with spray.

"This section discusses masculinity from a slightly critical standpoint. It's masculinity that is un-self-conscious, that does not consider the needs of others, that does not need a warrant for being. It doesn't worry about being liked or bending to fit into another's desires for it. But consider the contrasting admiring view of masculinity in this section:

34: They were the glory of the race of rangers,
Matchless with horse, rifle, song, supper, courtship,
Large, turbulent, generous, handsome, proud, and affectionate,
Bearded, sunburnt, drest in the free costume of hunters,
Not a single one over thirty years of age.

'Glory' and 'matchless' are words that celebrate masculinity. So do the descriptors of these men, who, by the way, happen to be from Texas."

"How do you know that?" someone asked. A couple of guys whistled.

"He says at the beginning of the stanza that he's thinking back to when he lived in Texas when he was younger. See?"

"Oh yeah… cool!" There were murmurs of pleasure and interest.

I could only imagine how Richard and his crew were flattering themselves. I didn't look at them.

A lanky Hispanic student with a faux-hawk and Buddy Holly glasses raised his hand diffidently.

"When I read Whitman, I felt like I was exposed to something really important. But the more I try to get it, the less it really makes sense. And all this duality stuff just makes it more bullshit to me, pardon my language. Like when he says 'I am everything and nothing, I am of one phase and all phases.' It's pretty but it doesn't mean anything. You know what I'm saying, Miss?"

There was a pause as I formulated my thoughts.

"It's like—here. In 17. And- oh. Um. 22. Just some examples, Miss. It's confusing."

I turned to Stanza 17 to see what he was referencing.

17: These are really the thoughts of all men in all ages and lands, they are not original with me,
If they are not yours as much as mine they are nothing, or next to nothing,
If they are not the riddle and the untying of the riddle they are nothing,
If they are not just as close as they are distant they are nothing.
This is the grass that grows wherever the land is and the water is,
This the common air that bathes the globe.

When I skimmed the stanza, the line about closeness and distance resonated with me. For a while, I had been trying to pin down my thoughts on Henry. We had been spending a lot of time together lately, and I felt that it was time for me to decide whether he was someone I wanted to be serious with or whether it was time to let him recede into the background. Jada too, to some extent. I had gone to church with her a couple of times now, and I felt swept up into something I didn't understand but which captivated me. But I was still watchful because both Henry and Jada possessed the same jarring quality that kept me from trusting them entirely. Paradoxically, it was exactly this quality in them that usually inspired confidence from others.

Henry was often defining and refining, whittling everyone down until all that remained of them were the categories into which he had melted them, little asphyxiated glops of bread at the end of a large meal. And he was so certain of everything and everyone, like the young men who did not think whom they soused with spray.

While Jada's personality was more feminine, she too was so close to everything that defined her—her church, her ideologies, and her marriage— that the end result was a blanket certainty which rivaled Henry's. She was bound up by the chaff of ancient judgments which she gratefully collected like Ruth, and yet she proclaimed her stiff unnatural movements those of a liberated daughter of God. I believed that truth was a matter of timing. What was true on one day may not have been the day before or continue to be the day after, especially when it came to matters of the heart.

They were too close, too defined, too certain of where they left off and everyone else began. But I admired them both for their appreciation of beauty, and I loved being around them because of the force of their individual personalities. They were both so easy to love.

I had to consider how to respond to the student, whose name was Edgar.

"It all comes back to the idea of dualities, I think, Edgar. They aren't easy for us to accept because oftentimes, they show us that our black-and-white ways of thinking aren't reliable. Sometimes, there is a middle. Sometimes, there isn't just one answer. One of my favorite writers, F. Scott Fitzgerald, put it best. 'The test of a first-rate intelligence is the ability to hold two opposed ideas in the mind at the same time, and still retain the ability to function.' And he wrote this, I should add, in a public confession of his nervous breakdown. Psychologists call this cognitive dissonance. I'd call it growing up, I guess."

Edgar brightened. "So it's like these ideas, they don't cancel each other out, they add balance to each other and keep each other in check?"

Yes, Edgar. Yes, they do.

After I had answered a few more questions, I let my students leave a couple minutes early. I had my book open to 22, where remnants of the class conversation still lingered. *What did it mean?* In the silence of my empty room, I read:

Sea of the brine of life and of unshovell'd yet always-ready graves,
Howler and scooper of storms, capricious and dainty sea,
I am integral with you, I too am of one phase and of all phases.
...I am he attesting sympathy,
(Shall I make my list of things in the house and skip the house that supports them?)
...This minute that comes to me over the past decillions,
There is no better than it and now.

So what united us all, Whitman said, was sympathy—the "house that supports" everything that the poet included in the poem. The earlier comment from one of my students about Whitman's call to break down barriers without feeling superior in order to do it was exactly right, I thought. I felt that perhaps he really did possess the foresight, as he claimed, to speak to future generations through his poem. It was of personal interest to me that Whitman used the image of a house to make this point about sympathy.

I had always rented increasingly nicer apartments as I grew older. Santiago and I had lived in a beautiful loft downtown. We'd never owned a home because we both always suspected that we would leave Texas. But there was this one house that attracted me. It wasn't that it would have been the only place I could have been happy; it had just happened to be the only place I'd ever actually seen that felt like it could really become a permanent home to me.

After my heartbreak, I had driven aimlessly through my tears down hidden back roads in an effort to escape my feelings. As I left behind all the familiar parts of town and the landscape became increasingly rural, I accidentally stumbled upon an unobtrusive but strikingly picturesque home on a lake. The highway was only five minutes away, but you would never guess that with all the visible wildlife and kept animals. There was a serenity, an unhurriedness about the place. This was the kind of place where you could spend evenings catching fireflies and listening to crickets, where butterflies would flutter amidst the violets and hyacinths. Something about the vivid greenness of the grass and the trees—the wild growth and tended gardens alike—gave me the fortitude to dry up my tears and drive home with renewed calm.

Perhaps for me that place was symbolic of everything Whitman embraced about the American experience—the human experience. It acknowledged and approved of all of the dualities present in this poem by its very existence because it contained elements of each of them. I wanted that house but at the time it wasn't for sale. And I wasn't at all certain that it wasn't just a fleeting whim of mine—a desire to assert my adulthood by undertaking that Texas rite of passage of owning a piece of property.

Reading Whitman's call for sympathy and his charge that there was no better time than the present in the history of time, I wondered. If there was no dividing line between oneself and everyone else, or if there was, you could still feel compassion for them without feeling superior, then I supposed there really was no better time than this minute for living. Or better place than this one either. Maybe there really wasn't any place like home.

CHAPTER FIVE

"But the disparaging of those we love always alienates us from them to some extent. We must not touch our idols; the gilt sticks to our fingers." --Gustave Flaubert

November--

*T*he center of the hourglass was the most constricted point. Swept along by the eggshell grains, I squeezed through, yearning for the all-encompassing again. Homecoming mums, each as overbearing as the mothers who made them, attached themselves to the jangling, ill-equipped bodies of young women. Texas daughters were burdened with this hopeful heirloom, a blossom of youth: the natural life cycle which, the mothers lamented, was cruelly short. If only, they sighed. Back when I was the fairest princess in the land. Once upon a time.

I went to Canada to see a best friend of mine right out of high school whose job had required him to move to Calgary. Somehow, the word "foyer" came up in conversation. Canadians pronounced it the French way—"foy-ay"—and having never heard it pronounced as anything but the Texan "foiy-ur," I was impressed. I felt like a rube. A foy-ay probably had sophisticated diamond chandeliers and dark wood floors. Foiy-urs, I knew from experience, were just entryways to common houses.

Having been raised in a lower middle-class home and having lived off ramen noodles and other cheap fare while working my way through college, I hadn't received the earlier "social education" many others had. But since I'd become a professor at the university, I had received quite a few invitations to black-tie affairs at dazzling venues and magnificent homes. The last few years had taught me much about the influence of money on education. I recognized the Bludworths' contributions to the school endowment and Jada's high-profile status in the community. But as I pulled up to their gatehouse for the women's bible study I'd finally agreed to attend (and only then because I was curious to see where Jada lived), I was still taken aback. I hadn't approximated anywhere near this level of extravagance. Rolling down my window, I pushed the intercom button and a woman's voice demanded "Yes" as a statement rather than a question. I announced my name and the gate opened, as of its own volition. Pulling through, I saw the house situated at the end of a tree-lined lane about a hundred yards in front of me.

Jada's mansion looked like a Gothic cathedral. It was all arches and turrets in a white stone and wine-colored brick combination. Her property was considerable, and her lawn was perfectly manicured. Even in this chilly late month, the sun shone down on a prolific front yard. There were Italian cypress trees and pruned shrubs; tall yellow milkweed, sweet alyssum, and copper canyon daisies along the entrance in a rock garden; and tall, thick pots of various wildflowers and almond verbena whose sweet smell attracted me from a few feet away. A large American Flag stood sentinel over the garden, its ripples and snaps resembling the sound of a snare drum beating out an irregular cadence.

As I walked up to her doorway, I could hear a little dog yapping. "Peppermint!" Jada's voice scorned. "We don't bark. We behave like a lady!" She opened the door with Peppermint, an overly groomed Yorkie wearing a shamed expression and an orange bow around its neck, in her arms.

"Well, hellooooo!" she said playfully in a falsetto voice. A murmur of women's voices tittered behind her. She swung the door open wider and invited me in.

I followed her lead through a large two-story foyer with a black and white marble floor, a massive crystal chandelier, and a crimson and emerald stained glass dome, all the while making small chit-chat. I began hearing voices down to the right as she swept into a commercial-grade kitchen with a buffet set out at one end. A pudgy gray-haired matron in a white apron was pouring out cups of coffee and overseeing the partakers' needs. Jada introduced her as Magdalena, her "right arm" and "dear friend." I supposed this meant that she was the housekeeper but I wasn't sure what that entailed, since I felt confident that more than one caretaker would be necessary on this estate.

Her buffet table was laden with fluffy pancakes and waffles. Also covering the red-patterned tablecloth were varieties of syrup, from butter pecan to blueberry compote. Glass bowls full of blackberries and strawberries were wholesome reminders of healthfulness; aerosol cans of Reddi-whip added a playful touch. Platters of quiche, scrambled eggs, bacon and breads ended the buffet line. Another corner of her commercial-sized kitchen held three different coffee pots with signs taped onto each of them that denoted their gourmet flavors: hazelnut cream, spiced pumpkin, and cinnamon swirl. She'd had out another pot with just plain coffee, Jada had explained. But you just never knew, did you? Another one was brewing as we spoke. Magdalena calmly substantiated that this was indeed a fact from across the room. And then Jada's attention was requested by a woman whose face reminded me of that same November morning: full of promise--a sunny smile that lit up the room, eyes like pools of warm liquid—but emitting a slight chill nevertheless, against all expectation-- her eyebrows were permanently arched into frosty disapproval.

Some of the guests were already seated and sampling the sweet concoctions, while others were standing around in cloisters, sipping coffee and catching up. A large area off of the kitchen, evidently one of her several living areas, had been transformed with tables brought in alongside the sofas and club chairs. I carried my coffee and plate to a corner table so far only occupied by a lone coffee, obviously waiting for its owner. Just as I settled into my seat, Lorena rolled in, sporting a yellow tunic over dark leggings. Her hair was pulled back tightly in a large beehive bump on top of her head.

I spoke first. "Look at this gorgeous spread!"

"Well, of course," she trilled," You don't win friends with salad!" She chuckled at herself. "I was so hoping you would be here! I just know your contributions to our study will be so insightful since you are an English prof! Don't you love *Real Housewives of Heaven?*"

Before I could respond that I hadn't read it, she saw another arrival and waddled over to her, calling to me over her shoulder that she liked my, um... sweater. I bit into my pumpkin quiche, trying not to let my discomfort show. A woman in head-to-toe denim with rhinestone cross cut-outs in various places claimed the coffee at my table and seated herself. She stretched out her hand and warmly took mine, introducing herself as Rhonda Something. I didn't catch her last name. I smiled politely and reciprocated.

"I look forward to these get-togethers, don't you? I get so inspired by the Word when we are all able to sort it out together and divine the true message of it. *Housewives* has helped me realize how very blessed I am to be able to be a stay-at-home mom with my kids. Of course, that is just one of the many blessings God has showered on me. Being in His favor has made my life so abundantly full. When we say the

Thanksgiving blessing, we always go around telling each other what we're thankful for before we eat, and I always worry that they'll think I'll never stop talking. You know how people get when they're hungry."

I responded that this was all new to me and explained how I had come to know Jada.

"Ah, I see. Well, we are so happy to have you. All of us just love these classes. They are Bible studies, of course, but they are also book reviews. We coordinate our book choices with scripture and choose our authors carefully. They also provide us with a Godly outlet for all of our emotions and pent-up questions to things we just can't understand. You know we have to be constantly reminded that everything happens for a reason. Let go and let God."

Her remarks made me uneasy because I wasn't ready to agree with her rather whimsical approach to life, but I was a guest here, so I simply said, "I am an avid reader myself, so I enjoy hearing others' interpretations of literature."

Looking halfway appeased she turned her attention to Jada, who had just sashayed over.

"Stella, I see you and Rhonda have met. Rhonda's husband is the head of cardiology at Regional Memorial. We are so lucky to have him; he is recognized on every *Who's Who* list of cardiologists in the nation!"

More confidentially, she added, "I wanted to catch you earlier to show you my collection of old European novels upstairs in my private study, but we don't have time now. We must get started on time since people have other commitments and engagements."

"Oh, I would love to see them. Maybe later?"

Jada smiled and nodded to me, then turned and moved to the center of the women. Exuding confident elegance in an espresso ensemble with thick fall-colored baubles in her ears and dangling from her thin wrists, she greeted us all and thanked us for making time in our hectic schedules for "fellowship." She emphasized this word with a clap of her hands.

"Let's all give thanks for blessings in his name." Everyone around me bowed their heads, so I followed suit. She gave a quick prayer which centered mainly on woman's responsibility as the weaker vessel to remain humble.

Jada sat down next to a beautifully made- up woman in her late seventies with pince-nez around her neck and a crafted scarecrow brooch pinned to her oversized burnt sienna sweater who began the discussion.

"Okay, ladies. As you know, we've volunteered to help make the Homecoming mums this year for the Fall Fundraiser. Now, most of them have been done, but there have been some late orders come in that we will have to fill. These mums bring in quite a bit of money every year, so those who can stay after the Word this afternoon would be greatly appreciated."

She pointed to a few boxes on top of some furniture in the other room. "We've got mums and garters of all sizes and shapes and colors. We've got cow bells and LED lights and feathers and stuffed animals. We've got feather boas and bubbles and many pictures of girls and their dates. We've got all kinds of thingumabobbers in silver and gold. We'll custom-make them according to what the customers have checked off on their order sheets. I know the girls' soccer team at one of the high schools ordered matching mums for each of their athletes."

One woman asked what mums were. She had only just recently moved to Texas with her husband. This sent everyone into fits of hysterical mirth. They scrolled through their phones to show her pictures as they explained the gaudy, oversized, completely ridiculous tradition that was itself not a little representative of the culture that had produced it.

The woman in charge paused and pushed back a wisp of hair from her face. She wasn't distracted from her purpose for a moment, and she spoke over the din in a pleasant holler. "Now I've been in charge of this for years on end, but I still remember when we used real mums for Homecoming." A few older women murmured nostalgically at this remembrance.

Jada exclaimed, "Like these!" She went over to a counter and brought out a fragrant bunch of white chrysanthemums in a painted vase encircled at the mouth by a bow of twine. The old beauty smiled.

"Yes. Just like those. But those mums don't make as much money and they don't last. It's much better now that the girls have something to keep in their hope chests to help them remember. Do girls have hope chests anymore? I'm just getting old and out of touch." She smiled self-consciously.

Everyone assured her with emphatic gesticulations that it wasn't so. They all relied on her energy and organizational skills to head up the team every year.

Satisfied, she smiled impishly and replied, "And I rely on you all to help an old grandma out. After the study, ladies. It's a gift to the community, really. And they're fun to make!"

Small groups of people began talking among themselves, reminiscing and extemporizing and telling stories about their own children's plans for the big event.

Lorena suddenly hollered, "Oh Jada, I've had too much sweet tea. Get it out of my sight!" Almost immediately, the entire room erupted into empathetic consolation. Take this cup from me-- Jesus' own words. I noticed, however, that Lorena continued to sip on her sweet drink absent-mindedly as she weaseled her way into multiple exchanges. I caught snippets of conversation: the eater's remorse someone was experiencing that very moment (but wasn't it so worth it with all this wonderful food, and anyway, how could anyone help it?), an ugly little aside about an absent woman's supposed success (but who was she fooling? We all know she *paid* for her new waist), a half-hearted compliment, a flippant joke. Jada looked down at her phone and then reassembled everyone.

"Remember we are working through *Housewives of Heaven* as a companion guide to *Proverbs* 31. Let's all get out our books. We had just finished Chapter Three, hadn't we?"

There was shuffling as all obeyed respectfully. As an afterthought, Jada instructed that everyone should get out their Bibles and turn it to *Proverbs* 31 too, as a reference for the discussion. I had misplaced my old bible, but I had had the forethought to borrow one for the occasion. Jada winked at me as she slid me an extra copy of Warren Wendell's book.

I was shocked by the back cover, which I had inspected immediately. For days beforehand, Jada had gushed about how wonderful the author was and randomly fed me little tidbits from the book that she could make relevant to our discussions, no doubt because she wanted to ensure my attendance at the study. Though I thought I hadn't heard of him, when I saw his picture on the back, I recognized him from some major political functions at which he had made his presence felt.

"You haven't heard of Warren Wendell?" Rhonda asked me.

"Actually, I have seen him many times before. I didn't realize he was the author I'd be studying!"

"Oh my goodness," Jada began. She was rapturous. "He's the biggest name in all the Christian book stores lately. His latest book series—*Housewives of Heaven*—I know, isn't it cute? Like the reality TV show!--accompanies major books of the Bible that center around women. He kind of translates for us how the modern woman can learn from these examples, as opposed to what society tells us the modern woman should be. For instance, his latest is the bride from *Song of Solomon*, but he has all kinds... Ruth, of course the *Proverbs* 31 Woman, which we have here, and Rahab the Prostitute. There are others, too. He's also a successful marriage counselor."

At this several women responded with bobbing heads. My curiosity was piqued at the term "modern woman." Granted, many here looked modern enough, but you didn't take marital advice from a two-thousand-year-old book and call yourself modern, in my opinion. I was realizing with more and more certainty that I didn't really think this philosophy or lifestyle would accord with me. I murmured something that seemed to placate everyone, and Jada continued by asking if anyone had anything special they wanted to discuss from their week's reading.

Lorena piped up, "When he talked about how it is so important for a man to have a routine date night with his wife every week, I thought, 'Thank you Jesus!' I took my pink highlighter out and couldn't stop highlighting his message." Everyone laughed. She beamed.

"God was speaking through him to me. I shared this advice with Billy that very evening. Billy said it sounded like an expensive idea to him but I told him that God would provide. And you know what? He has. Getting all gussied up for a for a good chicken fried steak and some country music has put some spark back into the bedroom and given new meaning to the word "submissive."' As she said the word, she sniggered towards Jada, who shifted in her chair and corrected her posture.

A woman to my right chimed in: "I know that's right, Lorena. My honey always says to keep your saddle oiled and your gun greased. I'd say that's good advice." Her bawdy laughter filled the room.

A more subdued lady in a lavender blouse reminded them with rectitude that heavenly housewives should also practice humility in their submission. "With all humility and gentleness, with patience, bearing with one another in love."

Jada nodded her head at this scriptural advice. "We all must bear everything in love. All of us here have some cross to bear. We must pray continually for grace and forgiveness. Don't ever doubt the power of prayer, ladies."

"Amen, Jada."

I peered at the table to my left and realized it was spoken by a woman whom I had noticed earlier because, well, she was impossible to miss. Her deep smoker's voice and tough exterior vaguely suggested to me possible membership in a biker gang. She was totally un-self-conscious.

She boomed out in a nasally voice, "God is so good, y'all! I received a blessing this morning. Well, today was the last day to sign the kids up for football with a scholarship. I was havin' to wait 'til Friday when Cody gets paid (he works for the city), but I didn't know how we would still have the extra 90 dollars for the boys. Lo and behold, I went on down to the Boys and Girls Club and explained to the lady in charge that I needed to be put on a payment plan (my cards being maxed out and all). So she said, 'Oh honey, let me put your application in the stack for scholarship submissions today. Shhhh! We won't tell a soul you didn't have it in on time. I've been in exactly your situation and know how it feels. It will be our secret.' Y'all, I had prayed on it this morning and since I believed it, I received it! God is good!" Her delighted laugh could only be described as the kind of cackle that impelled everyone to cough.

Everyone sang back to her "All the time!" in one chorus. After this witness to God's goodness, the women all broke into applause with exclamations of "Praise God!" while the recipient of this blessing beamed over their words. I later learned that she and hers had been recipients of many blessings from the church itself in the form of groceries, rent, and clothes for the kids.

While I knew these women had come from diverse backgrounds and incomes, I couldn't imagine most of them associating with her outside of this setting. Besides guns and death, God must have been the great equalizer, I thought sarcastically. Shame on these ladies for making a spectacle of this poor woman! She couldn't even guess how congratulatory they obviously felt toward themselves that they were able to muster up any genuine pity for her. It revealed how selfish, how condescending, the sentiment "There but for the Grace of God go I..." truly was. I didn't want to hurt Jada's feelings or seem ungrateful for her invitation or hospitality, but my cheeks were burning. I bowed my head and pretended to be absorbed in the text.

Twenty or thirty minutes of discussion and conversation and reiteration of Wendell's message passed. I didn't contribute, but I made sure to smile pleasantly so no one suspected that I was racked by negative emotions. Jada had us list out all the characteristics of the *Proverbs* 31 woman from the text and then list out beside them all the ways we could manifest those characteristics in our own lives this week. I had many practical questions to ask, but nobody else seemed to have any, so I worked on quietly.

Everyone else was relatively quiet too while they worked until the sober woman in lavender broke the silence.

"I am just going to ask this. I can't be the only one thinking it. What if I'm the only one in the relationship who is asking myself if I am kind, or strong, or diligent, or any of these things? What if I become the best woman I can be and there isn't any difference?" Her naked honesty encapsulated me and did not release me for a long time afterward. I felt my heart go to her.

All eyes were upon her. She looked upon each face in turn, genuinely seeking an answer. Finally, self-possessed, Jada spoke with absolute resolution.

"You may not see a difference. God never promised we would have it easy. He only promised we wouldn't have to do it alone. Remember what Paul says: 'So we fix our eyes not on what is seen but what is unseen. For what is seen is temporary but what is unseen is eternal.' 2 *Corinthians* 4:18. We may never know what happens in Heaven as a response to our behavior here on Earth until we get there."

Having accepted this answer as wisdom, including the woman who asked the question, all the women finished their assignment and began to share their ideas excitedly. Listening to them each relate pages from *Housewives of Heaven* to their own lives served to remind me that the best way and, increasingly, the only way to reach people had always been on a personal level. And in a way, I agreed with the import of the verse that Jada quoted, though I didn't quite feel comfortable with its meaning. I thought back to Pastor Sam's sermon of a few weeks ago on communion and storytelling. He was wise to bring the two subjects together.

We began in the nursery telling stories that would shape our children's morality and their dreams. As adults we continued swapping stories or parables in our music, religion, and all facets of life which perpetuated our own societal beliefs and morals. The only difference between youth and adulthood in this regard was that we tended to become more inwardly subjective than we started out as we aged.

So we fixed our hearts not on what we could see but what we could not—through stories, the unseen became itself eternal, yanking us out of the temporal and thrusting us into communion with generations of well-intentioned storytellers who haunted us until we believed; they entreated us to help them commemorate their embarrassment of having ever become old and wizened with a bacchanalian celebration, replete with an inviting aperitif before the ingestion of a feast of kindly pretenses which they had prepared for us all to gorge ourselves upon.

We all dug ever deeper within ourselves, hoping to find something within us that would shore us up for the baffling quest for the Grail (that immortal laureate cup!); blindly tunneling into remote subterranean fathoms of the soul without a care for how we should ever resurface in one piece; rupturing at once our pleasant but less celebrated realities—an inevitable casualty of the war on mediocrity to which all of us were drafted from a tender age.

I had always understood the importance of good intentions. But ultimately, I now thought to myself, anyone could say that they had intentions to do anything; the proof was in the—well, whatever was in the oven. No amount of graciousness from the hostess could truly excuse a bad meal experience if her guests were unruly or the provisions inadequate. Equally, the comfort of having a place among friends and loved ones as a guest at a shared meal shouldn't be an excuse to act however one would like away from the dinner table for the rest of the evening. In other words, communion *was* a story we told ourselves—and it was up to us to decide if we categorized it as fact or fiction. These women had chosen for themselves, but I had become painfully aware that it was no longer even a choice for me. I just didn't believe.

I didn't really pay attention to the rest of what was said. People told stories and prayer requests were taken and then a flamboyant prayer was sent up thanking God for his eternal wisdom. I knew all this was going on, but I was lost in my own thoughts.

A few women left right afterward, but most stayed to help with the mums. Jada was setting up stations with them and helping the older woman with the pince-nez sort out her materials. I asked her if she wouldn't mind if I went up to see her collection of European novels. She seemed to sense that I wanted to be alone for a minute. She graciously assented, explaining how to get to the turret from the second story of the house. I thanked her and made my way up the stairs.

Flinging a look behind me, I heard the bustle of women with a purpose and saw the lighted atmosphere contrasted with the darkness of the upstairs hall. It was completely still. At the very back of the hallway was a winding staircase that led up to the turret.

Making my way up the wrought-iron steps, I was childishly afraid. Jada's house was monstrous, and its gothic design imposed a feeling of foreboding upon me, a trespasser into this secluded attic. I advanced into the conical room, mesmerized by the effect of the natural light on the upholstered furniture. I could see particles of color floating in the beams. Those silvery particles carried a notion of the past. The room was lined with bookshelves, many of them full of antiques and old photos besides a lovely collection of books. I spied a section of tattered hardbacks with ornate red and white spines. I picked up a few of the more antique ones and noticed the publication dates were all around the 18th and 19th century. After thumbing through them, I figured most of them were aristocratic love stories by authors who were relatively unknown.

Some of the other shelves contained self-help books, many of them religious in tone. Another section was dedicated entirely to Nathan Firestone novels. I never could understand his popularity. Most of the movies that had been made from his books had received poor reviews. I read two of his books to give him a fair shot but soon realized that they held zero appeal for me. I wasn't a fan of Firestone, but I had never seen any of his books in hardback before, so I reached for one. As I opened the cover, I saw that it had been autographed by the author himself. It wouldn't have surprised me to find out that Jada knew him personally.

I put the book back on the shelf in its place and my eyes lit on a gilded frame resting on the built-in shelves. It was an embroidered scene of Christ beckoning a group of children to him. There were also old sepia photos, evidently of family, arranged in the shelves. I saw a couple of faded ones of adults dressed like they were young in the '60s with a little blonde girl I suspected was Jada; an unsmiling old couple, she with her arms crossed in front of her and his legs splayed, beneath the gingerbread ornamentation hanging over their wrap-around porch; and a much more recent photo of Richard in a football uniform, taken sometime during his high school years. One photo on a lower shelf was off to itself. A young raven-haired man in uniform with eyes like light blue steel and a portentous grin on his face emanated a bright charisma which still prevailed through the portrait. At the bottom was an inscription: S. Heath Bludworth. Heath. He was somewhat of a mystery, one of the many shortcuts to intimacy among the church women looking for something to confide. Lorena related to me that she had heard that he had killed over a hundred people in his life and that his guilt had given him post-traumatic stress. Another rumor circulated that he was only pretending retirement, that he was in fact up to his neck in the business of orchestrating top secret government operations. There was much speculation about his well-known proclivity for avoiding society: he had inherited a predisposition to become easily over-stimulated; he was an alcoholic of such proportions that he couldn't leave the house without a flask; he was a pompous elitist, a terminal patient, a habitual gamer and, it was suggested with only a slight upturn of the mouth, a vampire.

Combining our short conversation over a cigarette with the measly scraps of information I had gleaned about him from Jada, I had formed the impression that he was a difficult, confident, but still charming man. Perhaps Heath was the kind of man in whose presence one felt honored just to be tolerated. Sure, some people might not have known how to take him, but I was willing to bet he had a wry humor that was over some people's heads, that was all. Maybe, I conceded, he *was* a little too judgmental—Jada had mockingly quoted his cynicisms a time or two, but nothing he was supposed to have said was far from the mark. I settled upon this paper doll vision of Jada's husband as at least possible, as I had known another man—my Santiago—who had possessed these traits in varying proportions.

I wandered over to the window which overlooked the side of the house. Craning my head to the farthest corner, I could see down in their backyard a huge garden which looked straight out of a storybook and an Olympic-sized swimming pool. Just beyond it was a large, detached guest- house of some sort. I knew Heath spent much of his time there, in that nondescript building which could have housed anything or anyone.

I decided to return to the world of the living and offer my truly humble skill as a craftswoman. The hardwood floor creaked under my weight in places, and my irrational fear returned. I was again a trespasser in a place I should not have been, in the center of the sole dark stain on an otherwise brightly-hued November afternoon. Wasn't this how all horror stories began, with an unsuspecting woman prodding around among others' things in the most secluded part of a terrible house? My throat closed up, and I plunged down into the darkness, racing myself down each stair step of the winding case to the end of the dark hall. My heart was pumping blood to my ears, and

I took my breath in deep gulps. I purposely slowed my pace so that the women downstairs wouldn't wonder if I had knocked something over or think me silly for scaring myself. I tried to take noiseless steps, telling my body to behave, slowing my heart rate by sheer willpower. I focused on the light ahead of me. I couldn't quite hear the human voices beneath me that would remind me where I was, but I was in the proximity of safety.

A hand reached out from a door frame and grabbed me to the back of the hallway with a jerk. I was too surprised to scream. Living heat breathed against the skin at the neckline. A panicked voice behind me whispered rapidly but with conviction into my ear. The utterer pivoted in front of me, pressing tightly up against my body in the darkness as he did so. The halo of light behind him formed a sort of inverse chiaroscuro, where all minor objects were illuminated and he, the focal point, remained hideously obfuscated. He held me by each trembling arm and repeated himself with urgency. As if to penetrate through mistiness, he shook my body lightly to the pulse of each syllable.

There were times in our lives where all of us were pushed over a word precipice and we could never again find solace in viewing the world the way we used to. These words once spoken or read had the power to make or break a magic spell; our fall was broken by either a pink cloud of wonder or a thorny patch of fatal reality. And sometimes the same sentiments that once spun our castle of bliss could lock us suddenly into an ivory tower. I knew that this was one of those times for me. The words themselves were innocuous enough, but their impact upon me was earth-shattering, both because of their singular method of delivery and also because their possible meaning was beclouded by the numerous subjects to which their speaker might be referring.

With that, he slipped away down the stairs into the back recesses of the house. I was afforded a solitary glimpse of his face, only because I was so intent on knowing the identity of my assailant. It was

Heath. His eyes gleamed with the fury of his own intent, his cheeks skeletal in their pallor, his stubble replaced by uneven patches of frizzled beard. But for all of his strangeness of manner, he was still recognizable. Was his message a personal one, or was my being the one to hear it circumstantial? I couldn't tell. I could still feel the phantom of his body pressing up against mine, which was faintly tingling with the memory of his heat in places.

I flew down the stairs, frightened and deeply disturbed, but also stirred by primal emotions which were confusing in themselves.

Jada grimaced and asked if I had seen a ghost. All the other women were too busy to comment upon my absence or return. I told her I thought I had.

"Did you like my collection?"

"It was surreal." I affected a weak smile.

After faltering a moment, she merely said, "I'm glad."

In many instances in the past months, I'd wondered what she was thinking, what thoughts allowed her to respond to life with such poise, so foreign to me because of my burning desire--my obsession-- to know, to understand. At times, it was almost like she viewed the world through an octagonal kaleidoscope, the funhouse fragments whirling through her like a current. In one hemisphere she tried to knit together whatever she saw into a logical whole; in another, she wanted to cling to the eternal possibilities afforded by a mystery.

But this time, it was obvious that she was wondering about me. She scrutinized my face, her face screwed up in thought. Then, having at last decided upon some course of action, she rose to her feet and pulled me into the kitchen corner where the hum and sizzle of the coffee pots might allow us to talk privately.

"Stella, you know I've been worried about you for a long time. With what you've gone through—" She sputtered and began again. "I know that time is supposed to heal all wounds, but I just know that it doesn't always do its job so efficiently. Take it from me. I just want to know that you're okay."

"I'm fine," I said hesitantly. I felt anything but fine at the moment, but I hadn't had time to process whether or not I wanted to tell her about the encounter upstairs. I wasn't quite sure what had happened, really. Since she seemed to expect more of a response, I added, "It's still hard, you know, to not drown in self-pity and say 'why me,' but it's gotten a little better. I've got friends, I've got a good job, I've got things to be thankful for. I'm not awesome, but I'm fine," I repeated.

"Listen, you're not seeming fine. You know what's gotten me through all the trials and tribulations of my life? God. Church. These fine people who'd stick their neck out for me if I ever needed anything. You think I'm just trying to convert you. Well, I am. I'm worried about your soul, Stella, that's for sure, but more than anything, I've been so glad you have accepted my invitations because I know that God can do for you what He has done for me. He can give you peace that passes all understanding."

Peace that passes all understanding. That was the source of her ease. Except I wasn't sure it didn't pass over all understanding rather than transcend it sometimes. Willful ignorance of knowledge that brought conflict so as not to shake the immovability this peace inarguably provided. Drawing strength from the belief that only the mystical could preserve its sacredness over time, that its self-referencing omniscience easily included everything on earth in its sweep. But I didn't want a mystery. I wanted to know, to understand everything. I didn't believe God existed as Jada and the others imagined him. If I was going to hell for stuffing down as much as I could from the Tree of Knowledge, then God was hiding something He didn't want anybody to know. Niggling in the back of my mind were the words Heath had shaken me into remembering forever, words I wasn't quite ready to release, as I hadn't digested them all the way, couldn't wrap my mind around their full import.

"I told you I'm fine." I forced a huge smile. "Thank you for caring about me. Your friendship means so much to me."

She seemed disappointed. "You need to be saved," she insisted. I agreed with her there. But who was there available for heroism who wasn't flailing in the swamps of their own lives? Deep down, we all were, whether we recognized it or not. This democratic need for God didn't mean that he existed to fulfill it. I was glad for Jada that she'd found a way to navigate her own private terrain with confidence and security. It didn't lessen the danger, but it made the journey more pleasant. But as for me, I would not be attending any of these meetings where people begged for special favors from a personal god who loved a select few over the other billions he had supposedly also created. Not only did it defy common sense, but I knew I'd lose control if I heard the casually dropped phrase "everything happens for a reason" one more time as an acceptable warrant for the extant misery in the world, as the circular answer to any "why," as justification for the status quo. Santiago's suicide hadn't been divinely inspired, but neither had it been his own choice. He'd reached his limits on all sides: he couldn't go any deeper or wider, couldn't expand or contract any further. He'd been born with a certain constitution, a natural inclination, and there was simply nothing to be done for it but what he'd had to do. And even if that wasn't true, I'd never accept that there was a specific reason for his death which I would not be capable of knowing, or even worse, not allowed to know. No one could have saved him from his death, not me, not Orlando, not God. Oh yes, I was finished with Jada's God. But I wasn't going to tell Jada that.

"Where did you get those strawberries?" I asked by way of changing the subject, pointing at the half-eaten bowl. "They're huge!"

"Magdalena goes to the farmer's market on the other side of town. Okay. I get it. You don't want to talk about it. Just know that I'm worried about you. And don't say I didn't try."

"Why would I say that?" I asked her, thinking how very strange she sounded, like she knew something was coming that I didn't. I wanted to ask her, but the ladies summoned her from the other room to settle a dispute over whether this particular arrangement on the mum in question called for the addition of more school spirit charms or specific activity-related ones. She shrugged her shoulders apologetically and went to them.

Later that evening, when I had finally gotten to the safety of my own apartment, I logged onto Facebook. For the second time that day, I felt like a trespasser as I typed "Heath Bludworth" into the search function. There were no returns. I was reminded of a comment Orlando had made some time ago: "If they're not on Facebook, they're not really real people." I wondered.

PROVERBS 31
Epilogue: The Wife of Noble Character
[10] A wife of noble character who can find? She is worth far more than rubies.

[11] Her husband has full confidence in her and lacks nothing of value.

[12] She brings him good, not harm, all the days of her life.

[13] She selects wool and flax and works with eager hands.

[14] She is like the merchant ships, bringing her food from afar.

[15] She gets up while it is still night; she provides food for her family and portions for her female servants.

[16] She considers a field and buys it; out of her earnings she plants a vineyard.

[17] She sets about her work vigorously; her arms are strong for her tasks.

[18] She sees that her trading is profitable, and her lamp does not go out at night.

[19] In her hand she holds the distaff and grasps the spindle with her fingers.

[20] She opens her arms to the poor and extends her hands to the needy.

[21] When it snows, she has no fear for her household; for all of them are clothed in scarlet.

[22] She makes coverings for her bed; she is clothed in fine linen and purple.

[23] Her husband is respected at the city gate, where he takes his seat among the elders of the land.

[24] She makes linen garments and sells them, and supplies the merchants with sashes.

[25] She is clothed with strength and dignity; she can laugh at the days to come.

[26] She speaks with wisdom, and faithful instruction is on her tongue.

[27] She watches over the affairs of her household and does not eat the bread of idleness.

[28] Her children arise and call her blessed; her husband also, and he praises her:

[29] "Many women do noble things, but you surpass them all."

[30] Charm is deceptive, and beauty is fleeting; but a woman who fears the Lord is to be praised.

[31] Honor her for all that her hands have done, and let her works bring her praise at the city gate.

CHAPTER SIX

*"Yes, her will was fixed in the determination that life should be gentle
and good and benevolent whereas her blood was reckless, the blood of
daredevils. Her will was the stronger of the two. But her blood had its
revenge on her. So it is with strong natures today: shattered from the
inside."--D. H. Lawrence*

November-

*A pacific world lies at the bottom of the sea. Barnacles attach themselves
like rust to walls that still stand and streets that are now deserted.
Schools of fish dart in and around ruins of whole structures. Here, objects once
eroded by the pulling of the tide maintain their permanence with relief. Strands
of hair-like growth sway with the water. A crustacean scuttles across the top of
the ancient civilization like it was just another part of the rocky ocean floor.*

"No, sir, I wasn't aware I was speeding. It just felt so good to get
out on the open road for a little bit after being cooped up in the city
that I was getting a little over-excited, I guess," Henry said with an
exaggerated East Texas accent.

"Where are you headed?" The middle aged officer with the harsh military cut leaned into the window of Henry's oversized expensive pickup truck.

"I'm taking my beautiful girl here to the log cabin I just finished for the weekend. I built it with my own two hands. Took years."

The officer relaxed his official pose and began asking Henry questions about what kind of wood he used, told stories about a buddy of his in college who had built upscale chicken coops on the side, and sympathized with his penchant for rural areas.

"Y'all take care now. Lucky girl. I always wanted to stay in a log cabin. And drive the speed limit, if you can help it," he said with a wink.

"I've never gotten a ticket," Henry said smugly to himself as the officer drove off in the opposite direction.

I thought back to all the times I *had* been given one. It hadn't happened very often, but I never thought it was fair to lie to the police, or flash my breasts or play the damsel in distress, for that matter. All the things I had heard could get you out of a ticket just didn't seem like something a dignified woman would do. I always tried to be honest, apologetic, and fair-minded. The thought of Henry getting off scot-free because he was a member of the Good Old Boys Club enraged me. He was so cavalier. And I didn't particularly like being called "his girl," either. I wasn't his to possess, and I thought his proclamation was premature in a romantic context, too. Lately we had been clashing over everything, and I wasn't sure what had changed us, if we had really even changed at all. Maybe we had just gotten to know each other a little bit better. Maybe he'd gotten a little more demanding—a little less compromising. Maybe the change was in me. Whatever the reason, I knew I had become less willing to keep silent about all the perceived injustices in our relationship.

But since we were going to be alone together away from everyone else for the entire weekend, I thought it wiser to stay silent this time. Besides, it was the end of my Thanksgiving break and I wanted to make sure I had time to just relax before going back to work.

Henry was singing happily to "Peaceful Easy Feeling" as we sped into the afternoon. "I love this song. The Eagles are one of my favorite bands." He went back to singing along with the music and tapping his hand against his leg as he drove.

I pulled out some lotion from my purse and applied it to my arms and hands. My skin often became dry and flaky in colder weather. Then I looked out the window.

Henry had said we were headed to the Piney Woods, but at that moment, we were passing miles of undeveloped rolling hills, sparsely treed, with here an old windmill and there an old weathered shack that bespoke a Depression-era homestead. I remembered driving by these run-down shacks on country roads as a child and imagining each time that this one was the house belonging to the farming Gale family in the 1930's—it was in pretty good shape, I conceded to my young self, considering that it had survived a twister and famously landed on the Wicked Witch of the East.

As we neared the cabin, Henry spent a good forty-five minutes detailing the symbolism every hand-hewn log would hold for his grandchildren and essentially arguing how this feat of his made him a better man than any other around who hadn't built his own wooden legacy to himself in the middle of nowhere. I grew more annoyed by the minute. Didn't he realize what a ruthless egoist he sounded like? I pretended to listen but turned inward instead.

Would his grandkids really care about some old pile of rotten logs a century from now? It seemed to me that while some people were inclined to revere and even romanticize history (historical fiction was all the rage because it brought cinematic passion to what were otherwise useless worn-out facts), most people just wanted to focus on how to make their own mark on the world. Everybody dies, I thought. But maybe our common enemy isn't death itself; it's the blank slate we have ahead of us—the finite amount of time each is given in which to change the world, to make our mark, to die in good conscience. Those hills out my window, I thought, were like infinite generations fighting each other for the celebrity of lasting achievement. As far as the eye could see, they overlapped and spread out like waves of earth captured in a motionless image of movement. And possibly concealed under each mound were the buried remnants of innumerable lifetimes of achievements. Not to mention, I added with a shudder, the decaying fragments, the dust of dreamers themselves.

I became aware of a dark shadow in the back of my mind. Its silhouette—the shadow of a shadow—reminded me of something. Or someone. It unsettled me, and so I got to thinking of what it might mean, materializing in my mind without my conscious knowledge. The silhouette began to compact itself into a more solid form. As it took shape, I realized it was not a weeping red guitar but Jada's husband. Heath Bludworth was on my mind. Feeling simultaneously relieved and horrified by this mind-specter, I quickly turned my attention back to Henry. Surely log cabin building was a very unique hobby, and many people were proud of their hobbies. Why, Abraham Lincoln built log cabins, Henry said so himself! He had wanted to share himself with me, and here I was tearing him down in my head instead of being properly grateful for the opportunity to have a real Walden-like experience of my very own. I was forever going to be a captive of my own idealism, I said to myself, if I couldn't just accept the good in people and quit criticizing. Besides, my morbid streak was all too often the only blot on an otherwise perfectly good afternoon.

When "Hotel California" came on, we sang together in lighthearted tones. Henry said it was his favorite. I tried not to think that he seemed very pleased with himself for recognizing the ugliness of materialism, something that had been apparent to many of my college students for years already. Instead, I focused on how the baseball cap he was wearing formed an attractive shape around his face, and how the muscles of his forearms were showcased through the tap, tap, tap of his fingers to the beat of the music.

Finally we turned onto a long dirt road. The truck was bouncing up and down, and with each jolt, Henry looked more and more like a little boy. His eyes were shining and the breaths were shorter in between the words of his preparatory speech. I was infected by his excitement. Maybe this would turn out to be a marvelous weekend after all.

We pulled up to a tiny solitary dwelling in the middle of a forest. I thought perhaps it was a deer stand or a ranger hut or something. He jumped out. When Henry motioned me to get out of the truck and come along with him, I couldn't imagine why. It really didn't occur to me that this desolate shack was his beloved cabin.

"What do you think?" He was grinning like he was showing me the universe in his palm.

"This is it?"

Because of Henry's referring to it as "modern," and because of the ardor and reverence with which he always spoke of it, I had come to expect a log cabin style home—like a lodge in Colorado. I expected high ceilings and central air and at least two large rooms. But "modest" would be too grand an adjective for what I saw before me. It looked like a very good art project. A stage cabin, maybe, for the background of a recitation of 'The Gettysburg Address" or *Huckleberry Finn*. There was even a big stump in the front with an ax buried halfway into its ridges to complete the somewhat theatrical feel of the setting.

Henry grabbed my hand and led me around the outside of the cabin. I wrapped my tailored grey winter coat around me, shivering all the more at the prospect of actually having to stay here for two nights. Crunching through brown and dying leaves, he pointed out the aluminum "shingles" he had gotten from scrap his friend gave him. He fingered the wooden sign that hung down on the tiny wraparound porch. It read, "Henry's Hideaway." He never did have much imagination, I mused as he led me around back to show me the fuse box that lighted the cabin at night.

Smart-ass that I had always been, I asked, "You mean we aren't using kerosene lamps?"

He deprecatingly granted that he had felt a little guilty about that point but that it was impractical not to have lights, cheap as they were to install. "But I did decide that central air would have made this place way too inauthentic. So we'll build a fire tonight."

My disappointment must have shown on my face because he laughed, kissed me lightly, and told me to just wait until we got inside.

We walked into a single frigid room. There were woodchips on the floor. It was windowless except for a large one on the furthest wall which only thoughtlessly let in more cold air. An uncomfortable couch which looked more like a pew with a threadbare cushion on it, a wood-burning stove, a large bed which was made up with a patchwork ring-patterned quilt, and a rusty claw foot bathtub were all that Henry had set up in the way of furniture. It definitely did look quaint, but I still felt more like we would be camping than actually having the romantic getaway Henry described.

All smiles, he led me over to the bathtub and turned on the faucet.

"Put your hand under there. Surprise! Hot water!" He was jubilant. I had to admit that I was relieved. I could stay there for a couple of days and survive.

He turned the faucet off and kissed me again.

"And electrical outlets! I brought my IPhone and some speakers! I've never done that before, but in your honor, I thought it would add a special touch. We are gonna have so much fun. What do you think? Huh?" He looked at me expectantly.

"It's nice," I said noncommittally. I wondered outside of taking baths and chopping wood what we would be doing. I asked him as much. We sat down on the bed.

Indignantly, he retorted, "We get away from civilization. We breathe good clean air and relax. We live like people who knew how to live did it back in the day. When things were easier. Better. People just have their priorities all mixed up all the time nowadays. Entertainment, material possessions, mindlessness all around. It depresses me being around the masses. Their lives run quietly by corporations and lobbyists and they don't even care. They don't think about their health or their hearts. They don't even know why they do what they do most of the time. I think it would do everyone some good to pull out a social experiment like I did. I've thought about building on and just moving here, like Thoreau." His voice was raised in intensity.

I guessed when you spent so many summers in your youth baling hay you baled other things together, like people, out of force of habit.

"Don't you get bored?" I asked.

"Sometimes," he admitted. "But then I think about all the people who would be so proud to see how I've carried on their way of life in the middle of the 21st century. I think about how they lived their daily lives. I think about how much fun it is to look at ants and plant gardens and doctor sick trees. So simple and so fulfilling."

"If you like it so much, then why haven't you moved to the country instead of staying in town?" I asked.

"Oh, don't get me wrong. I dream of coming out here all the time when I'm somewhere else. But I have too much work to do and too many obligations at this point, I guess."

Something about our conversation reminded me of that house—my house--again. It was the only way I could relate to what Henry was saying. But my house was verdant and green and full of maternal vitality. It gave you the feeling of solitude without actually being too far from everything and I thought a person could go there seeking genuine inner peace and find it. Solitude didn't necessarily have to mean physical separation, after all. This cabin was shrunken in upon itself, isolated, and built upon dead growth. Henry was looking toward a past that was buried in our national consciousness and working furiously to resurrect it. I think he came here looking for peace, but he didn't strike me as the kind of man who would ever find it. I did, however, respect him for trying.

But I couldn't really believe that he had made plans to move here. He was naturally pedantic and enjoyed feeling superior to people, and he probably believed it made him more interesting to have this unique part of himself that he could pull out when he was lecturing people on the sins of our times. I think he was probably right about it making him more interesting. I had been attracted to his mindfulness, to the serious thinker and the idealist in him. But what had impressed others was that he must have been a man who actually lived by his morals. After all, he could prove it by the tangible fact of this cabin. It didn't hurt that he appeared boyish and athletic as a result, either. I had heard certain women comment upon how tan he was and how young he looked for his age. I was sure he liked that too. It was the truth.

I finally had the nerve to ask him outright what the plan was for the weekend. He shrugged.

"I've already told you," he said stonily.

Digging through my book bag which I had packed for the occasion, I held out a peace offering.

"I brought us these Sudoku books. I remember you suggesting I try it. I thought we might have some down time."

"I love Sudoku. It's the masculine version of the crossword. You should do some so you could learn to think logically like a man," he said jokingly.

"Don't get me started—" I began, but he leaned into me and kissed me passionately.

"I know, I know. I'm just teasing. Thank you. We can work on these in a while. I have some stuff to do around here first." He rose from the bed and as I was about to get up to help him, he held up a warning hand.

"I'm just going to get all the rest of our stuff from the truck and the groceries for dinner."

"You don't need help?"

"I can handle it."

Not knowing what to do with myself, I took out more lotion and rubbed it all over again. My skin was still scaly in some areas, like it was getting ready to peel. After that, I turned to the first puzzle in one of the books, grabbed a pencil, and began trying to fit the numbers into the grid. It was really easy. There were only a few empty spaces to fill. I was triumphant when I finished. Henry had just come back with his hands full.

"I did it!"

"Already? What level?"

"Very Easy."

"Oh, that explains it. Put the book away and come help me for a minute."

Once we got everything situated and music was playing softly, and dinner had been made and eaten, Henry grabbed the other Sudoku book and completed two puzzles almost immediately with a pen.

"See? These are insultingly easy!"

"Ugh. I didn't say I was the best in the world. I just wanted you to know I finished one."

"Yeah, yeah. We need some more wood."

"Okay. I'm freezing, so that sounds great." All evening I had shivered uncontrollably. The stove's fading warmth hadn't provided much relief, but I hadn't wanted to say so.

"If you're cold, I have the perfect idea. This will warm you up."

He came over to me and kissed me erotically. His aftershave was still fragrant. I was still unsure of how I felt about him, but we were here, and he felt so good, and he wanted me and I wanted him. So we had each other. He was always rough and dominant and wild in bed with me, but I knew he loved me to be soft and receptive and tender with him. There was never much question about our roles.

Afterwards, he left to go chop wood after he had run me a hot bath. I loved hot baths. Whenever I felt upset, I could feel the water running over me, pleasantly stinging my skin, and it could wash away my physical pains, my mental anguish, and sometimes even my broken heart. It gave one the feeling of having a sympathetic nurse who regulated your temperature, fussed over your welfare, and tried to make you as comfortable as possible. Even the creeping rust on the sides of the tub didn't seem to matter.

He came back in to get some drinking water after just a few minutes and grinned when he saw how I was enjoying myself.

"You like baths, huh?"

"I like water in general. It's calming."

"I have a lot of friends who are really into fishing. They say the same thing about the water. I was talking to Jada about this not too long ago. We were talking about fishing and water and all that. Yeah, and somehow, blue lobsters came up."

I wondered when he and Jada had had time to talk, but I figured he had probably run into her or done some work for her.

He continued, "She had never heard of a blue lobster. She didn't even think they existed. Like I would make that up. She said she wanted to eat one to see if it tasted any different. But it's so rare that only one in two million lobsters is blue, so the likelihood of that happening isn't very high. Anyway, it's due to a genetic mutation. The more it molts, the bluer it gets."

"Oh, I think it's cool. It's like some people's Holy Grail, then?"

"I guess. I think it's stupid, but that's just my opinion. I told her they all turn red when you boil them, so what's the difference?"

I looked down at my hands. They were pink from the heat of the water, which was rapidly cooling at this point.

"Henry, you have to let people have their own opinions about things. I think I'd like to see a blue lobster, too."

There were fifty different scenarios in which I might have appropriately presented slightly altered versions of Stella to someone. We had all done this to some degree: it was actually a healthy social requisite that we did. What disturbed me was that what I would have considered my "true" self was vastly different from those selves I sensed in other people where I lived. I guessed I felt like the blue lobster Henry talked about—when you boiled it down, we were all essentially the same, but it was obvious to everyone there was something different about the way I thought. I would have loved to submerge under the protective spangles of a sympathetic deep blue ocean—then maybe those old sunburnt fishermen couldn't find me, holding me up with white stripy hands for a sudden but conclusive review of my authenticity and a chance at glory. I, too, "should have been a pair of ragged claws scuttling across the floors of silent seas."

"On second thought," I said, "I think the lobster would like to be left in peace. Never mind."

Henry laughed. "It's just a lobster. Who cares?"

He really got under my skin.

"I do. You are reckless with other people's feelings sometimes."

Scoffing, he said, "Like you aren't? I've spent the last few years working on this cabin and you didn't even tell me you liked it!"

"I did too. I told you I did."

"You didn't mean it."

What he meant by this, I thought, was that I didn't stroke his ego and tell him how impressive his respectable experiment and his detachment from society were, how special he must have been to have done this all by himself. He wore this cabin very much like I thought Lorena wore her crosses. The shape of his philosophy was alright: circular and interconnected. It was the blinding hard shade that was all wrong. How could an infinite number of diamonds fit into a finite number of pre-made settings? It couldn't be done without discarding innumerable imperfect stones, and the final product would be garish to behold, a monstrosity that only someone like Lorena would wear, probably with a disorienting yellow dress.

"Henry," I said coldly, as I drained the bath and began to dress myself, "what you want is to teach somebody, but I'm already a teacher."

"What an ego you have! I brought you out here to show you a good time. I ran your bath for you. I built these walls you're staying in. Your insinuations about me are absurd. If you'll excuse me, Your Highness, I have to go finish chopping wood so I can heat this place for you tonight!" Ruffled, he flew out. I chortled aloud as I thought of quite a few rejoinders but recognizing both their tardiness and their futility, I decided to detach from the oxymoronic icy heat I felt with a few more Sudoku puzzles. Henry's I-pod was still on shuffle, and an upbeat song helped me lose myself in thought.

Placing my pen absent-mindedly in between my teeth, I set to work thinking about the patterns of given numbers on the grid of an Easy level puzzle. Within minutes, I had solved it effortlessly. Always up for a challenge, I moved on to a Medium level puzzle. It only took me a few minutes longer than the first did to complete. Proud of myself, and really enjoying the feeling of accomplishment each neat completed puzzle gave me, I flipped to a Hard puzzle in the book. I found that this would be a lot tougher than the first two right away. Trying to attack it from many different perspectives, I plodded my way through most of it.

Before I could finish it, though, Henry stomped into the room.

"Look, Stella. This is silly dramatic stuff. We always seem to get to each other like this. Let's just forget it and move on this time, okay?"

I had honestly forgotten where I was for a moment and what had been going on outside my own mind. "Okay," I said, trying to recover quickly. Really, I couldn't for the life of me remember what we had even been fighting about. I just wanted to get back to the grid I had been trying to fill in without seeming rude.

Luckily, Henry must have truly meant that he wanted to move on this time. After starting a crackling fire in the stove, he came over to me and coarsely rubbed my back up and down, peering over my shoulder to see what I was working on.

"You're on Hard already? It took me days to get to the Hard ones the first time!" Though I think he intended this statement to be positive encouragement, within moments, the import of what he had said must have taken hold of him. His jaw set in a hard line. His eyebrows furrowed. I had only glanced up in appreciation of his comment, and with no small amount of surprise, but when I saw his face, I figured what his next move would be.

Sure enough, he wiped his brow, picked up the other copy of the Sudoku book he had set on the edge of the bed, and with an obviously strained casualness, began to work an Expert level puzzle. He was so predictable. Unfazed, I continued filling in the last few sub-grids and took extra pleasure in announcing that I was finished.

"Should I move on to Expert?" I asked innocently.

"They're really difficult. If you think you can do it," he said.

"Challenge accepted. I think I have a natural flair for this game," I said. Looking over to see what his reaction would be, I noticed he was completing his puzzle in pen. Trying to make a concession, I told him that I thought he must be great at this game if he was confident enough to fill in the squares the first time he attempted a guess with permanent ink.

He laughed. "When you've done these as long as I have, you notice patterns and it's pretty easy to fill in the right numbers."

"I see," I said to him, but I thought to myself that I would take deftness before overconfidence any day. If he hadn't experienced any repercussions, though, maybe this crude method worked for him. We worked silently for a few minutes, except for the sounds of heavy breathing, writing, and the crackle of the fire in the stove.

"See?" he said. "Done!" He was jubilant.

"I just finished mine, too," I said.

"Let me see." He grabbed it away from me. Using his eagle eye to try to spot an error, he had to admit that I had told the truth.

"Okay. A little clean fun. What do you say?" He eyed me maliciously. "Let's race. Expert Level. First one to win gets gloating privileges."

I wasn't sure I wanted to engage Henry in his ridiculous competitive endeavor. But I would be damned before I would let Henry believe he was better than me without indisputable proof. I wanted nothing more than to poke a hole through his inflated ego because his challenge had just reminded me why I had been angry with him in the first place.

"You might want to use pencil for this one," I couldn't help saying. I wasn't normally passive-aggressive, but we were out in the forest all by ourselves, after all.

"I'm fine."

"Okay. I'm just saying."

"Turn the page. Let's do the one on page 66... Yes, that one. Okay. Ready? GO!"

Henry's hand was flying across the page before mine had even touched the pencil to one square. I was calculating in my mind; Henry was asserting his knowledge one region at a time. I was beginning to panic, filling in one light square after another with my guesses, darkening them each time I knew for sure that's where each number belonged. At that rate, though, Henry would be finished months before I was. I was stuck in one region, trying to find any way to logically deduce which numbers belonged in which order in the remaining white spaces. Suddenly, Henry threw his book so close to me that I almost got hit in the face.

"Damn it! Goddamnit! Ugh!"

"What happened?" I was shocked.

"I'm sorry, Stella. I didn't mean for it to hit you. I was just..." His face was scarlet.

"Well, it's alright. Get your book. I'm gaining on you," I said with an impish grin.

He glowered at me and abruptly left again. Confused, I picked up his book and opened it to the crease to see what had caused his outburst. There were violent scratches all over the page. He had written and re-written over a few squares so that the numbers he had finally meant to go there were merely alluded to in the margins. All of the squares were filled in except for the last two. Checking over his work, I realized he had two sevens on the same row, and a couple of numbers were left out of other columns. At first, I was exultant. I had won! Then a sick feeling pervaded my body as I realized that I had actually lost, only in a different sense. Henry could not be bested. If someone else won fair and square, he changed the rules. He had a compulsion to impose his will on everything, including all the numbers in the grid. But some things wouldn't be penned in that way. I wouldn't be; I couldn't continue going on like this. I didn't like who I became when I was with him. He forced me to see myself differently, from his own perspective. I didn't like being forced, and I didn't like what I saw.

The more I thought about how unfairly he had treated me, the more I believed that though this instance was small enough in the chronology of our relationship, its significance was colossal. It was a litmus test of the acidity of our chemistry, and the strip came out unmistakably bright, as it would have done in any other random incident in which we were involved. And with that, I decided, I was done.

I was on my way out to find Henry to inform him of the fact, believing he was probably pouting close enough to the cabin for me to find him. Before I left the warmth of the cabin, however, a haunting song came on in Italian. It sounded melancholic and otherworldly. I was apprehended by the minor chords and the chilling melody. I had to keep listening to it just to get a feel for where it was going musically. My eyes fell on a bunch of white mums in a vase next to the door. I had an epiphany.

I didn't know if it was the song, the mums, or the combination, but suddenly, I knew. Henry had brought Jada here to his cabin. I knew it positively because I had seen those same flowers at the church and at her house. Henry did have a landscaping business, but those flowers had a certain feminine fragrance and arrangement to them that could only belong to her. The perfidy the twine bow around the mouth of that vase revealed! I thought back, recognizing all the signs I had missed before.

"Sai, la gente e' sola..."

As from the darkness, the song played slowly and achingly on. I was temporarily immobilized, but in my brain, thoughts were materializing and lacing themselves into a tangible pattern maybe more quickly than they ever had. They were having or had had an affair. What tense was it? Did it even matter? I stopped breathing for a moment. I wasn't quite disgusted, but I was unsettled and inexplicably relieved. So many mysteries, little moments of discomfort, disparate micro-expressions, were unscrambled; so many more mysteries surfaced at the same time. I determined that my next course of action would be to get to the bottom of all of them if I could. I knew which mystery I was most interested in illuminating. The shadow of a shadow…. Yes, the entire Bludworth family had their secrets, didn't they?

As the song crescendoed, "Tu, tu chi sei diverso….Almeno tu nell'universo…." Henry walked in. He looked much smaller than when he had walked out, though his chest was puffed up in anger and embarrassment. I knew what he was going to say. I was going to let him say it.

"Stella. This just isn't working. Things between us are so difficult all the time. I just don't think it should be this hard, do you? We want different things." His voice was pleading, and his face was a mixture of fury and shame.

"Yes, you're right," I heard myself saying. "We want different things. You should find somebody more like you. Someone who likes to smile a lot and maybe who has your interest in flowers." I smirked.

"What do you mean?" Henry grabbed my arm.

"Nothing." I removed his hand matter-of-factly from my person. "Simply that you are right." I pretended to let him have the power position. He needed it more. Plus, it would only make things easier for me in the long run.

He stood looking at me, dazed, unmoving.

"Well, don't just stand there. Shall we go?" I smiled and, with great poise, began collecting my personal belongings.

We packed our things and were on the road within ten minutes. Neither of us spoke all the way home.

WINTER

CHAPTER SEVEN

"If you want to tell people the truth, make them laugh; otherwise, they'll kill you." –Oscar Wilde

December-

*E*very city is a lighthouse. It doesn't matter if it's New York or Seattle or Minneapolis or Dallas. People congregate in cities to make a lasting impression on each other, to happily and conveniently abide together. More boats answer the call, more people shifting uneasily, more red traffic lights and sirens and hot breaths of neighbors. Mother dearest lays out her terms: my name alone shall remain—you are too menny. There are no stars here. An Indian woman in a red sarong weaves her children through the congestion on the sidewalk. They walk into a dirty pizza kitchen. In front, a young man has trouble parallel parking his car in the lines. I become afraid: I realize I am nameless.

I had been feeling a nagging, grayish gloominess for days. Everywhere I looked there were barren trees and brown silhouettes of buildings and people bundled up in themselves. It was the season of frosty breath and smokestacks mingling together in a dull indifferent sky. One chilling afternoon I came upon the Mixmaster again, paralyzed by the rapidity of the confusing traffic changes that were made in the name of progress. Construction sites were raised and torn down as rapidly and as flimsily as a traveling carnival; exits closed, detours announced, and mere traffic signs unable to keep up with the furious pace of the city; and no GPS would be able to help you get back to where you needed to go if you chose the wrong fork of a highway, misread a sign, passed an unmarked exit. Many of these bridges crisscrossed over each other in the air, erected higher and higher to accommodate the sheer number of multi-directional highways that were smashed together at a convening point. As I traveled upwards on one of these bridges at almost ninety degrees, I felt the dread of being lurched jerkily upward on a terrifying roller coaster just before the stomach-dropping nosedive. And the dizzying loops and twists of this concrete labyrinth driven at seventy miles an hour were truly death-defying.

After being tail-gated by a few trucks in a hurry and honked at by cars whizzing around me, I made it safely past the most congested and convoluted part. I realized that I cared more about my survival than inconveniencing the people behind me. My heartbeat was erratic and my palms were still sweaty. I had been gripping the steering wheel with them tightly (while intermittently wiping them on my jeans so they wouldn't slip off), as though this one simple action would tighten my control over the situation. It was merely instinctual; I knew I could just as easily make a fatal mistake on the Mixmaster while paying attention as I could while playing on my phone.

I wondered if they'd ever stop construction on the roads. As soon as they finished one project, they began plans to tear down or reconstruct ten more. With nostalgia, I remembered the area as it had looked a few years ago. The city and its surrounding suburbs were no longer the same places my friends and I went out in at night during our college years. Everything was different now, and what wasn't changed felt different anyway. Though I had always tightened my grip on the wheel a little as my car mounted the pinnacle of some overpass, I remember that it had seemed a lot easier then to skyrocket through the maze, rolling my eyes impatiently as I zoomed around the creeping mass transit buses in the right-hand lane. We complained back then, whole carloads of us, that they should consider adding new highways, giving us easier access to our favorite places and wider lanes to help with congestion. We just hadn't lived through years of interminable gridlock yet.

I laughed to myself then, grateful that I was by myself and hadn't voiced that line of thinking to anyone else. They'd probably tell me that I sounded just like one of those coffee-drinking, chain-smoking old men who told stories to an audience comprised of other old men about the good old days, sending up a collective wail about the evils of the modern world.

But there were so many of those groups of old men in Texas, so many of them everywhere. It got me thinking again about those rolling hills, those waves of generations at odds with each other because one wanted a chance to leave their mark on the world and the other didn't want the mark they had already left destroyed. Soon enough, these older generations must say to themselves, the world will forget I was here—there will be no trace of me, of my generation, of my civilization, even my way of life. These policies, these landmarks, these traditions I have fought tooth and nail to create, to improve, to honor—I have poured my entire being into the blankness of my time—all my eggs in one basket—I cannot watch them pale before my eyes. Not while I live. The young will have their time. And then they will understand. So they will say in their turn. And so I had already begun to say to myself.

Hoping to lighten my mood, I called Orlando. A few hours later, I found myself watching him walk toward me in the very expensive Italian restaurant he'd suggested downtown, his very presence evaporating every concern except how I was going to get home.

Orlando was no blushing violet. At 6'3, he was slender and yet powerfully built. He had a strong jaw and, though he wasn't much over thirty, his thick dark hair was multi-colored, spackled with gray and white, which only added to his well-designed appearance. He was capable of an intensity that made his whole body concentrate itself into a pointy cusp, and his palpable strain in holding himself back from unexpectedly lobbing forward was intimidating. When he was in this state, the crescents of his smoky quartz eyes became illuminated by the totality of his absorption. As he whisked into view, I saw he was wearing a ridiculous long winter coat over an impeccable suit. He threw off the dense coat with a flourish and seated himself across from me at the inconspicuous table I had chosen next to a window.

"This isn't Paris and it isn't 1882," I said sweetly.

"It doesn't mean we can't appreciate style," he returned with a snap, patting down his coat against his chair. "And I'm always going more for *Midnight in Paris* than… well, now, wait a minute. Oscar Wilde's Paris wouldn't be a bad place to be. I could always use a little hottie like Bosie in my life."

"Who said you would be Wilde?" I joked.

"His friends said he was 'contaminating and self-indulgent.' I'll indulge myself on this one and don't you contaminate it for me."

"This place is beautiful. Toto, I don't think we're in Texas anymore," I joked. As I took in the glamorous décor, I felt like an old Hollywood starlet. Thick, oversized Mediterranean-style columns joined the high ceilings to the plush eggshell-colored marble of the entryway flooring. We walked into the large center room, upon which the largest lighting fixture I had ever seen, more artistic than functional, hung down like an ancient highly-wrought god. The lighting was dim and sexy, the plump dark blue cushions on the chairs complemented the contemporary- shaped silver lamps hanging every few feet on the walls, and each table was perfectly set with fancy folded napkins and a tasteful candle-lit centerpiece atop a thick white tablecloth. The rich dark woods of the furniture and the floors endowed an air of sophistication to the interior that both charmed and intimidated.

"Beauty can always be found by those who seek it out," he replied. "In other words, by those who are willing and able to pay for it. Besides, location isn't as important now that everyone travels and retail chains are playing red rover with mom and pop stores across the planet."

The waiter, an older gentleman wearing a tidy black apron, proffered our menus with matching tidy movements. Orlando immediately handed back the wine list and ordered a bottle of Barolo Monfortino Riserva for the table.

"Christmas is coming, the goose is getting fat," he hummed as the waiter walked away. Without any segue, he said, "You know, people fight about the silliest things."

Didn't I know? The memory of Henry's scrunched up face sent a pang through me. My disgust with him over lobsters and Sudoku must have seemed questionable at best to the uninformed observer.

"Take this wine I've just ordered us, for instance. There are actually Barolo *wars*. Once again, we have the traditionalists versus the modernists. You can guess where I would fall on that spectrum, cosmopolitan that I am," Orlando began.

I raised my eyebrows. "I don't know anything about wine," I admitted, "but here's my guess: that little bottle is out of my price range," and as I scanned the menu I added, "like everything else here."

"Don't worry about it. It's on me. Get anything you want. I'm in a generous mood this evening," he smirked.

I emitted an audible sigh of relief, a quick thank you, and then said with mock-seriousness, "Now, I'd be a polite dinner guest and ask you to continue killing me softly with your pretentious prattling, but I have too much to tell you."

"Estelle, you should never interrupt an animal when it's eating, an addict when he's using, or a narcissist when he's pontificating. Haven't you learned anything in the past thirty years?"

"Ha. I'm halfway serious. I've got gossip and drama for you tonight. I'll save the good stuff for after dinner."

Orlando thanked the waiter, who had returned with the wine and begun to pour it into our sparkling glasses. We ordered our meals and brusquely returned to our personal universe.

"Oh, this is delicious, Orlando!" I exclaimed when I had tasted the wine.

"You're surprised? My counsel is sought after the world over. And you thought I was just being pretentious when I tried to tell you about it. I am truly interested in the maturation process of such exquisite grapes!"

"Here we go again," I told him. "I'll leave the 'maturation process' to you and just enjoy the alcoholic results."

"And as for Luchresi, he cannot distinguish Sherry from Amontillado...." He murmured.

"What?" I didn't quite catch what he said.

"Spoken like a true Texan," he retorted.

"Oh-- come on. We both have our ideological and practical issues with this area. But that's kind of what I wanted to talk to you about. I found a house," I told him. "It's not too far from here, but it's quiet and calm and near the lake. There are trees. I'm not even sure it's still on the market but I've been thinking about it a lot lately."

"I'm not against the idea. In fact... yes, I think you could do that. You should." He was processing what I told him and finalizing his judgment as he spoke.

"Really? I thought you would be disgusted. I was bracing myself for a speech about how I'll never meet my potential or how ugly the landscape is or about the travesties of rural living!"

"While I do undoubtedly agree with all of that, it all comes down to your book bag. Let me explain. I'm surprised you didn't bring it with you this evening. It's a surrogate home for you, I think. You've been so uncertain, carrying around your now literal baggage, waiting for a place to finally set it down, that you haven't given yourself a chance to breathe. And while, in my opinion, there are much more beautiful places in the world, you haven't really enjoyed the beauty surrounding you right here because you're still waiting for something that probably isn't going to come. At least not like you think it is. We may not live in Paris. It may not be 1882 anymore. But Stella, we can still have a nice dinner and a lot of drinks afterwards at a fabulous dive bar around the corner, and you can enjoy it. Wherever you are, you're still there. It doesn't matter where you live. Or when, for that matter. And you will never be happier anywhere else—not even Paris---unless you can accept that life is messy sometimes. Like you. I mean, that dress is hideous but you're still my best friend." He curled up his lip in a smile and blew me a kiss. I looked down. I was wearing a glammed-out dress with an artistically rendered disembodied head floating across my torso.

"I'll help you decorate. You know what Wilde says... 'One should either become a work of art or wear it.' Seeing as how you aren't wearing it tonight"--he gestured to my dress-- "you should definitely become it. I think you are well on your way. Each person you meet is a material for your house. Build your home here. I'll find a way to make my own mark, maybe with sunflowers or peacock feathers or blue china!" Orlando giggled while he drained his second glass of wine.

I warned him jokingly, "You come near me with peacock feathers and you're not even getting an address."

"That's what *he* said. This from the woman who wore those awful peacock feather earrings that time we went dancing."

"Oh, God, I'd forgotten about that! And they got so soaked by the end of the night that they were stuck together and molting onto my shirt! Maybe that's why I reacted like I did! Subconscious memories."

"Probably. That night haunts my subconscious too, mainly because of my awful date—I can't remember his name, though. Oh! Our food is here, and just in time. I take back what I said earlier. It *does* matter when you live. I miss the days when you could light up a cigarette at your table without anyone batting an eye."

We were the perfect picture of friendship. I could hear the beautiful arias playing softly, which subtly colored our feelings on the subjects we talked about throughout our meal; when a joyful song played, we laughed and quipped as we drank our expensive Italian wine; when an emotional love song emanated through the speakers, we reminisced and savored another sinful bite of Tuscan food.

"You have to 'fare la scarpetta'!" he exclaimed near the end of our meal.

"I have no idea what that means, but I'm certain I'm about to find out," I said with an eye-roll.

"Language is such an interesting study. The Italians have a specific phrase for the act of sopping up the leftover sauce from a meal with bread. Fare la scarpetta, or in English, 'do the little shoe.' Skate on a plate, if you will. Haha. I learned that in Florence. I wonder if this means they hate leftovers or if they have shoe fetishes. Either way, I heartily approve. Now don't let your ten dollar sauce remnants go to waste."

"I can't eat another bite," I whined. I pinched off a piece of bread obligingly, but he slapped it out of my fist.

"Stella, it's okay to indulge, but as a single woman, you have to keep your girlish figure. You never know when having a small waist might pay off."

When we had finished, paid, and walked out into the cold December evening, Orlando donned his coat and removed a polished silver case from within.

"It's just a short walk to the bar we're going to. Cigarette?" he cordially offered as he hunted with oversized hands for just the right one from the pack.

"Why not?" I rationalized, remembering the pleasure that my last cigarette had brought me—the glow of the tobacco leaves burning themselves up in my fingers as I talked to Heath, the rich smoke even more gloriously enjoyable as I readily inhaled because of the self-indulgent nature of the act, the inherent self-destruction suggested by it.

He cocked an eyebrow, lit both of our cigarettes, smiled coyly, and slung his arm around my shoulder as he puffed on his treat.

"Look at all the lights. They are very tastefully decorated here. Those trees—" He pointed to some large oak trees whose branches and trunks had been wrapped with magical white lights. "They look charmed."

"Well, the city spared no expense, I'm sure. This is the nicest part of town. If you go into some of the neighborhoods, you'll find blow-up Santas and reindeer wearing cowboy hats. Oh—and don't forget the knock-off nativity scenes where Mary is Mrs. Claus or the Three Wise Men are elves. The serious ones are even worse. Joseph looks like a melted terrorist and Mary's lips are scarlet as a whore's."

Orlando guffawed. "Estelle, I am detecting that you don't like Christmas! Can it be that my best friend is a"-- he paused in mock horror-- "a *Grinch?*"

"I don't know exactly. I guess I'm just dreading so many things. This time of year is worse. Maybe it's the traffic. It's nice walking out here with you now, but imagine being in that traffic if we hadn't taken cabs." I pointed to the street where cars were lined bumper to bumper.

"Yes, traffic is always a nuisance. But there is a greater and more profound reason to struggle through holiday traffic; everyone is getting to someone they care about most in the world—and not just to get together, but to celebrate being alive, to be in communion with friends and family and eventually leave the roadblocks and the traffic and the noise in the past."

"Well, aren't you just Mr. *It's A Wonderful Life* all of a sudden? Where's your family, Orlando? I've never heard you talk much about them."

"I'm in a, uh—" He stopped. "I don't really want to get into it. My job takes up a lot of my time. I envy *you*, though. You have a few weeks off for the holidays. It must be nice. I'll tell you, if it weren't for the salary, I might have considered being a teacher."

"If you weren't so hell-bent on hob-knobbing, you would have all the time in the world to yourself. You can't tell me that bankers don't have enough time off to go home to their families for the holidays."

"I'm intelligent enough to recognize the necessity of networking. And it has served me well. Better than you know," he muttered.

"Okay. Welp. I still hate the holidays." I threw up my hands. We walked in silence for a few minutes. Considering why I had such violent feelings, I felt my anxiety level rising.

Around this time of year, I had often heard complaints about how Christmas had become meaningless because it was so commercialized. I thought that commercialization was exactly what made Christmas so unattainably merry. Every Christmas song on the radio inspired sugarplum visions of happy families caroling together; every Christmas candle flame immediately transformed a dreary middle-class three-bedroom directly into a mythical home where cookies never stopped baking and candy canes never got broken; every advertisement featured generous cups of Coca-Cola cheer and the white smiles reminiscent of the good homegrown folks of yore. Stories made the mystical and magical seem possible—they advertised the restoration of the happiness and comfort of our lost youth. And yet those of us who could not summon even the smallest excitement for the nearing of the holiday season felt inadequate somehow, emotionally indigent. We all wanted to believe. The price of that faith, however, was that we chased after those red and white glittering promises which, much like Santa's sleigh or the perfect family experience, were only real in the hope we had of someday catching a glimpse of them.

"Do you see that little place up there? The sign says *A Life and A Lover?*" He closed his eyes as if enraptured and sighed ostentatiously. "It's a little dingier than our dinner environment, but this is about as good as it gets around here if you want to smoke inside, which I definitely do." He looked down at his phone, which was vibrating. He turned it off and continued. "If I owned a bar, I couldn't have chosen a better name myself... though I've hidden away a few ideas just in case."

"Like what?"

"Well it depends on the place. Gay or straight? White or blue collar? However, anything I would open would be classy but decadent. No kitschy stuff. It's a foregone conclusion at a joint called *Third Base* or *Double Wide* that by the time the tab gets paid, someone is going to feel deeply ashamed of themselves. Personally, I always feel ashamed when beauty is entirely absent from an experience. Not of myself, of course."

"Oh, no, of course not," I snorted.

When we went in, the bar was about three-quarters full. We found an empty booth, slid into it, warmed up, and got comfortable. The prospect of more alcohol put us both in better spirits. A waitress came over to take our drink orders. I ordered a whiskey and diet coke and the waitress nodded. Orlando announced that he wanted something more exciting. "A Manhattan? No... a Chancellor Cocktail. Have the bartender look it up if he doesn't know it, please. It's exactly what I need to get the ambience just right in here."

"Hey—*I'm* here. The ambience is already amazing," I said, flaring my nostrils like I always did when I was trying to be funny.

"Like I said, the cocktail, please. And some better company," Orlando teased.

"You let your boyfriend talk to you like that?" the waitress asked.

"Oh, I could never date anyone who is wearing a clothing item with a face that's bigger than mine," Orlando told her with a self-satisfied grin.

"Good one," I admitted, looking down at the floating face on my dress.

The waitress smiled and shook her head. Orlando flirted harmlessly with her and, within moments, she was giggling and making her own jokes to us with shining eyes that promised that we were going to be the center of her universe for the evening.

When she had gone and returned with our drinks, Orlando let me try his obscure cocktail. I told him it was no wonder he liked it—it was sophisticated, complex, and not a little fruity. He threw the orange garnish at me and I feigned resentment.

"I may be mostly sophisticated but I'm not always, you know," he said.

"Yes, I know. And that's one reason you're so damn likeable. You can relate to everyone."

"Oh—I can relate, alright, if that's what you want to call it. I went on vacation recently—"

"You're always disappearing somewhere, aren't you? I wondered where you were off to."

"Sue me. I like to explore the world. I was at a friend's wedding in Mexico. Well, most of the wedding party was older, married, respectable people. Not really my type, in other words. The day before the ceremony, I was lonely and looking for a little company. Company, I repeat." He raised his eyebrows suggestively the second time.

"Yeah, I get it. Go on." I reassured him.

"We were staying at this gorgeous little resort on the beach where only patrons of the hotel could get past security. So I got on Groaner."

I groaned. "Gross. When you told me what that app was, I was disgusted at first, but then I thought—hey, it's revolutionary and kinda useful—and then I just thought 'nah, it's gross,' and I've been thinking that ever since."

"So I got on Groaner," he repeated without missing a beat but with the addition of a smirk, "around midnight after a full day of drinking and found someone local to hook up with. He didn't speak English. Like, at all. Which isn't really relevant to the story or for my purposes either, frankly. I speak enough Spanish to get by, but we didn't meet up for conversation. That's not what Groaner is for. So we were going at it in this dark water and floating out pretty far when out of nowhere this bright light comes on. We swam down the beach because we didn't want to get discovered, of course, but all of a sudden these two men with machine guns came yelling at us to get out. We did, and then we ran away as quickly as we could, or at least I did. I never saw the guy again. The dramatic exit is not to be underestimated, after all, I suppose."

"Orlando. That is crazy. I'm soaking in the crazy unreal aspects of your story right now." I was also soaking up the last bit of whiskey in my drink with my straw. "Mexico is really dangerous right now, you know."

He boldly asserted, "I'm not done. I'm used to danger, anyway. So I go to the wedding next day. During the ceremony I notice my knee is bothering me. After a covert inspection, I see this rash on it, and immediately, I'm thinking, 'Oh my God, I've got flesh eating disease from that poisonous Mexican water,' and I'm convinced it's spreading as I sit there. It's all I can do to not jump up and start screaming, but I make it somehow. I keep calm by drawing a circle around the affected area with an imaginary Sharpie to monitor its spread. As soon as the wedding is over, I grab my friend who has just gotten married and ask him to ask his doctor brother to take a look. He does. Turns out it's rug burn. RUG BURN. That I also, might I add, 'contracted' from a previous Groaner liaison."

"HAHAHA! You. Are. Revolting."

"I know, but I made you laugh." His smirk broadened. His phone vibrated again and he texted someone quickly.

"You always do."

Orlando straightened himself up, set his drink down, then asked me pointedly, "What the hell is going on with you and Henry?"

"How did you know anything was going on?" I asked.

"Because you haven't gushed about him in a while. My eyes are starting to cramp up because they're not used to going this long without the rolls which accompany the mention of his name."

"Why don't you like Henry?"

"The man has an Ego McMuffin for breakfast every day. I'm all for narcissism and vanity, don't get me wrong, but his is the dangerous kind. The oppressive kind."

"You know, I figured that out for myself, actually. And there's something else."

I told him about what had happened in the cabin and about my suspicions that he and Jada were having an affair. He leaned in, sucked in a breath, and drew out a "Whaaaaaat?" in a high-pitched squeak. "You know, I'm not surprised. Lots of women have the Bible in one hand and a carefully titled book like *A Missionary's Position* in the other.... Except it's rarely about evangelizing." We both tittered.

"Gail!" he called to the waitress, summoning her with his hand. "It just got real in here. We need another!" Three tables away, Gail, with whom Orlando was apparently on a first name basis, nodded her head, yelled, "Gotcha!" and disappeared to get us more drinks.

"But here's where things get, um, complicated," I began.

"Hang on... my phone again," he interrupted, looking down, frowning, and decidedly ignoring it.

"What's up with that?" I asked. His phone had vibrated almost incessantly since he had arrived. I thought of how often Jada's phone had distracted her when we were together and wondered, feeling momentarily ill, how often, unbeknownst to me, the person on the other end had been Henry.

"Oh, just the last few victims of my carnal embrace," he joked. "I can't be tied down just yet, but they don't stop trying."

"How could anyone resist you?" I asked, putting away my morbid thoughts and smiling widely at Orlando.

"They can't," he asserted before taking a big swig of his cocktail, "...apparently." He set it down and made a contented noise. Then he focused in on me, that palpable strain the only thing keeping him from blowing my hair back with his intensity. "Now tell me all about the complication... I'm dying to hear."

"Well, I got this weird thing in my box at work the other day." I fished around in my purse and pulled out what I was looking for. It was a gorgeous antique key. I put in on the table between us. We hovered over it like it was a problem that needed solving.

"Mmm... mysterious. Delectable. What does it mean?"

"With this, too." I pulled out the poem that had accompanied it. I read it to Orlando, who was at rapt attention:

"The Old Key"
My dear can you hear
The tik-tok of history clinking against your breast
The thirteenth door of the thirteenth floor
There's a lamppost past the cupboard
It only makes sense in the twilight glints
Of the periwinkle past--of
The mind, once upon a time
Put anything in it and it comes out real
You know we have to dream to find what we mean.
But this key-- this key
This old soul winking from the secret bowl
A strange surface from an ancient shore
Its owl face leaves a curious trace
Of its intention to release or fasten tight--
Turn a lock wind back the clock
Everything that can go behind the curtain is a sinister power.
How many have died who have touched it and cried
"Vanity, vanity, all is vanity"?
They tested their mettle and a part of each settles
Inside the number 13.
Imagine-- how tragic—you use all the magic
To see that what's behind the lock is your own dark backyard
The rabbit- hole filled, the moment distilled
And this old bronze key alone to remind you.

"Well?" he asked expectantly.

"Well, I think it's from Heath Bludsworth--"

"Jada's husband? You think he's trying to tell you something?"

"I don't know. I think he's starting a game with me. I mean, I don't know who else it would be from."

"You mean, he's flirting with you?"

"Maybe. I mean, this poem is pretty dark, and I've got no idea what this key might actually open. Probably nothing. It's too old, and I think it's meant to just stand for the shattered illusions of the speaker of the poem. But I understand pain. Heath knows that—he told me so once. He's got the most haunted look in his eyes--ghostly, I'd say. And they are so blue they're almost white. It's like he's got a quiet desperation to be near me, to connect. But now what? And is it really fair to think about Jada's husband in such a way even though she's got something going with Henry? And what if anyone found out? "

"Okay, Stella," he said, his tone shifting to a genuine seriousness, "Here's how it is. As long as you don't say it, you can still do it, whatever it is, even if everyone already knows. All too often I've maintained wonderful working relationships with people who keep what they think about me under the surface, and then… one inevitable moment of pronunciation and their sense of decency won't allow them to turn a blind eye anymore. You sound about a breath away from something wonderfully horrible happening to you. I envy you. Oh, to have an illicit affair that is both toxic and intoxicating at the same time!"

"So you think I should indulge myself, as you say?"

"Yes darling, but all the same, I'd like you to be careful. It's dangerous to catch any tiger by the tail. If he hollers, let him go."

"I've just never thought of myself as *that* kind of woman. I don't know if I could go through with an actual…" I choked on the word *affair*. "On the other hand, I don't know if I can stop myself." I pulled at the napkin under my drink and tore bits of it off as I talked.

"But you are that kind of woman… if you want to be."

"What do you mean?"

"We all tell stories to ourselves about ourselves in a way. And to others, for that matter. It's not exactly lying, but it's definitely an illusion of sorts because we believe it. Now you can't escape illusions because of how our mind works. But you can learn to recognize them. It's like me and this drink. I am literally sitting here drinking it (and loving it). But in my mind, I'm James Bond or The Most Interesting Man in the World. I am consciously not in a Tennessee Williams play or a train wreck of a child celebrity has-been because those aren't the stories I'm telling myself." As an immediate afterthought, he shuddered and said, 'That *would* be an illusion. Get it?" He winked and sloshed the remains of his drink against the glass.

"Well, metaphors have always been valid tools for communication," I began. But Orlando cut me off.

"No. Not tools for communication. Our actual thought patterns. Rhetorical theory-- uh--Recent therapy strategies--" He stumbled for a way to convey his meaning.

"Look here. My point is that everything is metaphorical, and thus illusory to some degree. If you can recognize *that*--that I am a metaphor-- then you can spare yourself the suffering that comes along with taking anything too literally. Some have good intentions when they perpetuate the literality of a metaphor—The Boogie Man is coming to get you if you don't behave, I will love you for better or for worse, everything happens for a reason; others try to get you to buy a house you can't afford, plastic surgery that doesn't make you happy, or insurance that won't pay out in the end anyway. Either way, we can't do anything about the illusions we all live with. It is within us to yearn for the wonder of a fairy tale. After all, we are all of us composed of stardust, Stella. But we are never happy with the results of a mythology once told; we must then try to live by it, make sense of our reality from it, and we inevitably strive for Godhood in the process. If you want to be moving forward, you don't have the luxury of being timeless. It's a beautiful sentiment, but timeless is another word for inert or dead. We can, however, take the facts of life as they happen and decide which metaphors we will use to shape our existence." He looked down at his suit and brushed off an imaginary piece of lint. He looked back up into my face and said, "That's the key. It's all a metaphor." He cocked his head to the side and gazed at me with intensity.

I jumped. *It's all a metaphor?* I thought to myself. Those four words, innocuous in themselves, were like little individual missiles threatening to explode into unfortunate realizations in my mind when Heath had whispered them to me in the dark recesses of his house. I had tried to dodge them, but the more I struggled to disentangle myself, the more they clung to my thoughts. I didn't know what Heath meant by them, but their enigmatic nature only increased the intensity with which I received them. Orlando glared at me with naked ferocity for a moment in response to my confusion and then forced a laugh.

"Did I say something?"

"N-No... I was just thinking about what you said," I stuttered. "So Walt Whitman was kind of right when he said he was large and contained multitudes? Because we are all that way? Everyone and no one at the same time?"

"Absolutely. Whitman blurred the lines between himself and others by conceiving of himself as a fluid concept, one which accepted all the selves he had been and at the same time made room for endless possibilities of future selves. It was then easy for him to see other people as just another possibility of what he himself might have been or might become."

So the generations fighting against each other, the different factions and sections that gridlocked real progress could be seen as one person fighting against himself, I thought. Out loud I said, "Society attacks itself like a person with an autoimmune disease. And no one is immune."

"Ha ha. So true." He only half-heartedly responded because he was texting someone back and in the short silence, I relived the moment that I felt Heath's hot breath against my ear. Just the thought of it made my body pulse and grow warmer. I knew I wanted his mouth close to me again and that I was too intrigued to stop whatever might happen between us. I wondered if I should tell Orlando about the strange coincidence but decided against it. He would think I was a little too eccentric even for an English teacher if I went into metaphysical musings about signs from the universe. There was a stirring at the front of the bar. The band was being announced and people were getting a little more rowdy, anticipating the excitement live music would bring to the scene.

"Well, Jada did make it a little easier when she talked about heathenism needing to be stamped out. What kind of woman talks like that? Queen Victoria? And starting her own brand of heathenism on the side?"

"Honey, that isn't her own brand. That brand of heathenism has been going on since the dawn of time," Orlando yelled. The band had begun. They opened with a Las Vegas lounge version of Nine Inch Nails' "Closer."

We tried to continue our conversation, but the content was too personal to blast, so our attempts to talk in the same vein were aborted quickly. After a couple of minutes, Orlando turned his back to me so he could watch the band perform. He listened for a few moments, then turned back around and shouted, "Who is this YOU that everyone keeps talking about in their songs? They must be a suave bastard. Everyone keeps singing about how YOU has done them wrong or they regret how they mistreated poor YOU but they have learned the error of their ways and want YOU back. Really, I must meet this fascinating muse!" Gail had brought us more drinks while his back was turned, so our laughter turned quickly to appreciation and the night began to slip into fast-forward.

We got up and met some people who were having a good time, Orlando charming them all. Even the men were impressed by his ability to make people feel entirely at their ease. Orlando commanded a room; that was certain. When the band took a break, he performed an impromptu lip synch to the jukebox's "Don't Stop Believin'" on one couple's table, replete with brilliant dance moves and perfectly timed humorous additions of his own. They were thrilled and when he was finished gave him hugs and high-fives. There was applause from the small audience he had garnered. At one point, he tried to pull me into his skit, but I wasn't drunk enough yet.

When we got back to our booth thirty minutes before closing time, I began to feel anxious again, looking around at the very crowded bar and the crumpled wet napkins on our table and thinking about going home again to my small, empty apartment. Orlando drunkenly leaned over and pointed at my hairline.

"Oh dear. You've got some gray hair. I've got some too, if that makes you feel better."

"I've decided something," I announced. "I'm going to buy that house."

CHAPTER EIGHT

*"But the brilliance, the versatility of madness is akin to the resourceful-
ness of water seeping through, over and around a dike. It requires the
united front of many people to work against it."- F. Scott Fitzgerald*

January-

A solitary cobweb clings desperately to a stone corner to preserve itself
against the godly vacuum. Screams of passionate approval follow the
"Rocket's red glare." The righteous patriotism of a moment gives way to a distant pyramid of respectable legs and midriffs. The deflated clock, exhausted
by centuries of use, finally flings itself against the heavy desk, sticking there
like over-kneaded dough. A quivering key longs to dig a hole and bury itself.
He stares at the cracked plate in horror, wondering how to make anything
matter anymore. And somewhere else, the curling vapors murmuring under
a spot of light in a darkened street remind the privileged watcher of what
must be done.

Jada greeted me at the door with a peck on the cheek. She beamed
up at me as she turned her face halfway inside and announced my

arrival to nobody in particular. She wore rhinestone jeans, a cashmere pastel sweater, and pink cowboy boots. The chic socialite deigning to play the man's woman. I supposed that, since the Cowboys were playing the Washington Redskins in the NFC East championship that day, she looked what could only be described as adorable. I wasn't at all sure I meant it as a compliment.

"Hey, your hair—it's like Jada's," yelled Lorena as I walked upstairs with Jada into the party. Thirty or forty people were smiling and munching on snacks and sipping beers. Lorena's voice wasn't nearly as loud as her neon yellow cable-knit sweater.

Jada smirked a bit, like she had already had this thought herself, but she patted me lightly on the back and told me change was always exciting.

"I prefer my dark hair, to be honest, but I've started to go grey, so I thought having light hair would help it all blend together better." I adjusted the Cowboys jersey I had worn with my skinny jeans, feeling self-conscious and a little defensive without knowing exactly why.

"I'll run to the ladies' room, if you don't mind," I said.

As I rushed towards the bathroom down the hallway, I was reminded yet again of the scare I'd had by the outstretched arm and the hot breath and the garbled words of a deep whispered voice. This time, there was nobody there. Almost everyone was in the media room, already enjoying pre-game festivities. But I had to pass by Richard's apartment and saw through the mostly open door that he was lying on his bed. It was no surprise that he was here for the football-themed party his mother was throwing, but I wondered why he was not with everyone else. I would have just ignored him but for the unfamiliar look of vulnerability that was clearly displayed on his face. He was pointing his remote toward the TV, apparently replaying a certain scene.

"Hey," I said.

"Oh. Hey." He didn't take his eyes off the screen except to see who I was.

"You gonna watch the game?" I asked.

"Hell yeah. I was just finishing a movie. One of my favorites. I used to watch it over and over as a kid." He scratched his nose.

"What is it?" I wanted him to look at me.

"Friday Night Lights."

"Oh—that's a true story isn't it? In Texas?" I hadn't seen it, but I'd heard about it from many proud people around here who felt personally affected by the story.

"Yeah. That's why I love it so much. It's true."

We both silently watched the screen for a moment. Billy Bob Thornton was talking to a kid in his car. In his best good ole boy accent, he was saying, "We all of us, uh, dig our own holes."

Awkwardly, I asked, "Is everything okay?" Richard, still staring at the screen, closed his eyes, nodded, and gestured with the remote toward the door. I mumbled a quick apology for the intrusion and promptly forgot about him.

The bathroom was spotless. Jada must have made sure it was company ready. She had a lot of day workers—housekeepers, lawn care professionals, and the like. There were real poinsettias on the sterile granite countertop. I sprayed myself with some perfume from my purse, rubbed my blush into my skin with my hands so it blended better, and pondered my strange new blond reflection in the mirror. Somehow I was ashamed of my new hair color. It was irrational, but it was undeniably how I felt. I'd dye it back dark as soon as I had the chance, gray hair be damned. With this resolution, I went into the party.

After making small talk with a few people I had brushed up against in various former times and places, I saw with some surprise that Heath had wandered into the room amid the comings and goings of others. Finally able to look at him up close again after feeling suffocated by his physical absence when he had been so present in my thoughts lately, I noticed how disheveled he looked, deteriorated somehow, as though all of his energies had gone solely toward the continual suppression of strong emotions. He scanned the room with narrowed eyes like cameras, scoping all around him without revealing anything specific within him, as though the natural light which was let into the great entertaining area by way of many elongated windows was taxing his overly acute sensibilities. Very probably the entire setting overwhelmed him, I thought. Jada had told me he kept mostly to himself when he could help it. I felt a stab of protective sympathy, like one feels for a stray animal whose mangy fur and visible ribcage betray the fact that it doesn't properly belong anyplace in the world. In fact, he was skulking around the fringes of the room, looking mistrustful and resentful of the people in it, and one could see in the worried lines on his face the instinct to burrow back into the safety of his dark solitude. By contrast, Peppermint was panting excitedly, zooming from leg to casually outstretched arm, hoping to get some extra attention from strangers even through the cotton of her Cowboys-colored dog jersey.

I overheard a still-beautiful middle-aged woman with very obvious fake breasts exclaiming how much she adored get-togethers and holidays. "Don't you always think that looking forward to holidays is as good as their arrival?" she asked Heath.

"I forget what day it is and holidays and all of that. I'm retired," he curtly replied. She grimaced politely and turned her attention to the couple nearest to her.

The occasional loud whoop or raucous laughter coming from the various small groups forming in the warm room interrupted the generally pleasant murmur of simultaneous intimate conversations. I had the uncomfortable sensation that every chummy contribution I attempted to make to each cluster of acquaintances fell short of the impression I intended to convey. But I was a social success compared to Heath. He was nervously fiddling with his wedding ring, glaring with seeming intensity at the big screen TV. A handsome jovial man with broad shoulders and an orangey complexion, noticing Heath's apparent interest in the patriotic pre-game hoopla, attempted a kindness.

"Hey, man, that could be you out there. You served for years, didn't you?"

"Yes." He looked sullen.

But the man was undeterred; his smile didn't falter.

"I'll bet you have some wild stories. Did you ever go to the Middle East?"

"Oh yes." Heath averted his eyes from the television and furrowed his brow, deliberately turning his head away from the interrogator. He rose as if to go run some recently remembered errand. The man was resolute in his attempt to "reach" him.

"What was that like?"

"It's lucky for me that nothing that the government has approved can be immoral," Heath sneered down at him. "And lucky for you that you don't have the faintest idea of what I mean."

And as if the man's golden face was a tight bulb, it suddenly burst into an exotic purple blossom. He excused himself and left the room. I searched Heath's face. It was dark and brooding. He had obviously not gotten any pleasure out of the exchange. I wondered if Jada was upset by Heath's unfriendliness. But Jada hadn't seemed to notice Heath's presence at all; she was laughing with her head thrown back at two women's insistence she didn't look a day over thirty-five.

Lorena, gathering momentum, began with an "ooh, ooh," and growing louder, ejaculated, "The game is about to start! They're getting ready for the National Anthem! Quiet, everyone!" And after reverberated hushes and murmurs of excitement--except for the occasional storyteller who hadn't any intention of deferring to the TV until he or she had gotten to the punch line-- people began to settle in, preparing themselves for a night of solidarity engendered by pure entertainment.

But as everyone else's eyes were glued to the theater-sized screen in the Bludworth's media room, I was suddenly aware that Heath was staring at me. He nodded furtively, as though we were privy to intelligence unbeknownst to all but us two. Nervous and brimming with uncertainty, he motioned that I was to follow him out of the room. Was this how your average affair started—so publicly and yet with an air of intimacy that seemed to indicate its inevitability and thus its relative morality? I felt wild for complete possession of him, but the very improbability of the fulfillment of my desire fanned its flames. What would I come to mean to him, and was I a good enough actress to indulge him enough in these first tender moments not to spook him from forming intentions for me that flattered us both? I was beholden to him already for making the first move. His sullenness and masculine reticence had been obstacles which, in visions, had hurled themselves against my determination.

But here we were in real time, in real life, and I was watching myself meekly follow him downstairs with blanched face and trembling limbs. I was cold with adrenaline and neuroticism. Heath pulled me into a dark corner in the back of the house. I opened my mouth to speak, but he shook his head firmly.

"Not here," he whispered fiercely. He kept looking around to make sure we weren't being followed, or to see if anyone had even noticed our absence. Then all of a sudden, with a sense of urgency, he pushed me out the back door and, taking the lead, grabbed me by the hand. Feeling a little apprehensive, my first instinct was to run back inside, but he seemed so intent after my acceptance of his unspoken proposal that my curiosity got the best of me. And seeing the distinguished grey at his temples and his handsome dignified features up close reinforced my desire.

My hand was sweating in the grasp of his clammy hand as he pulled me breathlessly along, and I felt exhilarated by the immediacy his attention to me conveyed. He was ushering me secretly through the yard toward the large detached studio about which I had often fantasized in the few quiet moments of my mind over the past couple of months. What did he do there, alone amidst his possessions in the environment which he had fashioned for himself over the years? And what would it look like? Would it show signs of an orderly and uncluttered mind—a clean, well-lighted place? Or would it be anachronistic, expensive heavy furniture reviving the Gent's Club days of Europe, rather like the study I'd glimpsed in the house? I realized I still knew next to nothing about the pale enigmatic man who was breathing heavily and tiptoeing with me to the edge of his own property.

We reached the door and Heath mumbled that he always kept it locked. As he fumbled for the key in his pockets, I noticed that the crumbling tree branches and decaying leaves which covered the cement entrance and the low roof were uncharacteristic of the magnificent house and yard which were also part of his estate. Rusty dirt-colored patches appeared in places, and under the eaves, various insect nests were comfortably installed. A few orange bird of paradise plants were in full bloom around one side of the building. They were spiky and vulgar. I didn't speak, and as Heath turned the key into the lock, he blurted out an apology. He'd been preoccupied as of late, he said, and it was well-known custom that he alone should have ingress into his personal workspace.

"I'm afraid the inside isn't any better," he pronounced without embarrassment as he swung open the door.

The building was half bachelor's apartment, half artist's studio. To the right of the front door were stacks of half-finished vases and pots, shards of baked pottery haphazardly thrown inside beautifully finished glazed containers, and a large pottery wheel in the space on the distressed hardwood floor. Paints and glazes of all brands and colors and sizes sloshed up against one another on an old home-made shelf against the wall. Random artists' instruments were flung all about the room, like someone had been unexpectedly interrupted in the middle of a murder rather than merely feeling the artist's fury to exorcise his genius. To the left, a modest bed, a dorm-room-sized refrigerator, an old wardrobe, and a rather tidy desk for all the impression the rest of the room gave me, were hints that Heath had spent many nights out here, doing whatever it was that suited him. A radio was playing the tail end of Ray Charles' "Hard Times." Above the desk and almost touching the exposed wood crossbeams of the ceiling was a surreal painting that seemed familiar to me. The rest of the walls were stark and completely devoid of art—except for three crosses which hung on the wall facing the entrance. Something about this place struck my imagination to the core. The man himself had had that effect on me, in a grotesque but not unpleasant manner.

Heath must have noticed my quizzical expression as I contemplated what the crosses were doing in his room.

"My wife is actually relieved to see those there. She doesn't recognize the malicious mockery they were intended to bestow." He laughed darkly.

"Hmm," I responded, uncomfortable but not surprised.

"That painting looks familiar," I said as Heath closed the door behind us, peering outside to see if anyone had noticed we had left the party. No one seemed to. We both exhaled.

"Salvador Dali. *The Persistence of Memory*. You are a Dali fan?" he asked.

"I have never seen his work. I've heard about his antics. His reputation reminds me very much of my best friend. But this is very thought-provoking art," I reflected.

"Yes. And the name. Oh, the name!" He looked pained for a moment and then turned his back to me as he went over to the refrigerator.

"I am old and tired, Stella," he began. He wasn't really that old, I thought, maybe in his early fifties, but he did have a faded quality which lent earnestness to his words.

"I know we have all the best party food that Pinterest can inspire in the house, but I couldn't take it in there for one more minute. I don't know that I've eaten in days. Pardon me." He pulled down a cracked china plate and lopped onto it a huge helping of barbecue from the fridge.

"Well, these cold leftovers aren't really fit for company, but if you want some..." His unfinished sentence was obviously only a courtesy. I politely declined. His fingers traced the crack in the plate. "I wonder if it hurts," he murmured to himself.

"If what does?" I asked, a little too loudly.

"Nothing—never mind." He looked agitated, like a man whose intense reveries have been disturbed.

"What is this desk in here for? Do you write novels—detective stories or romances?" I asked, trying to lighten the mood. I desperately wanted a revelation from him. I didn't yet have the nerve to ask if he was in the habit of writing love poetry to younger women.

A sad smile appeared. "Fiction is always about the past, but if it's any good, it's got to take the future into account too. It's hard for me to imagine scenarios that aren't dying or already dead." In the background, the radio was softly playing Willie Nelson's version of "Midnight Rider."

I did not think he expected a response. I wanted to fold him into my breast, caress him, and tell him that it just wasn't so. But he was lost in thought again, and I began to wonder why he brought me out here, away from the party if it wasn't for--. Maybe he was waiting on me to say something. But I didn't know how these things went, and I wasn't the type to abandon all caution and just throw myself onto someone.

I absentmindedly glanced over the papers on his desk. Scattered across the top was some research on Thomas Hardy, the Victorian novelist and poet. I often felt like a Hardy heroine, my life filled with poignant ironies and the unceasing naturalistic struggle against unfair and yet inevitable outcomes. But I wondered what Heath could want with Hardy's biography. I picked up a sheet and pretended to read it.

"Are you interested in Victorian literature?" I asked.

He shrugged his shoulders and began to shovel mouthfuls of cold leftovers into his body.

A shiver ran through me.

"Do you write—poetry?" I hoped I sounded neutral.

"I admire it as an art form. I'm sorry to disappoint you, but I must admit I don't write anything. It's all evidence that I can't afford to have lying around." He plucked the sheet of paper from my grasp and shuffled it in with the rest of his papers, hitting them together against the hard edge of the desk and then defensively shutting them into a drawer with a bang. He went calmly back to eating, only this time with a sinister gleam in his eye. After a moment of silence, he put down his fork.

"Listen. I didn't bring you out here to discuss poetry or art. There's something I need to-"

Finally, I thought. "Not even this one?" I interrupted, spotting my chance. I pulled out the poem with the key from my purse.

Heath, who was already as pale as any man I'd ever met, became even more ghost-like and colorless. Sheer terror lined his face when I handed it to him. His eyes looked like pendulums as they sped from one side to the other when he read. At one particular line, he gasped. His terror turned to rage.

"Where did you get this?" His voice was a violent whisper.

"I don't know what you mean. I got this in my mail box at school. I thought you were flirting with me, playing with me—" I shook my head as I explained and shrank instinctively away from him.

"Playing with you?" He convulsed as though possessed. His voice sounded thick, like speech was becoming increasingly more difficult. He began to simper, and I could no longer understand one word of what he was saying.

"Heath, are you okay? I think we have just had a misunderstanding. I don't know what's going on! Should I go get someone?" Over my incessant and confused blabbing, he began to laugh. It was a demonic laugh filled with hatred and madness, a boundless laugh which caused my blood to curdle and paralyzed me to the spot. He came closer to me, one deliberate footfall at a time.

"Oh I'm not really the romantic type," he said plainly. "The horror, the horror, they say. But these are just words. The things I have done—have been made to do! What I have done without even knowing it! But I am beginning to know it. Maybe they are beginning to know that I know."

"Who- who knows it? What things?" I stuttered.

Here was a wounded animal backed into a corner, by whom, I didn't know. The romantic Mr. Bludworth I had conjured in my mind was shredded into limp scraps by the defensive claws of a desperate beast, a deleted file replaced by a much more sinister prototype. Did Jada recognize her husband's insanity? Had she seen him like this? Had she run into Henry's arms for protection? Heath's eyes went dark and he snarled.

"This is not a game."

He lunged at me with a fierce and unexpected energy and strength. This time, the ghost had been possessed by the flesh. I was impassioned and petrified at the same time.

"Help me Stella!" he shrieked. "Is this what you want? Is this what you need from me so that you will take me seriously?" He was howling and shaking me with clenched fists. I coiled my soul into a globe and retreated into the safe warm core of my body. What remained exposed stiffened into the frozen paralysis of the preyed upon.

"Huh? HUH?" He screamed. I felt warm moisture where his wrathful tears hit my skin. His face smashed into mine, a forceful mockery of a kiss, his lips and nose like a wrecking ball to my own. Pain seared through my head. I reeled back and fell onto the floor, writhing away from him. A glorious scene of the dark universe temporarily threatened to unravel my consciousness. When I was able to see again, he was there, standing over me, silent, satisfied. Then, inexplicably, he was Heath again. His face was expressionless except for the perpetual sadness which had always been there. Awareness crept back into his tone.

"Oh my God—Stella. I'm so sorry." His eyes brimmed with tears again. "I cannot control myself. Literally. And you've no idea how I try, how I've tried. I'm a desperate man. I need someone on my side. I know you will think I'm dangerous. And I am—but not to you. Please just listen for a minute. I'll tell you what I can."

He gently picked me up, brushed the dust and paint peels off of my clothes, touched my face where it still stung with cold but tender fingers, and looked into my eyes with the intense jealousy of the experienced for the oblivious.

"I want to die. I want to—no, I need to kill myself."

A puff of breath escaped from my lips, but my stingy heart was too busy pumping blood back upon itself to help my tongue form a convincing rebuttal.

"I know you must think I'm crazy. But you're my last hope. I have to fit the pieces together before I go... I need you to tell me what it's like, for Jada's sake—"

When he could see I was still reeling from the shock of the blow, shrinking from his touch and not understanding one fragment of his speech, he hardened his face. He walked stiffly to the door, opened it, gestured to me that I was free to go, and mumbled apologetically.

"That's it, then," he said, his shoulders drooping as I began to shakily walk out.

"You're going to let me go?" I asked.

"Yes, of course," he said, swallowing hard, then added, "but then I couldn't tell you about my dream. I dreamed of Santiago."

He had gotten my attention. I stopped and turned toward him. "What about him?"

"Come sit down. I swear I won't touch you again. I just need..." -- here he pressed the pads of his fingers to his forehead and massaged them into his skin—"...to know they will be okay."

In that moment, I recalled all the rumors that had circulated about him. I knew he was retired military, that he'd had top clearance at one time, that he preferred a reclusive lifestyle. Maybe he was dangerous, maybe desperate: probably both, whether he was conjuring up morbid hallucinations or truly reaching out for help. But as terrified as I was to go back into that shed and shut the door behind me, I was more curious to know what he had to say, what he might confide in me. And the allure of being able to hear Santiago's name mentioned again like he was still alive, an active subject, was too strong for me to resist. I went in and calmly sat down, resolved to accept the consequences of my interest.

He recounted his dream. "I was making pottery, here, on this wheel." He demonstrated by giving the pottery wheel in the center of the room a spin. "I could feel the cool wheel under my palms in my dream, spinning as I manipulated the clay. I was calm, like I always am when I'm working out here. It was such a familiar feeling, that calm, the wet clay, the motions of creation, that I had no idea I was dreaming. Suddenly, the wheel morphed into Santiago's guitar, and—"

"How did you know it was his?" I asked.

"Because I'd been to concerts of his before. He was—well, I just connected with him. His music was healing, in a way. I felt like someone else could understand my pain and had found a way to voice it through song."

I nodded my understanding.

"So then I looked down and I was playing his guitar, the red one he always played. I didn't know how I was doing it, but I was magically able to emit the most beautiful sounds you've ever heard. I smiled in disbelief, genuinely delighted that I had found this ability within myself. And it was effortless. I looked around for an audience, someone to hear my song, soaring on the heights of elation, like you do in dreams, when I saw him. Santiago. He was standing a few feet away from me and wordlessly pointing to the guitar in my hands. I felt a little guilty at first, like I was encroaching on his territory or something. I tried to give it back to him. He shook his head firmly and just continued to point. When I looked down again, I realized the guitar had become my hands, and it was playing of its own accord. In horror, I tried to reach out to Santiago, to get him to help me, but he just kept sorrowfully shaking his head."

I waited silently to see if there was more.

"That was it," Heath confirmed. "And it scared the hell out of me. It was like he felt such empathy for me but there was nothing he could do. It was out of anyone's control."

"That's a strange dream. It's probably just something you ate," I said, rising to leave again, trying not to show that I had been affected by his description of his dream.

"Stella. Please sit." By this time, he looked far more like a victim than a threat, so much so that I was assuaged and sighed out my consent as I reseated myself.

Visibly relieved, he began. "I can only imagine how insensitive you must think me, how imbalanced. But after all you went through with Santiago, who could be a better choice for me to come to with this horrendous decision? You're friends with my wife; you teach my son. You can look out for them after I am gone, if it comes to that. And I'm afraid it must."

"Do you ever find yourself eating dinner," he continued, "sitting at your desk at work, maybe, taking a shower or driving somewhere— and there's just enough of a lull for you to feel —and I mean really feel, just *know*—that you're alone? That you are really and truly all alone in this universe? Or maybe you remember all of a sudden that you're going to die? That those you love will die? I think we all do. That's why we are so glued to our phones and our televisions all the time. We don't want to be reminded of how unpleasant it is to know we are alone and that we will die. People around here would tell you that you need God if you felt that way. And I think they are right. But I suppose they probably feel exactly like that too, sometimes, or they wouldn't go searching for religion in the first place. We do need God. To give us something to look forward to, you know. But just because

God should exist doesn't mean he does. We can't just will something into existence. Believe me, I've tried."

Ah, contact doom. That's what Orlando and I called it—when death's silvery hand reached into your gut for but a moment and then changed its mind—that time. I knew very well what feelings he was referring to. I had even had some of those exact thoughts. All too often lately I had been unable to enjoy much. I thought it had been solely because of my girlish feelings for this afflicted man. But a quick analysis of my recent state of mind proved that my restful feelings were laced with existential panic and not a little of that old-time Puritanical guilt.

I nodded my understanding. He seemed to be waiting for a response from me, but when I said nothing more (because really what was there to say?), he resumed:

"We mourn because when we die we shall be forgotten, and yet we also mourn because when we live we cannot forget the ghosts that haunt us. It's all so very, very sad." And he meant it. He looked as if he was about to weep again.

"The bliss of oblivion is necessary for any kind of life at all. Even for basic functioning, I guess. Being able to forget. And I—I cannot forget. Suppression only works for so long. And that is my tragic flaw." He winced.

"So silly. Those words. Like I'm a hero and I could have beaten the odds if only for this one bad habit. There's never just one. And I was never going to escape my fate. *I remember everything.* It's the rumination that kills. The grinding of the jawbone of God in my head… that's what makes me tragic."

I was feeling alarmed. Heath wasn't making much sense. I had visions of a porcelain man dusting up shattered pieces of himself—here a finger, there a forearm—with no more fuss than if he had dropped a cheap plate on the kitchen tile. I opened my mouth as if to ask a question, but he arrested my attempt with a shrug. The time for my contribution to a conversation had apparently passed. His was a monologue now—a verbal shrine to a personal past to which only he could bring form.

"My time in the military seemed somehow what I was destined to do. Yes, I chose to enlist, but I always felt somehow expected to do it. And it wasn't just my parents who expected it. I can't really explain it. But who can ever explain anything about their life? I spent many years doing things I thought at the time were for my country and its freedoms, but now I realize it was all policy dictated by special interest groups. People think I am just bitter and cynical. I am. But I am not ashamed of that. Anyway, it doesn't matter. Nothing does. The people in power pull the strings and we must perform, whether or not we like or even know the tune or the steps. I cracked up when I realized that in the navy, in my marriage, in my mind... I was never fighting against people or countries but ideologies. How can you triumph over an idea? But I will not give up so easily. I have figured out a lot more than they think I have. They never counted on the resourcefulness of madness."

Having held on to the word "marriage," I tried to assuage him by asking about how he and Jada met.

"Hmm? Oh. At a wedding. Years ago." He said the words automatically. But then he really remembered. His past came to life for him in living color. His face softened. "She wasn't like she is now. She really wasn't. Change is inevitable, isn't it? But oh, how cruel time can be. I was home from the naval academy to attend a friend's brother's wedding. I must've been about twenty-two. She was softer, fleshier, when I first saw her. Her face didn't have nearly so many angles. She was sitting with a group of her friends. I noticed her because she looked just like Faye Dunaway or Jacy Farrow from *The Last Picture Show*. She was wearing a proper dress, but the look on her face betrayed a sort of hard-boiled resolution in her that went all way down. She was the daughter of a judge whose family happened to come from oil money, she'd said. I guessed she was wild. But I found out afterward that she married me for tradition and safety. *Some* things about her stayed the same, anyway." He snorted.

"I've changed, too, though." He looked down at himself. "Oh, how the mighty have fallen." A slight pause, then, "To be or not to be. I'm full of allusions, you know. But you appreciate them?" Sure, I did, I told him. I was an English professor.

"Well, then."

"Is there anything else?" I asked him, ready to make my exit.

"I've killed people, Stella."

I froze.

"I've killed a lot of people. It wasn't me, exactly. It has something to do with my position in the military. They had a hold on me, like in a bad horror movie. But this is real. I'm remembering things, just small fragments and bits of terrorizing and being terrorized, of certain words and memories that I can't trust. But I'm starting to believe that I'm a monster. And my family may be in danger. I just need to know. It's been a while since Santiago's death. Will they ever get over it? Do you think they ever can? You can't tell them anything I've told you for their own protection. But will they ever forgive me if I commit suicide?"

"I-I don't know, Heath. I am sorry. I can't help you!" I made a dash for the door. He rose up with lightning movements and grabbed my arm right before I reached the knob.

With genuine desperation he asked, "But do you think they can? If it's for their own protection?"

Shaken up and feeling horribly ashamed of both of us, I broke from his grip and raced out of the studio without looking back, hearing him still shouting after me. As I came closer to the house, I could hear jubilant cheers from the warm interior. Too emotional to risk going in without betraying my overwhelming sense of guilt and fear, I decided to go around the side of the house straight to the front where my car was parked. I was almost running by the time I opened my car door. After sobbing hysterically until I had regained my composure, hands still trembling, I called Orlando. I simply couldn't be alone tonight.

CHAPTER NINE

"It wasn't so much the darkness of the night that bothered me but the horrible lights men had invented to illuminate their darkness with." - *Jack Kerouac*

February--

*T*he bartender shakes up a Mardi Gras cocktail in slow motion, releasing a spray of bubbles at the molecular level. A pearl necklace; creamy polished eggs press down on her collarbone. The Rubik's cube clicks, locks, clicks, turns. Tornado warning sirens —a pinwheel in a yard spins so fast the carnival colors blur into a brownish spot against the darkening skies. I am without, looking in on myself like crunchy leaves falling into a moving stream. Minutes writhe in waves like hungry serpents, forming circles which collapse upon each other until there is nothing but space.

The More Distant Past: A Mardi Gras Party in February
Winding around the residential forest on the way to the Bludworth's party, I pictured the area as it must have been, just horse country. During my grandparents' time, most places around here were still

rural and home to farms and humble horse ranches. White farm-houses and red barns had blown away like grains of sandy soil in a dust storm and given way to monster estates in varying architectural styles set off the road, buttressed by old oaks, pines, and manicured gardens. The slim silhouettes of the Italian cypress trees along the driveway in twilight felt a bit sinister, like shadow guards standing at attention. The house itself was Gothic and imposing: the stone turret on one side bespoke Old World mystery. Nevertheless, the cathedral-ceilinged entrance shimmered with soft golden light and I could see through some of the windows lining the front of the house outlines of people clustering and breaking apart.

"It's like something you'd see under a microscope," Orlando mused.

"Ha. Like a bunch of atoms bumping against each other. Is it gas that expands like that? Maybe this party is a gas."

"If there's alcohol, it'll definitely be a gas, as they used to say." He winked at me and took my arm.

We approached the oversized wooden door, manned by a hired member of the catering company. The fresh-faced, courteous young butler guided us in while taking my satin clutch. He offered to take my beaded Portuguese shawl, a proud purchase I had made on my last trip overseas. I had never found quite the right occasion to wear it, but the rich dark purple of the shawl added just the right contrast to the lavender dress I had selected. Orlando had assured me that my eyes were like the hollows of emeralds. I decided I would keep it. It was a chilly night. The grand living room toward the back of the house was already filled with lavish but tasteful decorations, a huge wet bar staffed by four chaotic young people, and all kinds of prominent and expansive men and women flitting in and out of the French doors which led to the illuminated gardens. Curiously, I led Orlando outdoors, where we ran into Jada breathlessly stepping past us.

"I knew you'd come." She squeezed my arm twice. "I'm so glad. So this is the famous Orlando?" She looked him up and down.

"You'll have to entertain us later this evening, I hope. Stella thinks you hung the moon. She tells the best stories about your adventures together. I thought I would love you before I met you, but I'm certain of it now. You're just charming!"

"Maybe I did hang the moon," Orlando grinned. He bowed slightly. She touched a stacked sapphire ring to her jeweled bun, making sure it was in place.

"You schmoozer! Hee hee. I've gotta run—I'll be back." She twirled past us in her tangerine cocktail dress and then stopped and turned to us, letting her fingers compulsively trace over the rhinestone trim which sparkled along the straps and the bust of her dress as she spoke. "I've heard that Dad is already wheedling for a drink. 'I'm 77,' he says. Raging Ruby, his wife, thought she found his whole stash but just last week she found him face down in the hallway with a bottle of Gentlemen's Jack and laughing about the bruises. He shouldn't be here tonight but he's my father, you know?" She emphasized *father* like she was in cahoots with him.

"I have to go convince Dad to behave and quit trying to get a rise out of poor Ruby. It's the sole pleasure he has left, I guess, if she has anything to say about it." She pivoted and went into the house. The speaker system, which piped pleasant music into all the rooms and out onto the terrace, was playing a light happy song with an accordion in it, which transported me to April in Paris.

Thoughtfully, Orlando said, "She's more beautiful than you led me to believe. A pity." We walked toward the swimming pool, lit up from within.

"Yes, it is. She reminds me of Ophelia. 'O, you must wear your rue with a difference.' I wish I knew about the language of flowers, what each one is supposed to mean--Ohhh! Look!"

The garden was illustrious. The lava heat lamps erupted in luminous streamers of light upon the Cuban Cigar Bar, near which a group of business men sitting with their legs lengthened and crossed comfortably at the ankles were laughing and smoking with their scotch. These gave way to strings of bright lights which lined the walkways of the most gorgeous personal garden I had ever seen. I had told Orlando about it but lit up this way, it showed up more beautifully than an enchanted dream of a garden. It was only a sliver of the size of the Boboli Gardens of Florence, but I had felt the same emotional proportion then as now in response to true natural splendor.

"But there's a spot on your painting—" Orlando pointed to an indistinct corner at the back near Heath's detached study. A faceless pair of trousers was working toward deflowering a faceless pink gown. "Let's see who's here, shall we?" He picked me up like a doll and almost flung me into a bronze statue of a longhorn that seemed to be sniffing flowers like Ferdinand. It was an extravagant piece designed to pay homage both to its location and the money that bought it.

"I do need a drink," I laughed. He shimmied his shoulders playfully and raked one hand through his thick hair.

"Oh, yes, Stella." He scrunched up his eyes and pretended to stretch out feelers.

A pair of older women walking by and whispering indulged him when he invaded their space and placed his hands near a lipstick-stained sweating glass. "The drinks are really strong here. I sense it..." His voice shook with mock-somberness like he was receiving this message from beyond. He really was voluminously charismatic.

One of them cooed, "Yes, Handsome, you aren't kidding. They're even making Old- Fashioneds and Mint Juleps at the bar inside! Can you imagine these young 'uns knowing how to make them so well—and so strong? " She leaned into us and gave us a loud friendly cackle. Her teeth were mustard-colored, like her earrings.

"Well, Maggie, they probably just looked it up on the Internet! We don't live in the Dark Ages, you know," said the other one, rolling her eyes. In the soft light, a hand decorated with a large cuff bracelet and river blue nails went up to an expectant coral-colored mouth and back down again. The ice clinked back into place. She too was basking in Orlando's glow.

"Oh I knoooow, Lee Ann," she said, making each syllable of the name its own sentence out of irritation. "What I meant was that... well, even the mint sprigs and the cherries will make you tipsy. And they're fresh, too." She batted her false eyelashes at Orlando. He was absolutely in his element.

"I'll go straight inside to try it! You ladies look lovely. Thank you! Enjoy this wonderful party!" He patted them on the back, ushering them toward their unknown destinations. The first synthetic beats of a billboard hit played a little louder over the scene before us.

We weaved our way past a few tight groups and lone wanderers looking for something or someone, past the businessmen with their deep coughs and unconscious laughter, and past the crawfish boil directly across from them, where Richard, in his waistcoat, was sucking the heads off as quickly as he could. He stopped to carefully pump a beer keg, but some foam still overflowed onto his shiny patent leather shoes. He acted unconcerned. The crawfish were piled high on the tables next to various appetizers on red and white checkered tablecloths, and a wine bar was set up in the back. I noticed that a lot of the faces I had seen when I had been here before were standing around this area. Most of them were probably Jada's housekeepers and lawn care men. They formed one big clannish group and laughed very Hispanic laughs. The women had strong shimmering hair. They wore more ribbons and sequins and neon jewelry than the others. Orlando stopped to say hello and selected a crawfish. He ate it in pieces and almost spit one out because he was laughing so hard when two gardeners (I supposed) told him some hysterical anecdote in Spanish. As I watched him, I wondered what his life had been like before he came here. I thought to myself that he was my best friend. He was the closest thing to magic that I had ever known.

He rejoined me shaking his head and snickering. "What was that?" I asked him.

"Oh, just something about this one guy's wife. She saw Jesus in a tortilla her daughter made and wouldn't talk to her for a month. I saw Satan once at this five star restaurant. He said he came there for the company, so I bought him a drink. I'm a gentleman so I won't tell you what happens next. Speaking of drinks..." He trailed off and grabbed my hand. "Let's a-go!" We made a beeline for the bar. Crossing back into the house, there was a gush of warm air. Above the music and the hum of unconnected fragments of murmured phrases and various reactions, there were clinks of glasses and soles of shoes tapping hard floors and souls of people tapping hard liquor. I felt born again.

The Future Which Has Become the Past- Jada's House of Mourning in April

Jada answered the door cautiously, opening it just a crack until she recognized us. Visibly relieved, she swung it open all the way and beckoned us in.

"It is so kind of you to come. It's been kind of everybody, I know, but I'm exhausted. I thought you might be another well-meaning group of strangers. I was just about to sit outside on the terrace and enjoy this lovely spring day."

"We should have called," I apologized. Henry glared at me. "We won't be long," I continued. "I just wanted to bring you this." I held out the foil-covered casserole dish apologetically. "I'm an awful cook—"

"I'm sure you're not," she interrupted me. "You are both very welcome here. Of course I didn't mean you." She accepted the gift graciously if not a little disinterestedly. But her smile was sterling. "Come in, come in!" We did.

"Follow me to the back here for a minute." We trailed her through the large living area to the French doors, where she deposited us for a moment, disappearing into the kitchen. Henry took the opportunity to mutter, "Told you."

I threw up my hands as quietly as I could. "I'm so over you, Henry. The only thing you've ever had over me is that you're a man." He threw his head back and laughed a great belly laugh.

Jada came back out sans casserole and led us out into the breezy spring afternoon as she scooped up a pair of sunglasses and a hat from a terra-cotta table situated just outside. Her oversized glasses added the last touch of unbelievable chic to her ensemble. I marveled that even in mourning, she looked like a middle-aged Chanel model. She was wearing a billowing navy shirt and underneath a red and white striped tank top with a horseshoe shaped neckline, white linen pants, and a wide-brimmed navy straw hat with a red sash. I looked down at my own dark cottony keyhole dress, afraid that I had been too literary with my selection. But I always proudly wore the turquoise set I pulled out of the jewelry box whenever I was feeling sentimental. They had never lost their enchantment for me. The rectangular drop earrings and rock ring were hand-forged by my favorite great-uncle, who was a jazz trumpeter and a world traveler and published a great many books on architecture in his lifetime.

We walked out to an intimate sitting area with a heavy round patio table from which blossomed a huge lime green umbrella. A pitcher of iced tea, glasses, lemons, and a centerpiece of Cadbury eggs graced the table. Either she was already expecting company or she just liked to be prepared.

Birds were chirping happily; in the distance, a mockingbird sang. All around the terrace and pool area were reminders of Heath. His hobby had added much to the loveliness of the yard; different shapes, designs, and shades of pots and vases colored the landscape with a variety of blooms. Splashes of pastels filled the pots, while snapdragons provided warm, dazzling dashes of color against tree trunks.

She poured us all a glass of iced tea, a polished gold weave ring clinking against the pitcher. We made small talk about our Easter plans for the next day. Jada made a point to show Henry her Easter lilies and irises which she said older generations called "flags." This began a conversation between the two of them about gardening techniques.

She snapped her fingers. "That reminds me! Henry, would you go around to the front of the house and take a look at my Italian cypress trees? They've got brownish spots on them and I can't figure out what's causing them. Rogelio's been gone for a couple weeks to Mexico and since you're here, maybe you could help?"

Henry loved when women asked him to do anything for them. In his haste to leave, his braided belt caught on the edge of the table. Jada pretended that she didn't notice and complimented him on his melon-colored Polo shirt. He nodded an acknowledgement and left us to ourselves.

She took down her sunglasses. "I've always liked you. You seem to have such a genuine sense of self. I envy you that. We are so different, and yet... and yet, there is something that binds us, isn't there? I know about your little infatuation with Heath, but none of that has ever mattered. I think you know I'm being honest when I tell you I can understand." She paused. Very carefully she enunciated each word, "And I want you to understand. For God's sakes, I just need *someone* to understand!" She gave an intimation that she might become hysterical, but she didn't. She gazed out into her yard like Queen Elizabeth at her coronation. I wondered if her flowers had taken on new meaning to her since the funeral. April was the cruelest month.

"You know why I like flowers so much? Because they show us how beautiful God intended life to be, you see? All the fairytales my parents read to me when I was small had flowers in them. But I'm still here when the last petal falls each time, trying to figure out what to do with myself. That terrifies me. Do you get my meaning?" Her eyes were operatic rubies. I told her I thought I did.

"God put me here for a reason, and He never gives me more than I can bear. Maybe my problem is that I'm just too strong." She contemplated what she had just said. She took a sip of tea and set it down on the table a little more forcefully than she had expected, I surmised, for she apologized and then put her glasses back on. The red sash on her hat flew out behind her head with the breeze.

"Heath hasn't been the man I married for years now. I think when he's back there in solitary—" she corrected herself with a mournful look toward his abandoned studio, "*was* back there—making pottery, he was trying to put something back together in himself that he never had the power to recover. But things have been worse in the past two years. It was like a horror movie. It began with confusion. He didn't recognize me sometimes. I thought he was showing signs of early dementia. Then his irritability increased. He was always a little touchy—sensitive—but he was really scary sometimes. Richard has hated him for years now. He would wake up with nightmares and tell us the most..." she searched for the words, "grotesque and disturbing stories. And then he disappeared for hours on end." She leaned in to me and crossed her legs tightly, fidgeting with her wedding band.

"My suspicions at the time were many... and they all proved to be unfounded. I still don't know where he went. But I shudder to think about what he was doing. There's so much that I don't know. If I could just..." She stopped, at a loss for words.

"What stories did he tell you?" My curiosity was insatiable. Did they have to do with me? Was his conscience pricked after all? I casually plucked a Cadbury Egg from the centerpiece and began to unwrap it.

"Oh—" Jada craned her head as though she was about to merge into oncoming traffic and told me that was it was too complicated. It was obvious that she was on the brink of something; she had deliberately sent Henry away. But here he was, triumphantly soaring into view.

The Past

There was a line. Luckily, Jada came back with Henry on her heels. We exchanged hugs and pleasantries and Jada motioned a bartender to meet us at the side of the bar. There were perks to knowing the hostess.

She ordered, and we heard a disconcerting crack as the yolk of an egg was professionally drained into the bottom of a romantically shaped crystal glass.

"Raw eggs? What kind of drink is that?" Orlando was horrified.

The bartender wiped his hands on a towel and turned a cardboard signature drink sign in our general direction with a smirk, mixing and pouring and scooping all the while. We read:

RAMOS GIN FIZZ
lemon juice
lime juice
sugar
cream
gin
egg
orange flower water
cold club soda

Orlando's face was a rainbow of emotions as he skimmed the ingredients and Jada explained the history of this colorful drink.

"They invented it in New Orleans in the 19th century for Fat Tuesday." She pronounced "day" like "dee," which gave it a melodious ring. She continued, "Actually, I found it online and thought it'd be festive. Try it. Here—have this one." She picked up the red and blue napkin on which it was served and scooted it over to him. He held up a hand in protest.

"I'll order my own. Aren't you worried about the health risks?" And to the bartender, "I'll have one—without egg."

But it wasn't festive. It looked like a frothy vanilla protein shake. The ingredient list had me picturing Mardi Gras floats and motley colors. The egg just took over the glass as its own.

Jada laughed. "We're all corn-fed here. Comfort food—well—" she continued bashfully, "a little comfort drink now and then, too—are a southern tradition." She picked off the fresh orange garnish, took a small sip, and made a satisfied groan.

Henry, without pause, took a sip of her drink and gushed, "Delicious!"

A triumphant smile, a swish of the hips, and she was off, drink in hand. "Y'all have a good time, now, okay?" she called behind her, and then she was swept into a whorl of admirers. Henry watched her leave, promptly ordered a scotch on the rocks, and thanked the bartender for his service. He removed the straw and took a chunk of ice in his mouth, cracking it with his teeth and swirling the dark amber liquid in his glass. He looked down into it and watched himself take another swig.

"I always have a good time." Orlando turned to me. "Estelle, darling, I'm going to head over to the Big Table" ---he jerked his head toward the outside—"to see if I can—"

Lorena brushed by us, her short legs moving quickly but her speed obviously impeded by the flip flops she was wearing. The thongs were decorated with huge fake daisies and her toes were busy keeping the shoes attached to her person. She wasn't paying attention to anyone; she was staring down into her cleavage like they were crystal balls or her personal GPS, adjusting now one side of her low-cut dress, now the other. Rather than simply giving her arms coverage because she had inappropriately selected a white pullover sundress smeared with black and yellow polka dots, the lemon chiffon cardigan she paired it with made her outfit the attire of a prepubescent girl on her way to an Easter Sunrise Service. She had to be at least in her early forties.

"I guess someone's walking the rounds tonight," I had to hold back a full-fledged belly laugh. I didn't like that woman. Orlando rolled his eyes, grabbed his drink, which I suppose he had decided wasn't really that bad since it was already half drunk, and laid a hand on my arm.

"I---"

"I wouldn't mind a cigar myself," Henry mused. "If you're going that way, I'll introduce you to some people." Orlando sucked in a breath with an ambiguous look at Henry and cordially agreed to accompany him. He tucked a tendril of hair behind my ear and smoothed it into place.

"I'll be back, okay? There's plenty of eye candy here to keep you busy." They left.

It didn't take long for me to figure out who Orlando was talking about. There was a rowdy group of Richard's football buddies within arm's reach of the bar. Probably the only thing keeping them from transforming this area into a scene from Animal House were their tuxes and the stiff formalities which the beginnings of an evening like this one still required. A gaggle of tan, long-necked sorority types in their prom gowns boldly approached the young men with their heads tilted at coquettish angles and their bangles sending thrilling tinkles into the air. They were reminiscent of the pyramids of midriffs and toned arms and firm thighs of the football field, and a remnant of sweet glory still mingled with their floral perfumes.

I scanned the room to see if there was anyone who could save me from the awkward embarrassment of drinking alone. Though I recognized a handful of teachers and professors and even a few members of the Board, I didn't see anyone who could ameliorate my momentary wistfulness. Everywhere there were waves and diamonds and metals. I thought one glamorous woman with her hair tightened into a flawless French twist might be running for Congress; there were other telltale signs, like the volume with which anecdotes were delivered, or the intricacy of a hand-stitched design, that this gentleman or that power couple had been invited for calculated reasons.

Near the doors, lengths of tables were set up along the walls, and they overflowed into the adjoining rooms -- offering such a dense variety of lush aperitifs that the density with which these tables were packed with food justified the collective description of a smorgasbord.

I sampled a deviled egg and a marinated olive. The two tables I was standing in front of were laden with shrimp cocktail, spinach artichoke dip, expensive meats and exotic vegetables on skewers, pimento cheese and bacon crostini, cheese fondue, goat cheese with peppers and almonds, and tacos verdes. Other tables had more Texan fare: chili and cornbread, racks of ribs, and charred meats. I followed the food trail into what seemed like a formal living room, where I found a dessert table. Should I try a specialized cupcake, tangerine crème brûlée, or a tangy slice of pineapple upside down cake? Slicing into the yellow icing of the cake, I was slightly startled when I felt a light caress on my back. The grandmotherly woman with the pince-nez from the bible study smiled up at me.

"Hello dear. How are you this evening? What a party, huh?" She clacked her teeth together in approval. "Jada always outdoes herself... I wonder, have you thought more about joining my women's mission outreach?" She pointed to a group of people who were seated on plush leather couches. Pastor Sam was talking to an eager young couple in mauve, a few feathered women without their spouses, and some aging men whose servility, I thought, came more from the inevitable creeping dependence they were beginning to feel than actual gentle dispositions.

I didn't know how to evade her question without sounding disingenuous or rude. How can you triumph over an idea? I continued to plate my slice of cake, giving myself a moment to think while I scraped the icing from the knife onto the side of my red plastic dessert plate. I heard Pastor Sam timidly explaining church plans for expansion and possible future mission trips for which he would soon be posting positions on the website. He was self-consciously nursing a beer, just the possession of which lent him a rebellious bravado, which for him, was expressed solely through a brighter shade of color in his cheeks.

"You know, I think I'm going to begin an outreach of my own, with a humanitarian focus," I said.

Her sweet smile faltered slightly. She opened her mouth to speak but I continued with a false start, "I- -um." I didn't know how to put it so she would not lose her goodwill toward me.

"There's a lot of sadness in the world. I'm learning that people mostly just need sympathy from someone: someone to give them permission to find their own passage to happiness. And if not that, then, well, at least someone who will try to understand." A thought occurred to me. I looked directly into her eyes, which were watery and tired.

"We have our own callings, you know. I wish you only the best in pursuing yours. Cake?"

She paused for a moment, as if she was thinking this through. She searched my face, and then accepted the offering with kindness.

"Thank you. I think I know what you mean. God bless you in your calling as well, sweet girl. God bless you." She bestowed a rhythmical three pats upon my shoulder and then went to join a group of elderly people who were whispering dryly but contentedly across from the church folks. They were sentimentally intimate; an image of a rocking chair on a front porch at sunrise came to mind. I liked looking at them, but this room was not for me. Not yet. Besides, my drink was empty, and I was interested in trying one of the cloudy but refreshing looking mojitos I had seen in the bejeweled hands of strangers.

The Future

"Spider mites," he yelled as he came up. His voice adjusted itself as he came closer, and so did our faces. "Just take a heavy duty hose and spray them off. That should take care of them." He sat down and helped himself to a handful of Easter candy.

"How can I prevent them from coming back?" Jada sounded worried.

"You can't," he said matter-of-factly. Then, chewing, "Well, your garden is so beautiful you might put two angels with two blazing orange swords in front of it to keep them out. Worked for God, right?"

"I think it's been proven that it won't prevent snakes from coming in, though," I quipped.   We all laughed. "You know, I really liked your friend Orlando. Why had you been hiding him from me all that time? We must have almost met a thousand times before. Such a pleasant guy!"

"I've barely spoken to him lately. He's like that—he falls off the grid a lot." I glanced at Jada meaningfully.

"He must have found someone interesting or maybe he's busy with work. I can't even guess." There was a comfortable silence as we all thought back to that night, the night of the party. Things were so different then for all of us.

Suddenly, Jada snapped her fingers. "Henry, I know you've just sat down but I want you to do something else for me. Go over there to the extra garage. I've got tons of Heath's pots—all shapes and sizes and different glazes, too—stored in there. I want you to take anything you can find a use for, ah, tools too. Otherwise, it will be ages before I can get them out of the way. I thought you could do something with them. They're extra. Stella and I will be right here when you get through."

He knew she was trying to get rid of him. But the thrill he felt at the prospect of snooping through the remains of Heath's sleepless nights overcame him. "You're sure?" A false note of concern for the impropriety of it all.

"Oh yes." A false note of the guarantee that her partiality toward him trumped convention.

As soon as he was out of sight, her face fell. "I'm going to sell this house." She rubbed her temples as she said it but there was certainty in her tone.

"You are?" I hadn't thought about what she would do next. I guessed it made sense.

"Yes. It's too big for me to live in alone. Richard has his own life, you see."

"But he comes by pretty often, doesn't he?" I tried to soothe her.

"That hardly matters. He's going to marry Heather now. I'm sure they'll get their own place soon."

Trying to be casual, I verified what I was hearing. "Lorena's daughter?"

"Yes. Richard got her in trouble. It was all Lorena and I could do to help them see reason, to do the right thing. They wanted to have an abortion. But they're just scared kids. They'll be alright. Of course Heather will have to drop out, at least for a while. And Richard will have to give up the football team in order to get a job. He wasn't happy about that. I told him neither am I, frankly. But I think everything really does happen for a reason. They have both been coming to church regularly since it all happened, like a real family already, and everyone is really accepting of them. I think Richard might even become a deacon soon. He's a changed man. I think the Lord got a hold of him and I'm delighted about it all. And of course Lorena reminds me every chance she gets that we are family now." I thought she suppressed a sigh. I could have imagined it.

"Where will you go?"

"Oh, I'm sure I'll eventually get a much smaller place. But I've decided to go to Africa for an extended period of time."

I couldn't believe what I was hearing. My jaw literally dropped. "Africa?" I could only repeat her.

"Pastor Sam asked me right after the funeral. He took me into his office and we prayed together and then he just came right out and asked me. He said he thought it would help me move on and that I would be perfect at helping to start a sister church there. I would assist in the building itself, which I've never done before but which will be good for me. And of course I would evangelize—hand out pamphlets, make friends with the natives, that sort of thing. I'm very excited and I've made up my mind that I'm going to do it." Words tumbled out of her.

"When I was in high school, we read *The Scarlet Letter*. My teacher was a young lady, whom I now realize knew next to nothing about life yet. When we finished the novel, I asked her why Hester stayed in that terrible community. Why didn't she just leave? She didn't do anything wrong, after all. It wasn't her. My teacher told me she didn't leave because she probably couldn't afford to go with a young girl to feed. But I think it was because she realized she would carry the past with her wherever she went. But I won't be like that. I'm free now, and I won't ruin my life looking back."

Oh, Jada, that's what you think. You can't escape the past because you can't escape yourself. The past is only what you made of it. Wherever you are, you are still there. And whenever, too.

The Present Which Has Become the Past-On the Road to the Future in April

Lorena was the first one to call me with the news that Heath had died. I could feel my pulse throbbing out of my neck. Simultaneous silent conversations crowded my mind—every actual word I began died away on my lips. She made sure we hadn't lost the connection, inserting herself firmly into my consciousness with speculatory tones about plans, pities, and prayers.

I went to the funeral. I was relieved it was a military memorial service. I couldn't bear to see Heath made up like a rodeo clown, smiling honestly for the first time in his adult life. He wanted to be cremated, Jada said tearfully, because he'd had claustrophobic tendencies. She wore a string of pearls that must have been an heirloom. She fingered them as though they were rosary beads for a solemnly beautiful mourning ritual. Tears and dark blue uniforms with white buttons and warbles of patriotic hymns are almost all I remember. But there was one more thing: I remember everyone kept looking upward with reverence as the passive service progressed.

Henry called me unexpectedly a few days later. He wanted me to go visit Jada with him. We decided on a time but I canceled at the last minute because I couldn't face either of them yet. Henry and I had not been alone together since our brief relationship had abruptly ended, and I was certain Jada would not want to see me. I changed my mind a few hours later. He sounded exasperated and told me he'd move some things around in his schedule, which wasn't easy, he wanted me to know. We made plans for early the next afternoon, which was the day before Easter Sunday.

"Did you call her?" were his first words to me after I let him in.

"No. I thought it'd be better if we just made it look like we were in the neighborhood. Kept it casual."

"There's protocol for occasions like this, Stella. You should have called her." He formed an expression of intensity.

"Relax, okay? I baked a casserole. She'll know we were thinking about her. I didn't figure I could count on you for *that* one, but you could have called her yourself." I slipped on my blue and silver sandals and searched for my keys.

"Well, *you* could have gone to a bakery or something. Let's hope she's home and looking decent and feeling like company."

"Getting something pre-made didn't feel right, or trust me, I would've. And when has Jada EVER not looked put together?" Henry grinned stupidly. He thought I had just paid him a compliment. He looked down at the little table next to the front door and spotted the Rubik's cube amid a pile of random junk I'd taken hurriedly out of my pockets over the last few months. He picked it up and started twisting the squares.

"Are you driving or am I?" I laid down the gauntlet. Henry habitually insisted on driving. I wasn't about to concede to him that macho head-of-the-household symbol of control again, not now that our dynamic had changed entirely.

He fumbled with the cube, glanced over at me, and shrugged unconcernedly. "You can drive." What he seemed to mean was, "You think I'm going to argue with you over this small petty matter. But you have always been mistaken about me; I am magnanimous and a gentleman. Perhaps you should practice some quiet introspection." A cathartic daydream of performing violent acts to various parts of him afforded me enough momentary self-control to collect myself entirely. I sighed noisily and ordered him into the car. He checked his appearance in the small hall mirror and began to flirt with himself. I came up behind him, pretending like I was going to choke him. He winked at us both, his looking glass reflection and me, popped his collar, and ambled out. After making sure I had everything, I locked up and followed Henry out into the sunshine.

I drove, noting how many bluebonnets were out in the medians and near the highways. It was always strange to me that the bluebonnet should have been chosen as the Texas State flower. It didn't seem big enough, or the right color somehow, though I marveled at how a large field of them could seem like a mirror of the sky itself.

The Past

In the large room, men and women came and went. I dreaded the inevitable awkward confrontation I would probably have with Heath. But he was probably in his study. He didn't much like parties because he didn't much like people. After a few rounds of small talk, I made my way to the cigar bar outside. Heath had been there, I was surprised to hear. And Orlando too, only momentarily, they said. After this remark, the table was eyeballs and elbows. Henry brightened up for a moment when he saw me. He asked me if I knew where Jada was. I didn't. After announcing to the entire group that he had a surprise to top off the evening which must be revealed in the presence of the hostess, he plunged himself back into a deep discussion (for what other kind was there with Henry? He was exhausting) with two plump red-faced men. They seemed amused. Henry was oblivious to their reactions, probably because the scotch was obviously having its way with him.

But where was Orlando? I extracted myself, politely murmuring a few excuses to the present company. A well-to-do rancher type with a Sam Elliot mustache and a big Texas belt buckle veiled his ogling with a tight smile at me and a tip of his banded cowboy hat. With everyone dressed to the nines, it was easy to imagine we were in Manhattan or L.A., but then there were telltale signs of Texas everywhere if you looked for them. They were all over this guy. He was nearing handsome; the full-blown dignified cowboy, so romantic on the screen, had often become a scarcely recognizable inspiration for the amiable down-home advantage which the more savvy modern Texas businessmen at this party hoped their boots gave them. I wasn't convinced that he was the real McCoy, but I indulged him in a daughterly smile, and then broke away from his athletic eyes in an attempt to drink in the ambience of the party and to spot my missing friend.

I found Orlando in the gentlemen's study. The first time I'd seen it, I thought it must have been fashioned after the 19th century hunting lounge in which humbugs with curling moustaches fondled globes and displayed the stuffed heads of big game which they had brought back with them from safari. The walls were towers of expensive volumes with picturesque ladders on wheels attached to the shelves and a padded bay window which was arranged so as to seem inviting: there were decorative pillows which nevertheless were too crisp to have ever been lain upon. In the corner of the green and burgundy room a solid mahogany desk had been pushed to the side, presumably to make way for a dance floor, and against which more clusters of people were talking and laughing. But only a few people were dancing. Jada's small voice reemerged from my memory: Heathenism must be stamped out. I got the feeling that this dance floor wasn't her idea.

I recognized the back of Orlando, and as I approached him, too late he moved just enough for me to see over his shoulder that he was speaking in low muffled tones to Heath. What could Orlando have to say to Heath? Surely he wasn't confronting him about what I'd told him of the other night? Then what...? All I could make out beneath the din of the music and the delighted whoops of the crowd now gathering around a particularly gifted dancer and the general roar of the party were the words "too close to the lamp post."

And then the recognition in Heath's eyes must have alerted Orlando, for Orlando spun upon his heel as though he expected a sneak attack. I will never forget the impression his expression had upon me, the sole intended recipient I was certain was Heath. The upper half of his face was deeply sympathetic—his eyes were just like the munificent eyes of Christ surveying the suffering world from a crucifix as depicted by centuries of religious imaginations. But the lower half of his face was the image of a large predator disturbed mid-meal; his mouth curved up in what could only be described as a cautionary snarl.

Sorrow had traumatized Heath's face: his eyes were subterranean cataractic pixels now that he had popped into the world again from the dimness of his monastic refuge, and his complexion, the color of oxidized wine, emphasized the deep lines carved into his cheeks. He smelled like wet newspaper. After all the preemptive emotional responses to this meeting had played out like a collection of old films in my mind, the only emotion I felt in the actual moment was sympathy. He was scared, and more than ever, he looked like a blurry re-print of himself.

Orlando, what have you done, I thought. I could fend for myself; I was no nineteenth-century woman. I made up my mind to let him have it once we were alone, but I knew I could never stay angry with him for long. He was too sleek to be caught in any untidy flare-ups of emotion. Sometimes I wondered if he had specially sharpened his personality to a supernatural degree of proficiency as an effective shield against the shamefully personal.

So we all smiled stupidly at each other. What else could we do? Heath stared tragically into the folds of my shawl while Orlando said something hilarious. I couldn't read the scene; I was floating in between my mind and the moment, searching for something hard, something real. Luckily, after just a few more moments of bloated conversation, Henry rushed in and beckoned us to come along. It was time, he said. He had found Jada, he said. Heath's face darkened; he suspected, as we all did, but it didn't seem to matter anymore.

Whatever had taken hold of him was far larger than any one being. We gratefully followed Henry into the hot scramble of the central room where everyone was gathering for this special revelation.

The Future

"As sudden as Heath's death has been, everything happens for a reason. Maybe this is it: I have a calling."

"But—but—what about Henry?" I could see him, his chin raised a little jauntily, saying something to her about being thrown over.

"I'm not telling him yet. He was a weakness for me. That may be another reason for me to leave here for a while. I can find my purpose again without distractions."

"Won't you be lonely?"

"Aren't we always, Stella?" She looked down into her lap. "When Lorena found out I was going she started scheming to figure out how to come along. She'll probably take a leave of absence if she can get her bills paid while she's gone. We'll both fly back for the baby's birth, of course, but then… well, we will see what happens. I plan to be gone for a while."

"What does she do? I don't think I've ever known."

"Do? She doesn't do anything. Oh! You mean—Oh. She's a middle school cheerleading coach. And I think she teaches something else too. Social studies. That's it." After a moment, she pointed to some yellow flowers. "I love those yellow irises, don't you? They bloom so tall and so bright just so people will notice them, admire them. We all just want to be loved, don't we?"

"Are you talking about the irises or Lorena?" I couldn't help asking.

She smiled faintly and removed her sunglasses again, folding them up. She squinted into my face. For a moment she had the same tragic look in her eye that I'd seen on her late husband's face. I noticed she had a couple of light freckles along her hairline. They were endearing.

"I know you're probably thinking all sorts of things right now, but I have been meaning to explain something to you. Now I can't take anything back and neither can you. But we can come to an understanding, like I was saying earlier. And I can understand the appeal—after all, I remember telling you myself that Heath reminded me of your Santiago in ways. You didn't know Heath, though. I did. And with him, every question only leads to more questions. I don't even know how he died exactly. Because he had been a Navy Seal and an officer, he had access to top secret information. The results of the autopsy I requested myself were not released to me. It was classified, was all they would say, no matter how I threatened and pleaded and pushed."

"Oh, Jada—" I pushed back my chair to go to her but she held up a warning hand and continued with a flame in her eyes.

"You cannot begin to imagine what anguish I have felt, what sorrow I have both witnessed and borne…. and the bitterness. And not just since he died—for years beforehand. I won't lie—his obvious distress and insane mood swings placed a lot of strain on our marriage, as you noticed, I suppose. But you misread him. He always loved me. And we talked about your little infatuation with him. He had that effect on many people. That's why I married him. The mysterious is always either appealing or petrifying. In this case, he was both." I completely understood that. I had felt exactly that way when he lunged toward me in his studio.

"But you couldn't know, not like I learned, that he didn't get out of bed some mornings, and didn't come to bed at all most nights. And then there were those dark hours where his eyes turned black and he acted like someone I'd never met before. So even I do not know the truth for certain. All I can tell you is what he told me… in fragments and at different times, so his moods affected my understanding. Sometimes he was desperate, sometimes he was angry; my own opinion is that every bit of it is the paranoid imagining of a weakened mind that has finally cracked up."

We both inhaled sharply. I said, "Okay. Tell me." And she began.

The Present

The hard sun streamed into the car, lighting up the tin foil which covered Jada's casserole. The glint hit me right in the face as I drove. "Henry, can you please…?" I pulled down the sun visor and blocked the concentrated beam with my right hand.

"Oh, yeah. No problem." He moved the dish to the back floorboard, then pulled out the Rubik's cube and returned contentedly to work.

"Thanks. Much better. You brought that silly thing with you?" He had almost gotten one face of the cube to turn bright yellow.

"I've never solved one. Of course, I haven't really tried since I was around eight."

The car was silent except for the hum of the motor and the *click click click* of the toy. We drove on like that for a while. A stoplight turned red more quickly than I had anticipated and I hit the brakes. Henry's body lurched forward slightly and fell back against the seat.

"Oh, come on, Stella. I knew I should have driven. Women." He shook his head disgustedly. *Click click.* He was focused on red now. He peeked out of his window, then straightened up and pointed to a two-storied strip mall that we were approaching.

"Shut it. That was totally out of my control—"

He talked over me. "We just finished that job. I'm pretty proud of it."

I had just enough time to see patches of impossibly green grass and large blooming magnolia trees which looked plastic against the sharp edges of the building as we passed. His obsession with perfection made everything he touched seem a little less interesting to me. Still, there was something commercially pleasing about his work. There was a reason he was in such high demand; you always knew what you were getting with him.

"That's pretty."

"Yes." *Click click click.*

Stella's Thoughts

Heath was one of the only people I knew who understood fluidity. This quality allowed him to evade and to survive but there were parts of him which eventually fell apart like lean meatloaf. Yoked to a sense of relative purpose, others might imagine they have built up a fortress against suffering. "I am." This is their world, their meaning, their vision. But Heath's soft-boiled revisions of himself splashed up against the obstructions of millions of hardened shells. Everything then became for him a symbol for something else... a different time, remembered or imagined, an aspect, a fragment... He was made up of incarnations of space, and nobody knew what he was grasping for.

The Past

Henry whispered to a young girl dressed in a catering uniform and she left. He hopped up onto the bar and announced to the glittering room that tonight they would be a part of something both extraordinary and absolutely unremarkable. "And that's the point," he said. Jada stood beneath him, looking up in wonder. When the same girl returned with two other crew members, both carrying large sterling trays bearing tiny slivers of hors d'oeuvre, she tilted her head back and laughed. "You didn't," she mouthed with glossy peach lips. Henry beamed down warmly and smugly upon her.

The Future

"He started becoming obsessed with these movies. If he wasn't in his studio, my husband the Mad Potter, he was in the media room, watching *The Bourne Trilogy*, the *Manchurian Candidate*, you know the kind. Those CIA conspiracy movies. They got into his head. He started 'remembering' things, as he put it. Devil worshippers, flames, and ritual torture. I was certain it was symbolic for something he saw or something he did when he was in the Navy. He was a sniper, you know. He swore it was real. He remembered. Eyes, he said. Snouts. Teeth. A forest. I prayed for him every day. Then he said it was the government. They did it to him. They used the costumes as a cover-up, in case he remembered. I thought maybe he was truly demon-possessed. He was crippled by these wicked memories, he said."

The Present

"Oh my God. Of course!" I exclaimed. There was a long line of cars ahead of us. I slowed to a crawl. The odometer didn't even register that we were going more than five miles an hour. "There must be construction or something." My heart sank. I hated traffic. I thought hopefully of the quiet house by the lake.

A frustrated grunt. "Yep," he agreed. His lips puffed out in concentration. There was still some orange and yellow in his blue.

"Henry... what are we going to say to her? And how are we going to get through this? You and me and Jada. Things have been complicated between us all."

"Don't be so dramatic. Nothing is complicated." He was focused on getting all the blue squares aligned. But the cube was not cooperating. There was still one orange square in the middle.

"What if there was a wreck? We're never going to get out of here."

Stella's Thoughts

Sensitive temperaments all too often experience contact doom—that anxious dread which suddenly constricts our soul into a compact solitaire, that hard chill--- the natural consequence of a brush with the eternal. Between the dangers and the disappointments, moments which will later be regretfully laid out with reverent fingers are suffered through and labeled "passable" and that is all. Over the years, a sort of sensual inflation has crept into the general consciousness, the brilliance of old Hollywood glamour dissected into billions of stars. We want to feel to the superlative degree in order to believe that the epic storylines we have arbitrarily pieced together, mixing facts with bits of cultural confetti, are not elaborate fantasies but imminent reassurances of our splendorous natures. But sometimes real life is senseless—the stubborn facts won't conform to our conceptions-- and then how does one cope? A hero with a red cape stretching out his arms toward us is enough to make us smile again.

The Future

"Memories of summer camps when he was a boy. His parents waving goodbye with the American Flag whipping behind them like a red cape. They packed him a picnic basket with cake. It was hazy, he said, but it was still there in his mind. They made him go. They knew, and they still made him go. At the camps they almost killed him every year. When he was almost dead, he blacked out. Then they whispered to him, important things they didn't want him to know about and didn't want him to forget. They sent a grandmother in an apron to make him feel better and ask him a bunch of questions. He searched out flowers to look at when they drove him home."

Stella's Thoughts

I watched "Citizen Kane" with my mother and cried for hours on end when I figured out what Rosebud meant. I knew exactly how old Mr. Kane felt. I didn't have a sled growing up, but I did have a red radio flyer wagon that I felt pretty similar about. Christmas is based on the same lie as the rest of our childhood—the red and white promises that were so present, so close to us when we were young dissolve into memories of a domestic perfection we never truly attained, of a close-knit family gathered around the Christmas tree singing carols with hot chocolate to go around. With distance comes wisdom, and the ability to become fond of our parents, despite their having made us believe for so long that they were horrible parents for not delivering us into an eternal fairytale.

The Present

Henry's tongue was sticking out in concentration. It certainly didn't seem like he was enjoying the Rubik's cube anymore. He was challenged, and Henry never liked to be truly challenged by anything. He was hunched over the cube, twisting more quickly now.

I couldn't resist. "You're getting sloppy," I told him.

"Just drive," he murmured.

A smile rose to my lips. "Someone's getting crabby."

"Yeah, *you* are." *Click click click click.*

I turned the radio on and tried to find something I liked, switching past various commercials and laughing deejays and played-out songs and traffic reports. One of the stations mentioned a stalled out car in the middle of the road slowing everyone else down for miles. *I should have been a pair of ragged claws...* I switched it off.

"Damn it!" I hit the steering wheel with my fist. Henry ignored me. We inched forward and then stopped again.

Stella's Thoughts

Like the puffed-up weeble advertisements which have become so popular all over the city we have a center at which we rest comfortably. Any forward leaning or backwards tipping can be corrected by taking a big huge whiff of fresh blue oxygen and slowly and consciously losing our wayward momentum until we are quite still. We can then only hope to become cool assessors rather than raging addicts subject to the effects of a hallucinogenic laboratory of rabid emotion.

The Future

"It started with the witch-hunts and was so successful it continued even into Vietnam. The damn government, he said, like it was one word. Torture, rape, anything to make him black out so they could deposit their secrets into him. He was the chosen vessel. He had a guardian angel but it wasn't the grandmother. The angel commanded him with a phrase handed down by God. He had to whisper the words to other people sometimes, and sometimes, he had to hurt people so he wouldn't get hurt again."

Stella's Thoughts

Jada had her own web. It had its own purpose but like the World Wide Web, its threads held up the whole. Her broken relationships were entangled in it, surviving due to the cocoon she had woven around her family members. Her web had served to support her broken shell of a husband, her family honor, and her various charities. She had spun the truth so long it no longer seemed like a fairy tale to her. It was her vehicle to safety, a woven bridge which twisted and flapped precariously over the abyss.

The Present

"Can you see anything out your window?" I asked him. He broke away from the cube, rubbernecked as far as he could, and then looked down at the cube again, furiously moving the squares.

"Nope." His face had turned dark.

"You know, I'm surprised you haven't solved that thing yet. You're so good at solving things." I could feel myself slipping out of control.

"Better than you," he said. *Click click click.*

"I beat an Evil level Sudoku puzzle the other day." I was provoking him. It wasn't true but I knew his competitiveness would kick in.

"No you didn't."

"Yes I did." *Click click click click click.*

"Congratu-fucking-LATIONS!"

He opened the window and threw the Rubik's cube out with force. It shimmered metallically on the shoulder of the road.

The Past

"Here's a photo of what you are about to eat," Henry glowered. "Before we prepared this tonight, I made a bet with a friend that I could prove the existence of the blue lobster. The chef can not only vouch for its existence, but posted a YouTube video of its preparation because she was so honored to have the opportunity to cook it. The blue lobster is a one-in-two-million natural phenomenon. The funniest thing about this whole overblown affair is that you wouldn't know the difference between red and blue when it's cooked. There isn't one."

Stella's Thoughts

White picket fences are meant to keep us tucked away, safe in our childhood beds dreaming childhood dreams. We are inside, we are all together, we have manners and traditions and jokes and we understand each other. They can't get in, those who can't understand us. The American Dream.

The Future

"He almost killed me once. He was afraid of what he did when he didn't remember." She leaned in like she was herself a conspirator.

Stella's Thoughts

Jada, like a true native Texan, was building her fences. Maybe she recognized how threatening wide open spaces can be. I can see Jada eternally dribbling dirt into another of Heath's empty vases slowly like sand in an hourglass with a fresh bunch of flowers beside her.

The Present

I braked far harder than necessary, considering our lack of speed.

"Get it."

What? No. I'll get you another one."

"Get the goddamned cube, Henry. That was mine. You take things that aren't yours and then act like you don't understand why people get upset. Get it now."

He acted like he was going to yell again, but after seeing the look on my face opened the car door instead. He fell out, scooped up the cube, and stalked back to the car, plopping it in my lap as he slammed the door shut.

"You better not tell anyone," he commanded in a low voice. "She's in mourning."

Stella's Thoughts

I couldn't exactly approve of her leaving, but I thought Jada would be comfortable in Africa; the climate wasn't much different from Texas. There would always be beasts that freely roamed the plains and the vast deserts and the riotous forests; and there would always be the resentful sun restricted to its orbit and gunmetal and fences. *Thus, the cyclical violent histories of each region had inevitably bred the fanatical, the untame-able, into the colorful spirits of their peoples.*

The Past

"Enjoy!" He soaked up the applause and leapt down. Jada playfully shook her finger at him and then embraced him. Her golden arms were still thin even when pressed flat against Henry's shape. I came up to them. "You must have paid quite a price just to prove a point," she said.

The Future

"I'm telling you, he was lost a long time ago." The mockingbird replied from far away.

Stella's Thoughts

I was assigned a project on the mockingbird in third grade. I still remember Miss Harding's expression when I told her I wanted to do the state gemstone instead. All my friends did too, she said. I couldn't draw a bird very well. She told me the mockingbird had the prettiest song of any bird and that was why we chose it to represent Texas. I was proud of my project in the end; I thought the mockingbird must have the best sense of humor of all the rest. Now I wonder if they aren't little avian bodhisattvas, trying to spread their enlightenment to the rest of us.

The Past

"Not really," Henry said, chuckling, "I have friends in high places. My landscaping business reaches to the coast." Jada slugged him lightly on the arm. "Oh! You!" She took the proffered piece on a napkin and thanked the server.

Stella's Thoughts

Illusions at a magic show are specially created for the front row, for those closest to us; those at the back can either slip out once they have found the smoke and mirrors or stay and enjoy the entertainment. But those who are wise to the fun must shut it up inside themselves like the earth receives the dead because not many people can forgive someone who, by revealing the trick, spoils the evening for everyone else.

The Present

Suddenly I felt sorry for Henry. I had behaved badly. He was staring straight ahead like a petulant little boy. There was nothing for him to see except brake lights, and the horizon over them. There was at least that.

"I'm sorry, Henry. I'm just upset."

"I'll say. Get a hold of yourself. You've been acting like a bitch all day."

The Past

"So you found a blue lobster after all," I confronted him. "You should have left it alone."

The Future

"Heath said the Big Bad Wolf had found him and he was glad."

The Present

I took a deep breath and tried to think calming thoughts. We were moving forward again, even beginning to pick up speed. Maybe we were past the worst part.

The Past

"Stella," Henry sighed. "It's just a lobster."

The Present

Henry and I never would have worked out, I thought to myself. Never.

The Past

Jada looked questioningly at Henry. Heath and Orlando were slowly making their way toward us through the madding crowd.

The Present
"At least we're really moving now," I said. We were climbing up a large hill. When we got to the top, we gasped in unison.

The Past
I saw Orlando take two servings from a tray a few feet away. He gesticulated with his body when he spoke to the young man, who convulsed with stifled laughter. The tray wobbled. Orlando handed one to Heath, who looked like he was going to be sick. He had begun to weep silently. He threw the napkin down and took his portion into his hands.

Stella's Thoughts
We all have an immeasurable ability to love—we just have to lift the boundaries our parents and their parents before them set on our swollen hearts.

The Future
"He said his own personal Red Scare was over."

The Present
Stretched out for miles in the distance were pairs of angry red brake lights.

The Past
It was scarlet.

SPRING

CHAPTER TEN

"Do I contradict myself? Very well then—I contradict myself. (I am large; I contain multitudes.)"—Walt Whitman, "Song of Myself"

May-

I *am outside but there is no wind. Suggestive twilight transforms my solid cornflower uniform into a chaotic print of varying shades. Paralyzed, I cannot even shrug my shoulders as I stand on a checkered plain. The Red Queen materializes.*

"Are you ready now, Mary Ann?" she says in exasperated tones, as though she has already been kept waiting for centuries.

"I-- don't. My name is Stella. Ready for what?"

"Why, to play of course!" It somehow suddenly occurs to me that I am standing on a chessboard square. A battlefield.

"I don't want to play. I want to go home."

"Why, Mary Ann, you certainly are acting like someone else this evening. You usually revel in making the first move."

From behind me, "Let her forfeit if she likes. She'll want to play again, naturally." The White Queen looks down at her nails, unconcerned.

"I think there's been a huge mistake. I'm not Mary Ann, and—"At this the Red Queen begins knitting together strings of invective to hurl at me and the White Queen laughs.

"And I suppose I'm not Mary Ann, either, right?" The Red Queen screams.

"Next thing you know, I won't be!" The White Queen's indignant shrill.

"We are all Mary Ann. That's you, you know. So you'll have to make your move." A wave of a powerful hand and the board is filled with life-sized images of me, masquerading as chess pieces. Horrified, I search for answers in the eyes of the Red Queen. But she has my face now. And so does the White Queen.

"Well?" They wait, oblivious to my terror.

"Is this—chess? Am I supposed to move two spaces as a pawn? If I win, can I go home?"

"Idiot," I shriek, wearing a flaming red headdress and pointing my scepter menacingly at myself. "This is hardly a game of chess! Who ever heard of such a thing?"

"She can't even count," I add, unable to contain my mirth. "There are nine squares. Obviously. Not eight."

"But—I read about this somewhere. Surely I can win if I know the rules of the game."

"Or you can lose." I bark these out from behind myself in a deep voice atop a gorgeous stallion.

"And if you lose—you'll never get back home," I taunt from across the board.

I stagger to the ground, feeling lost and overwhelmed by confusion.

A diffident whisper says, "Don't get lost in the 'I.' Think of it like 'She.' Stand back from yourself. That's your hint."

"Quiet, you!" A cacophony of voices fall violently upon the whisperer.

Suddenly, an earthquake shakes all the pieces in their places into cowed silence from the center of the board twenty feet away. A great chasm opens up and moves like a mouth as my deepened voice booms out from within,

"They're right, you know. You have to play. But you can be the board. Then it doesn't matter if you win or lose, Stella."

Tearfully, I say, "You know my name?"

"I know everything. I have the advantage of watching it all unfold. You can't pretend with me even if you try."

Passionately, I look into the chasm in desperation. "How can I get home?" I ask the board.

"You are already there," I say simply.

When she opened the door, she saw him leaning against the side of the apartment across from hers, one leg kicked up behind him casually. He snuffed out the butt of his cigarette across the back of his shoe and asked her where he might discard it safely.

"Orlando. What a present surprise!" she exclaimed.

"Ha, ha," he retorted mockingly. "I just came along to see how you've been. You've hardly answered any of my calls. And your texts have been sorely lacking in entertainment value." He grinned.

"Now I know you're packing and all of that, but come on. Are you keeping a delicious secret from me, old girl? You have someone on the side?"

"I've been through a lot," she said, shutting the door behind them. She gestured to the half-filled packing boxes set up next to all the shelves in her living room, kitchen, and study. She stepped over a pile of unmade cardboard to make a point.

"And I have been busy. I still am." She went over to an open drawer in the kitchen where she was filling a taped-up box with heavy utensils. "I've just been thinking about things. I'm excited about the move, but I have so much left to wrap up here."

"You've never used that a day in your life," Orlando smirked. He pointed at the potato masher she was transferring from the drawer.

She shook it playfully at him. "Oh hush. Why don't you make yourself useful or something? I've got plenty I could delegate. Besides," she added, "I'm going to have to break down and learn how to use all of these things sometime. Who knows? Maybe I've let my fear of the kitchen keep the world from knowing their next Iron Chef."

"You may be onto something. Some people get over their phobias by controlled exposure to what they fear most. Snakes, spiders… egg timers." He grabbed it from the drawer and held it in front of him.

"Is there a reason you're here, or did you just come over between boyfriends?" she asked.

"Estelle!" He held his hand to his heart as though mortally wounded. Then he relaxed his pose, his tone grown serious, "Actually, there is. I'm here to tell you something." He shook the egg timer again and thrust it onto the pile in the box.

She froze. Her brow crinkled in concern.

"What is it?" She led him to the couch in her living room, where she moved two large boxes to the floor in order to make space for them to sit down. They sat.

""You've always sought after the truth, Stella. That's one reason I've been truly drawn to you, because we have that in common. And because I esteem you so highly, I'm going to tell you the truth now. Directly and honestly. Not many people can handle that. I'm not going to beat around the bush or sugarcoat anything or try to make you laugh. It won't be easy for you. Can I trust that you can handle it?'

"If you're coming out to me…" she laughed uncomfortably.

He took her hands into his. "Stella," he said with gentleness.

"Okay, okay." She was quiet, expectant.

"I am leaving here in three or four weeks at the most. For good." He waited to see if she understood the import of his words. She didn't react.

He said, "Remember, I am your friend. But I am not just a banker. That was my cover. I was sent here by a covert government agency two years ago on a special assignment. I can't tell you anymore than that, but I've got another assignment now. And so I have to go."

Her mouth twitched. Then she grinned and slugged him on the arm. "Come on, man. What do you have to tell me? I don't have all the time in the world. I'm kind of busy right now." She gestured with a wide sweep of her arm to the half-packed apartment.

He lightly grabbed her arm and continued, "You've got to know that I do love you. You are very important to me. This life is a lonely one, and you are a kindred spirit."

Her face fell, full of confusion, as she reached out for a large roll of bubble wrap and started popping, violently crushing one air pocket after another.

"Aren't you going to say anything?" He waited patiently.

"Get out."

"Oh, come on, now, Stella. I know you have questions. I really can't answer them now, but I promise you I will someday. Someday. And I'll miss you horribly."

Orlando came over to her and hugged her tight. She wanted to push him away, but she couldn't do it. She was overwhelmed by the news that he wasn't who he said he was, by the loss of her best friend, by all the unexpected changes that had already occurred in her life. He held her closely while she sobbed. After a few minutes, she broke from his embrace and tore off a couple of paper towels from the holder, blotting her reddened eyes. Then she left the room for a moment and disappeared into her bedroom. She returned with Santiago's guitar, holding it out from her body like an accusation against Orlando.

"Remember your promise to me. Remember the love we had for him. You can't just leave now." She threw the guitar at his head. He ducked. It scraped against a corner of her wall as it banged discordantly against the tiled floor, echoing hollowly as the vibrations from the strings grew further apart and finally died. They both stared at it.

"I'm stalled out, Orlando. I'm stuck, and you're just dropping this bomb on me and expecting forgiveness and then what? How am I supposed to live here without you around? How am I supposed to keep going at all, alone with this knowledge in this place? You tell me *that* because I really don't see it. How?" The tears streamed down her face again.

He was calm. "No. Santiago was stalled out. Heath was stalled out. Remember—there's a difference between total inertia and an interlude. Know the difference. You're just idling in traffic in the aftermath of their tragedies. It's not the same. Look behind you to see how far you've come already. And I know you've got lots of miles left on you, Estelle."

"I can't." Her voice was small, panicked.

He paused for a moment to formulate how to respond to her. He noticed a Rubik's Cube on her desk. He fiddled with it for less than a minute and then threw it to her.

"It's solved."

She looked down at it, amazement momentarily overpowering her fury and her pain.

"How- how did you do that?"

"It's simple, really. You just memorize a few different algorithms and it's a cinch. Works every time. It's a neat party trick." He half-smiled.

She was enraged.

"Life is not a game, Orlando. You can't just quarantine the problems of life onto a neat little grid with a magical formula or the right phrase or whatever. You can't predict or explain people's behavior! You just can't!"

Almost as if he hadn't heard her, he responded to her earlier question. "You're a star. That's what your name means, right? You'll build your home on the twinkle you give off. You are rather a diamond in the sky."

"What does that mean?" she sniffed.

"Merely that your reflective capability will serve you well. You asked me how you will deal with this knowledge. If you avoid the pain it causes you, you will only push it down further inside of yourself, where it will fester until you will someday unexpectedly be forced to confront the reality of it outside of your own terms. And it will have grown exponentially in its ability to hurt you because your fear and anxiety will have only strengthened it every moment you have refused to accept its existence. It's a black hole, Stella. Don't do that to yourself." He looked into her eyes.

She looked down at the floor.

He tried again. "Listen. We all deal with pain. Everyone experiences contact doom, right? A questioning of their own purpose or worth? Fear and anxiety? It can make your future seem like it's streamlined into a single stifling direction. But there is a way to turn the small stream back into the entire ocean again. It's all a matter of perspective. Let me think how to explain it." He paused.

"Okay. Let's take a mirror. It's got a frame around it. Most people think of themselves as what the mirror reflects, what is shown back in the mirror. But let's say the mirror is able to reflect the sum total of everything you believe yourself to be. We will call this the reflected self. Your environment, your experiences, the people you know, the words you hear in relation to yourself—all of this makes up the reflected self. Most people stop their thinking here and that's all they ever are to themselves. It rarely changes, and often, they limit themselves to that self. They will even be more likely to actually behave as they believe that self would be likely to behave. But think of the reflective quality of the mirror. It's smooth and calm. It's the reflective self. Instead of a mirror in a frame, think of this reflective self as the entire ocean. It has the fluidity to accept and reflect back the entire sky. It doesn't reflect in a judgmental or exclusionary way. It just calmly reflects everything exactly the same. Which one is the truer depiction of self—the reflected self or the reflective one? The waves can carry you literally anywhere in the world—once you shatter that framed mirror and go stand on the beach for a while. I've always found that people who live by the ocean are more self-aware, anyway. Good luck in Texas," he said with a wink.

"But my house is right by the lake. Second best thing, right?" she said feebly.

"Like anything else, finding this reflective self inside of you is a matter of experience. It takes a lot of practice and time to absorb the pain and not get too attached to it. If you just let it go through you—accept it fully as a part of the entire world, as a part of yourself—I've found that it helps in the long run. Pain is a natural part of life. But if you see the big picture, where you want to go, what your end goal is, then you can decide whether the pain is particularly worth it to achieve that goal. In other words, if you've got your heart set on dining at a world-famous restaurant, it's worth waiting hours for the ultimate satisfaction of having tried it for yourself. So it's no use screaming at the manager. The wait is just part of the experience. In fact, the food probably wouldn't be that good if one could just slip right in on a Friday night. Just try to be objective about it. Give yourself room to breathe. Become the ocean rather than the mirror that selectively reflects whatever it feels like reflecting."

"You can objectively notice what you are thinking without accepting it as the only truth. This is how you can distance yourself from your overwhelming feelings—annoyance at the couple waiting next to you, your stomach growling, boring small talk with your date. But it is really just as true that you are part of a very lucky crowd who will shortly be served gourmet cuisine, in the midst of the wonderfully torturous throes of anticipation, who will be able to recommend it to others as one who has experienced it for oneself."

"You really have the capacity to treat anything as a metaphor for something else, don't you?" Stella glared.

"We all do. That's one reason it's best to be reflective and not reflected. Symbols are tricky little bitches. They turn us on our heads, and then we're down the rabbit hole, not knowing up from down anymore. Words are nothing but symbols, Stella. Illusory. Dangerous. Or," he leaned back and threw up his hands, "really completely meaningless. That's what I'm trying to get at."

"Okay. So what?"

"So dwell in the space between the words. The pages themselves. Give yourself room to breathe. Become the reflective self. When thoughts, feelings, or bodily sensations arise, they are naturally associated with a specific time period in your life. Even complete fantasies that never really even happened can become harnessed to a frame inside of one's linear concept of time. But the reflective self transcends both time and space, because wherever you go, you are still there."

"You can't change reality, but you can change how you view it." She looked up for confirmation.

"Exactly. And you've already accepted that, I can tell, since you've put down your book bag and bought yourself a real home."

"But that was before all of this... all of this ugliness." She sighed.

"Oh I don't know. From the plane, Texas looks like peanut butter—it's sticky and spread out flat like paste and you can't get rid of it. That ugly has always been there." Orlando said.

"When I think of Texas, I think of a fiddle and a steel guitar." Stella was contemplative.

"Oh Stella, country living is alright. I need more excitement in my life than contentment, but for many, being away from the chaos and the traffic is worth living about twenty years behind. And Texas is special. I think people come from all over to the metropolitan areas of Texas for the possibilities: great jobs, cheap housing, and lots of networking opportunities. But I suspect that the practical ones will find when they get here that Texans are and have always been a little too preoccupied with the impossibilities of life."

She wondered what he meant by "impossibilities": did he mean that Texans all loved a challenge and were wont to prove everyone wrong? Or was he referring to something entirely different? She asked him as much, and he merely smiled enigmatically.

"A life without truth and beauty isn't worth living. You know how I feel about that. And there are all kinds of truths, and myriad artistic ways of expressing them. But sometimes, it's unkind to talk in riddles. The desperate need clarity so much that the weaker-willed of these can accept any answer that will alleviate their desperation. That's one reason I decided to be so forthright with you."

"I know what you mean. When life hands you lemons, just add a pound of sugar water every time and make lemonade. Because that's healthy advice, right? I guess there is something to the fluidity of water and going with the flow." She thought back to what Heath said not too long ago about the resourcefulness of madness.

"Help! I'm surrounded by lemonade!" she said, throwing her hands up like a hostage, trying to make light of what she was saying but failing.

Orlando, not taking the bait, said, "When life hands you lemonade, then, just eat it with a salad. I mean, I don't know what to say."

"But you don't win friends with salad." She was bitter and mocking.

"Then when someone hands them a salad, they can learn to make whatever else they want with it. The good thing about salads is that they're versatile. Everyone can add their own toppings." With a sigh, he said, "Get rid of the frame. All it does is limit and overwhelm. The feelings you have, the thoughts you believe--those are just leaves on the current. The current is the thing."

"You can't tell me *any*—"

"Nothing," he interrupted. "For both our sakes."

Thinking furiously, she rose and slowly walked over to the kitchen counter. In the back of her mind, she was trying to put pieces together. Pieces of a puzzle. Wordlessly, she began to pack again. He followed her in and caressed her hair.

"You can do this. We can do this. I'm going to dedicate every ounce of time I have left to being here for you. I'll help you pack, I'll get you settled, and we'll throw one last party—"

She grabbed his hand from her head and tightened her grip on his wrist.

She was deliberate with each word, looking directly into his eyes. "I'm going to let you do those things. But I want to be clear that this will be a process. Don't think that I am magically okay. I'm not. But I know I will be. I will be okay and you will be okay. I don't know if *we* will be okay. I don't even know if I will ever see you again once you leave, so it doesn't really even matter." She tossed his hand back at the rest of him like she was giving scraps to a dog.

"It does matter to me, but you won't see me again after I've left. You will just reflect where I have been. And I hope before then, you will have accepted what I've told you so you can finally be at peace with where you are and what you are. A diamond in the sky."

They were both silent. She taped up a box and slid it into a corner. Something inside of her relented. Moving onto the next one, she said, "So. Here's the tape gun. How about you make me some boxes?"

He grinned. "We have a lot of work to do, Estelle."

"I know. I'm lucky it's Labor Day weekend because then I can get a jump start on moving in my things without taking away from my summer vacation. I'm not teaching this session."

He looked at her blankly. "You still mix up Labor Day and Memorial Day? Really, it's easy. One goes at the beginning of summer—that's Memorial Day, and Labor Day comes at the end of it."

"I guess I always thought of it the other way around. I never thought about Memorial Day as a beginning. Funny how perspectives can change everything. Still, it has such a serious name."

The government had pronounced that Memorial Day was supposed to be a time to honor the fallen men and women who had died serving their country. But for Stella, Memorial Day brought with it associations of the retired whose daily affirmations included reminding themselves of their own worth through their legacy---of years put in at work, children, or tangible things that one could produce at a moment to prove that they had done something extraordinary with their time. Maybe that's why she had always thought of it as the end.

Why did we celebrate the ability to venerate past sacrifices that only brought us pain? Well, she sighed, it would happen to us all. Sitting on the dock of the bay and resting our bones. But if summer was just on the other side of remembrance—how much easier to release from the sting. Her muscles relaxed as she anticipated the lush creamsicle dawns, the call of the common loon from the wooded lake by her new home, and the days that stretched out as far as the horizon itself. Orlando was right—it was the beginning of something.

Her grandmother, the one after whom she had been named, had brought out special plates with poppies and bluebonnets lining the edges for their large family dinner every Memorial Day. One year, while she was helping set the table, Stella asked her what they were for. Grandma said she had finally gotten Grandpa to take her on that trip she'd been asking about for years beforehand. They'd gone to a really popular place in Fredericksburg that grew all kinds of native flowers, and she'd seen these plates in the gift shop. The poppies were for remembering the fallen troops, and the bluebonnets were especially for those from Texas. She was proud to have them displayed on her table.

Young Stella didn't understand why she was proud. They were just plates, she said, and besides, when people heaped their plates with food, they couldn't see the flowers anyway. Her grandmother constricted her into her cool blue apron, kissed her, and told her that someday she would understand. And if she herself didn't like to have nice plates, she added, she could start a holiday tradition of her very own. Stella nodded and extended an olive branch by noting her approval of the fireworks show they went to every Fourth of July. That tradition she understood.

She smiled to herself as she remembered the exchange. Her mind reveled in the details, vivid yet after all these years. Her grandmother's silver hair. The smooth spoons she plucked one by one from the clangorous bunch in her hands and laid them in their places near those plates. The old lace tablecloth, faint outlines of leftover stains increasing rather than decreasing its beauty in Stella's eyes. Lilies from the yard in the center of the table, their fragrance overpowered by the savory smells of casseroles and fried chicken wafting from the oven. And the sounds of Grandma's youth playing softly from the stereo in the living room.

Holidays. Holy Days. They were holy, regardless of what was being celebrated or mourned. That we all celebrated and mourned together had to mean something. Eternal memories bound to a temporal moment. But when the day passed, when the date on the calendar was observed, we continued to observe ourselves in others' lives through those overlapping memories we knitted together into what we had gotten comfortable calling "what matters most" year after year. But what did matter most? That was a matter of personal deduction.

Stella had become exquisitely sensitive to the receptiveness of those around her—the close red currents of emotion she found in some were balanced out by the coolness of the space others carefully left between themselves and any situation. This thermal perspective forced her to consider first the impossibility of any two people in the world sharing a total mutual understanding and then the paradoxical congruence of many beliefs which society demanded of its members. Yet it couldn't be through beauty or language or mathematics or even morality that we might all be penciled into the same grid, she thought. For herself, she believed that though vision had evolved differently in every creature, we were all transcendentally and eternally linked into a tight coil through the compassion with which we all could view another's personal struggle against mortality. What was God if not logic, language if not nature, business if not God? All of the boundless means through which men and women confined themselves to a single cause evoked a picture of a tormented beast in an enclosure, searching for a way out. No, she thought; better to distance oneself from all of that suffering.

And yet... and yet there was a way to create too much distance. Heath, behind closed doors, relegated to muffled party sounds and cold leftovers on cracked plates. Orlando, pretending that the body was just the brain's hilarious punch line, that anybody was even remotely capable of becoming a predominantly rational creature. Life was not a game to be solved in seconds by a bombastic ringmaster, even such as Orlando. He was not a psychopath, she knew. He was one of the few who could recognize the significance of things. He just saw the significances without always appreciating the things themselves. But she knew that people experienced life primarily through the senses, and that made every atom of every person sacred. Holy. There simply wasn't any church in the wild. Just the will to keep living. And the best way to touch eternity was through the stories that memories at the table and photographs would inspire our loved ones to tell, over and over again, year after year. Stories of loss, of strength, of triviality. Of bitterness. Of amusement. Of revenge. Of sacrifice. Of love. Of the meaning we spent our whole lives creating. Left, right... left, right... the rhythm of the upright life was a procession of infinite concentric circles on parade.

"I hate to interrupt you when you're obviously very deep in thought, my dear. Tell me about your house. You've yet to get down to the details. If I'm going to help you make it beautiful, I'm going to have to see what I've got to work with before we can transform it into a work of art. And we've no time to lose!"

"It's got high ceilings and a wooden door. It's made from brick and wood and stone—you know the look, like a cottage—and Henry's already promised to landscape it for me—and oh! Let me just show you! Of course! I'll show you the listing online, if it's still there."

"It certainly sounds like, well, an *interesting* combination of styles and materials. But then you always were a little eclectic." His analysis was only leaning toward favorable.

Excitedly, she sat down to her computer. She pulled up the view history on her search engine to see if she could find the real estate site without too much effort. A long listing of all the websites she had visited in the past came up. A flood of memories overcame her.

All the people she had met—the emotions she had felt—the significances she had gleaned—the decisions she had made—here they were, words on a screen. But to her, they were everything. She stared unmoving until they were again just words on a screen, almost nonsense, the way one repeated them over and over in one's mind until they lost their individual meaning.

"Here it finally is, Orlando," she said as he came over and stood behind her in front of the screen.

"My home..."

EPILOGUE

And there I am, free to create any meaning for my life I choose from this moment on. Accepting that the ultimate meaning is worth the inevitable emotion, not turning back, but darting through the gridlock, mindlessly humming a tune while I wait, because, let's face it, there will still be waiting sometimes. But she will continue inching forward, under the expansive sky, fluid, bright, and alive, because now that she is free to choose her own direction, she understands that the "forward" she means can't be found on the GPS.

Viewing our planet from our fishbowl outside of time and space, you can see what I mean. There they are, all the people on God's green earth, sitting at their tables or sitting in half-circles on their mud floors or around their campfires. And they all have one major thing in common. Don't be too hard on them, asking why there are still wars and philosophers and churches and governments. Society hasn't gotten any less truthful, like some have been heard to suggest. If anything, it's gotten more truthful, and that's at the root of all of its pain. It's no wonder they can't see their way out of it from there. They've got a lot on their plates, preparing to celebrate the diverse rituals that flood their own lives with meaning. Birthdays, marriages, sacrifices, funerals, rain dances, feasts, national holidays, yearly events. Eventually, inversely, their lives become symbols of these rituals. The metaphor, the parable, the story: it's what we come from and what we become, from one side of the bottleneck to the other. It doesn't matter where you are, or where you go: there you are. So change the details of this story; they're not important. Make it about you; it's okay. It always was, anyway. The absolute truth is that we relate to everything and everyone through comparison, and there is no absolute ideal when you compare two different things, or 8 billion billions. When you're comfortable with that, you might find yourself moving forward again, one meaningful fragment of a gorgeous incoherent whole. A whole which is but one eye of an ancient statue, a polished rock in an alabaster face. And the face might be smiling.

"The whole philosophy of Hell rests on recognition of the axiom that one thing is not another thing, and, specially, that one self is not another self."- C. S. Lewis

"Into this Universe and Why not knowing
Nor whence, like Water, willy-nilly flowing;
And out of it, as wind along the Waste,
I know not whither, willy-nilly flowing."—The Rubaiyat of Omar Khayyam Quatrain 32

"No matter how dreary and gray our homes are, we people of flesh and blood would rather live there than any other country, be it ever so beautiful. There is no place like home." – L. Frank Baum

Luis

"No small talk," Lucille instructed cab #7654. "I want to take it all in."

"As you wish," responded the soothing automated voice. That was the last she would hear from him before he announced their arrival at her destination. She half-nodded to herself with satisfaction, though driving on the left-hand side of the road took some getting used to.

Her eyes drifted through the white heat of the Caribbean, observing the palatial resorts dotting the shoreline as far as she could see. The water itself was crawling with sloops and body boards and various types of water crafts. Grace Bay was a slightly more bustling version of the fictional island paradise she had erected behind daydreaming eyes her whole life long (but not a whit less sublime for that... after all, any place that wasn't peopled nowadays wasn't a place worth visiting). The sight roused her into a pleasant expectancy; suddenly all things seemed possible again. But though the plane ride had been much shorter than she had anticipated (she had forgotten how much more comfortable life was bound to continue becoming in the most surprising of ways, at least to her), she was still a disheveled old woman with fly-aways sticking out from under her hat and the humidity of the tropics causing her clothes to stick to her body in bothersome places. She would need to take a cool shower and a nap, she decided, no matter how anxious she was to find her old friend and then... Well, and then? She let a string of age-old questions and conceivable scenarios flow through her mind, just as she took in the images of passing eateries, casinos, and displays of handicrafts, artwork, textiles—in, then out, observing the stream of color without judgment. By the time her cab turned into the Romanesque pavilion of her resort, she had become quite serene (the brilliance of the flowers lining the beds of the entrance delighted her— the climbing bougainvillea was most magnificent). She grabbed her oversized bag with the manuscript tucked away into it and her luggage was unloaded onto the Auto-carrier which would deposit her belongings right to her room. She wondered what would happen if they were to find something questionable in someone's bag during the security check. There weren't any actual people involved anymore. Well, it was just one of the many things she didn't know about. Technology was like a genie: it could make your wildest wishes come true, but you surely had to be careful what you wished for, and once out of the bottle it was impossible to stuff back in.

With these thoughts, she followed the direction of the conveyor belt to the dome-shaped lobby. The high open ceilings made her feel the gust of cool air, a welcome greeting to her tired mind and body, even more intensely. A hive of vacationers were ambling through the lush, landscaped resort. She observed couples and groups of people with accents representing the whole world in this one place and thought to herself that it didn't really matter where you lived, not really, that people went to places worth going to. She smiled to herself. A panorama of changing tropical scenes in 4D provided a lovely backdrop to the check-in counter. After scanning her security chip a few times, she was directed to the lift that would take her to her floor by smiling exotic faces.

Her oceanfront room was so extravagant that when she opened the door she said aloud to no one in particular that she didn't need all of this (but what a room! Her boys would never believe that while they were at work and corralling their kids, she was here in a place like this), but she would make do. The interior was designed to complement the sunlit water which the curtained edge of her room opened up into. It was as bright and skillfully decorated as the beach itself, clean lines with accents of fantastical shades of various blues and greens and yellows. Her luggage was already waiting for her in front of the heavy marble top buffet which spanned an entire wall. She poured herself a glass of water from a crystal carafe and absent-mindedly watched the Info Screen recommend various water sports, night life locales, and cultural tours. She took off her traveling hat, set down her bag, and began to unpack. After getting settled, she took an invigorating deodorizing shower and situated herself on the plush pillow mattress of her canopy bed. The thick blades of the over-sized ceiling fan lazily revolved over her as she slept.

She awoke to the pleasant sound of a micro-vacuum in the hall-way outside her room. Glancing at the digital time in oceanic blue on the monitor, she eased off the bed and stood in front of the mirror, fluffing her travel-weary gray hair and wondering what Luis would think of her appearance now. She knew she was a nice-looking older woman, but she was seventy-six. And how had the years treated Luis? She almost dreaded seeing him changed. Memories could lose their freshness when compared to the reality of the present. Maybe she shouldn't have come. Well, it was too late now; she was here. Perhaps she would eat a good dinner first and then see her way to Luis on a full stomach. She freshened up and set off to explore.

Walking down the beach a little, she stopped at a multi-colored square-shaped restaurant with an enormous conch shell on the sign (authentic cuisine was her favorite part of any trip. Why, you could get french fries and chicken wings any place) and ordered pecan en-crusted conch with orange sauce. Her dinner was accompanied by an island band playing a few yards away on the white sand (almost all of the buildings were open so you could still smell the salt water and hear the waves crashing). She swayed her upper body to the drums as she ate. All the people laughed and talked to each other so it was hard to tell who was working and who wasn't. She noticed that there was a thatched-roof bar within eyesight. She decided that sipping a mojito on the rocks overlooking warm Caribbean waters would be too picturesque to pass up. So after her meal (which was truly exceptional) she walked carefully through the sand to the bar (she had never seen so many palm trees or cacti in her life) and ordered a drink from the bartender.

As she looked out over the coral horizon with the sun sinking into the ancestral turquoise water, she thought about the past. She and Luis, once so young with the zenith of life before them were now beyond it, one day to return to the waters of their origins. And she was satisfied. For her part, she had enjoyed her life. She felt like the old cedar chest at the foot of her bed at home: full of beautiful memories she had collected over the years, boring to some but magical to others, and always hopeful that the lid would raise yet again for one more precious deposit. She thought of the Oscar Wilde postcard and smiled.

"Oh ma'am, that smile look like trouble," the bartender teased as he wiped down the bar. Besides a small group of people talking and smoking cigars at a far table, she was the only customer for the moment.

"I've been known to raise hell in my day," she retorted with a laugh. "But my day was a long time ago," she conceded.

"Where you from?"

"Texas."

"Big Tex-uhs, huh? You a cowgirl? You like horses?" His smile was friendly.

Diego loved horses. "Hah, many of my friends and family do. I wouldn't call myself a cowgirl. But you're right about the big part." She took another sip of her drink.

"Yeah, everyting be bigger in Texas, everyting. I got a friend say I can visit him whenever I want dere." He tidied up his bottles so they were all facing him as he talked.

"It's a short flight now," she said. She studied him. He had traces of handsome in his face. His teeth were natural, which wasn't common these days, though they were still blindingly white against his dark skin. He wore a loose white linen shirt (little curls of chest hair were visible at the open throat), but she could still tell that he was tall and thick, and his bald head was a not unpleasing contrast from the light salt-and-pepper beard he wore. His manner was easygoing, but he seemed to be absorbed in his work. He reached down under the bar and brought out some limes and papayas to cut up.

"What's your name?" she asked him.

"Lenny. Yours?" He wiped his hands on an old ratty towel and stuck one out to her. She shook it.

"Lucille. Are you from here?"

"Oh yeah. Dis be my home. Aways has been, aways will be." He flung his towel over his shoulder and began to cut the fruit.

"I can see why. It's breathtaking. The flowers, the water..." She trailed off.

"De mos' beautiful place in the world," he said with pride."Most people say de claritee of de water be de mos' strikin' paht. But I say dis place bring claritee in udder ways. People come lookin' fah it he-uh. De flowuhs... dey a whole language in demselves. De col-uhs, de shades... dey say everyting bettuh dan a word evah could. Dey..." He looked off, holding up the knife.

"Dey don' need to explain nutting. Dey be emotion outside de body, I guess." He shrugged and went back to cutting up the fruit. Lucille contemplated this. She had always felt that this was true. Flowers were so necessary. She liked Lenny.

" But even if it waddn't like dis, it still be my home. I got tree daught-uhs and dey perfect modder. Bote parents still livin'. I guess my life be pretty good. People who live he-uh is called Belong-uhs."

"Belongers?" She repeated the word to make sure she'd heard right. It was a meaningful word. Everyone belonged to a certain time and a certain place. Perhaps the tombstone was the real meaning of life. A name, a couple of dates, all the memories represented by the dash in between them, and an epitaph that attempted to explain what was already plainly written above it.

"Yeah. From he-uh. But we all real friendly." His genuine smile radiated over Lucille, and she basked in it.

"Yes, you are," she said. A couple of people came in and ordered drinks. Lenny smiled and served them and then they walked down the beach.

She continued, "You must see every type of person from everywhere here. What stories you must have heard and what characters you must meet!" She shook her head trying to imagine as she surveyed the beachgoers and passersby. Even though it was almost dusk, there was still some activity along the shoreline and around the resort.

"You know it. Crazy people. Wondahful people. From all over de world dey come. Cose we have some local people like dat, too. De captain live right ovah dere." He pointed vaguely down the beach and lit the candles in jars which were placed in intervals along the bar.

"He an artist-- he paint de best pitch-as you ever saw. Everybody love him. Dey buy his paintings and listen to his stories. When he come to de bar, I aways laugh my guts out. He can talk ol' stories wit' de best of 'em. He a good man, too. Paints pitch-as for little kids and be givin' it to 'em fah free. I never met no one like him. He's not from he-uh, but he be a Belong-uh."

"What's his story?" she asked politely.

"I don' know. He come a little while ago--few ye-ahs--and he was a big businessman. Lot of dem come coz we don' have tax on commerce. But den he grown a be-ahd like me and start to paint. And talk ol' stories. And mainly dat be what he do."

Her heart leapt. Surely—well, there was a way to find out.

"I'm looking for an old friend of mine who lives here, actually," she began. "I wonder if you'd mind pointing the way to this address. I've just arrived a little earlier and I don't quite know my way around," she said apologetically. He accepted the postcard and then looked up at her with wide eyes.

"This de captain's address! You know Cap? He nev-ah—I nev-ah met a ol' friend of his!" He rambled on in his surprise and her suspicion was confirmed by his reaction. "You will know his house by the peoples dat's laughing from it, but he-uh, jes in case." He scribbled down directions on a napkin for her.

Dear Luis, she thought. Precious, serendipitous, magical Luis. Captain Luis. Captain My Captain.

"Tell me about him. We always be wantin' to know round he-ah," Lenny said. "He merr-ed? His stories be true? Did he aways be de same?" He stopped and leaned into Lucille. "Oh, Miss, dere be dat wicked smile again on yuh face."

And she thought to herself that sometimes life was full of personal symbolism if you could recognize it. Maybe it wasn't mathematically precise, but it was satisfying all the same, like looking at a well-kept flower garden. She thanked Lenny and gave him the largest tip she'd ever given anyone. Then she scuttled off as quickly as her old legs would carry her down the horizon.

She heard breaking waves and casual voices yelling to kids across the sand. Strolling onto the beach she took off her shoes, lifted a bit of sand with her foot, and thought about everything and nothing all at once. Her eyes adjusted and readjusted as she searched for him in the dusk.

He ascended through the waves of the twilight air from the beach where he docked a white sailboat. He could've passed for a sun-darkened old-timer coming in from fishing (*Santiago* was her fleeting thought). He wore a straw hat, and his beard was long. The frayed edges of his cut-off shirt revealed the deep tan in his still shapely arms. He hadn't seen her yet. He flicked the ash from a cigar, shook it off from where it landed on his flip-flop, and walked inland toward where Lucille was standing (so this was how it was going to happen, on the beach, in the sand, toes dirty with surf and kale and grit). And when he saw her, he laughed uproariously and enveloped her in a great bear hug (she smelled his earthy body, the stench of his armpits and his cigar). She inhaled deeply and embraced him tightly, like the old friend he was.

"Mmmm, my friend! Finally, you came, Lucy in the sky with diamonds!" he exclaimed with great mirth as he released her. His voice boomed out like a man with much greater body weight than he possessed.

"Let me look at you. My, how good it is to see you, darling! Gorgeous as ever." He held her by her shoulders and looked full into her face, the smile lines around his face creasing into ripples. He kissed both of her cheeks.

"Oh, you too. You too." (He did look hale.) She was overcome with happiness.

"Come, Lucille. Let me take you to my humble abode." He grabbed her hand.

"If it's all the same, I'd like to stay right here for a while," she said. "I love this place." She set her face against the breeze and felt it lift pieces of her thinning hair, caressing the sagging skin of her cheekbones.

"Oh yes," he said soberly. "Of course, of course. We will sit." With a happy grunt, he plopped right down and waited for her, the butt of his cigar lighting up again in the darkening salty air. She was a little more cautious with her landing, but she found herself comfortably installed near the edge of the water (though how she would ever graciously get up again was a concern for a hopefully distant future). It was a beautiful evening.

With a deep sigh, she turned to him and asked, "Do you ever hear the mermaids singing to you?"

He shook his head and smiled. "They know it wouldn't do any good to sing to *me*. But we *are* getting older, aren't we?"

"I thought of *The Old Man and the Sea* when I saw you, to be honest."

A laugh rumbled from his belly. "Oh, no, darling. I'm old and I live by the sea, but I'm still the Captain," he assured her with a wink.

Thoughtfully, she grabbed his hand and held it to her chest. "Oh, how I have missed you, Luis." She looked pained. "I never truly got over your disappearance."

"I know." He turned away from her. "But, you're here now. Isn't it pleasant?" He sucked on his cigar.

They told each other about their lives in all the years they had missed. She talked about her children, the death of her husband, and her achievements before retirement. He brought out some rattan chairs with pillows for their backs along with an array of food and drinks from his hut. He told her about a couple of his long-time lovers, the countries he'd visited, regaled her with hilarious stories. Then they reminisced about their shared memories long into the night.

Finally she said, "You promised you would tell me someday what it all meant."

He leaned back and stretched his body. The beginnings of a paunch showed through the clinging fabric around his middle. "Well, old men are expected to give confessions, I suppose. But, for myself, I don't need to confess. Are you sure, Lucy, you want to know?"

"Yes."

He tucked a tendril of hair behind her ear. "Then I shall tell you."

She waited. He breathed out heavily through his nose and began.

"The subject was Cole Bentbrook. He was an integral part of an experimental project known as Janus. Janus started during the Red Scare and the participants were still being monitored for years following, though there were no more new recruits. Cole was part of the last wave of participants. There were many others like him, and each of them was assigned a "guardian angel"; I was one of those. My job was to ensure they didn't get out of line—that they didn't endanger the success of the project in any way. The subjects had been taught to dissociate from their personal identities. Their alternate or "synthetic" identities could only be summoned through a short phrase specific to each of them which had been planted in them through years of hypnotic suggestion. They could be tortured by national enemies and never give up any valuable information. They could pass any lie detector test in the world, simply because they wouldn't know they were lying. And they were taught to obey any directives they were given when in this hypnotic state of synthetic consciousness. We have used them for different purposes: messenger, assassin, and undercover agent, whatever we needed. And they have often proved to be a smart investment."

"The theory was that these men should have had no memory whatsoever of any involvement with the project until that phrase was uttered by an operating agent given express permission by the chain of command to utilize one of these weapons. In the early stages of Janus, outrageous amounts of under-the- table funding employed the top experts of the day in multiple fields, and the forecast for the success of the project was favorable. In fact, mostly it went well, at first. But the older these men got, the longer they lived with dual identities, the more flimsy the barrier between the real man and his synthetic personality became. The brain works on overtime to try to knit all the fragments together into a coherent picture, which, for these men, was precarious at best. Mental illness and nervous breakdowns were common byproducts that had to be watched for in the subjects. It was almost as if their bodies were rejecting an implant. There were a few awakenings. We weren't sure how it happened, but those men were remembering things they shouldn't, even though the utmost precautions were taken to avoid that possibility. They were piecing together certain facts and repressed bits of memory, and it directly endangered the entire organization. It literally drove a few of them insane. When that happened, as it did to Cole, the subject had to be put down for everyone's protection. I had hoped that he could put it to rest. He had made it to a successful retirement, but he had a strong subconscious, stronger than most, and when I realized what was happening, I ended his suffering. And he did suffer. Believe me, Lucy. Can you imagine suddenly recalling that you had been tortured by men in masks hundreds of times, year after year, and then recognizing that you had been a man in a mask many times yourself? Every night a different nightmare collage scrapped together from fragments of murders you have committed, of secret meetings in dark alleys and abandoned buildings, of a whole separate reality that you have been living without any inkling of its existence for most of your life? "

Her hands were clenched so hard it was painful to relax her fingers. She winced, aghast.

"The stories Cindy told me—he was tortured into dissociating?"

"Oh yes. It was crude, but they didn't know any other way to create a solid barrier between the two personalities. As it was explained to me, they believed that if they used the brain's natural defense mechanism against extreme amounts of pain—dissociation---the synthetic personality they had created would be more likely to stay undetected by the subject's conscious mind, and thus the risk of abnormal behavior in their personal everyday lives alerting anyone to the subject's participation in the project would be lessened. They set up camps for him to go to every summer as a child. His parents knew about it. They were patriots, giving up their only begotten son for the good of Americans everywhere. He was given false memories in order to help him 'make sense' of it' in case he did begin to remember."

"There were others?"

"Yes."

"When did you—I mean, you were so young back then."

"They recruited me out of Stanford. I was 23. I had been on Janus for several years already."

"No."

"It's all true." His tone was gentle.

"It so happened that I came to Texas for my assignment right before Diego—well, you know. We met up when he had heard I came back. I had actually requested the assignment to Cole because he was so close to where Diego lived. I was in love with Diego, you know. He was my closest friend—until you, of course. It was only through the strangest coincidence that you even entered the picture. I thought I could learn more about the Bentbrooks by your access to Cindy through the University. The possibility of you having Tom as a student had also crossed my mind. I pushed you toward them for my own ends."

"Then we weren't even—friends?" Her mouth scrunched up as the last word rang out an octave higher. Hot tears noiselessly slid down her face (whose voice was this? The sound of it was like a frail old woman's to her ears).

"Oh Lucy, you always were a very real thing in a very false world. Every ounce of me adores you. Our friendship was—and is-- very real."

She was quiet.

"Was it you who sent me that poem? I knew it wasn't Cole. He told me so."

"Yes. I had to get you closer to Cole so I could assess the threat risk he posed without raising his suspicions any further that someone was watching him. He never knew who it was, but he felt my presence in the wings. I didn't think you would have the nerve to confront him about it, but I was convinced that if you did, it wouldn't matter by then anyway. I would already have all the information I needed to make a decision. I sent him a warning, too, but he didn't heed it. I told him that Cindy was having an affair, that he could catch her in the act, but I actually led him straight to you at the university. I had hoped that you could distract him, give him something to look forward to, hold him together."

She sucked in her breath.

"You killed him."

"I had to."

"You're a psychopath!" But even as she said it, she knew it wasn't true. She wanted it to be true (that would be so tidy), but she remembered Cole's suffering, their conversation not long before he died. It was a foregone conclusion (would he have felt the same way had he really known that Luis was going to take away his power of choice?).

"But I'm not without feeling. It was precisely because I cared for Cole that I released him from his prison. He would never have been any good to himself or anyone else. He was completely shattered from the inside out years before I came along. I'm a killer, but I'm no psychopath. My feelings are always genuine, I assure you."

Lucille moaned in agony. She covered her face with her hands. A cluster of grains stuck to her brow. She rubbed them with one finger, feeling the grit on her skin, back and forth, back and forth.

"If I had just known that before. I could have saved him from you. I could have saved him from himself. Cindy—oh poor Cindy!" Her words were muffled by sobs which had been delayed for decades.

"There was nothing to be done but what I did. It was a terrible scenario. I know you feel used. I know you feel shock. I know it hurts. But trust me: the United States government not only authorized the death of Cole Bentbrook, they ordered it. They had to clean up after themselves. It was the responsible thing to do. And trust me: it was the most humane thing for Cole, too."

He whispered again, "It was the only thing to be done."

She shivered, even though it was a warm night. They were silent together, listening to the waves lapping over each other, fighting to reach the farthest distance inland until all were inevitably pulled back by the tide. They had long been the only people remaining on that part of the beach.

She said, "You were my best friend—you saved my life. But you killed what I loved. Both are true. And I can't reconcile that." She didn't look at him.

"Yes," he affirmed.

With an undertone of anger, she said, "And I remember you told me that Diego was timeless. I took comfort in that; he was too golden, too good to be long for this earth. But then you told me that to be timeless was to be inert, that we always had to be moving forward."

"Do I contradict myself?" Luis said with a small smile.

She looked reviled for a brief moment, but then her shoulders slumped in defeat. She wasn't as naive as she had once been. "No, I don't think you did. I think you were right. You taught me so much, Luis. We are all God; not one will ever attain Godhood. God creates; God destroys. So do we. So does life. Each one, forever and ever."

He wrapped an arm around her and pulled her to him.

"Amen," he said.

Draping a mortal with the mantle of eternity was the most rapturous form of true experience—of really living—there ever was. She thought this to herself as she looked out over the elemental water, the sands of time, the ancestral stars, and finally over at Luis, the Captain of it all.

ACKNOWLEDGMENTS

W e would like to extend a huge thank you to Ryan Obermeyer for the beautiful cover of *Dressing Eternity*; to Samantha for her generous legal advice; to Parker Zangoei for his support, dedication, mad editing skills, and kindnesses; to Peter Mosley for his critical insight; to Keri Puente for her attention to detail and her honesty; to Michael and Lindsey Zangoei for their motivational interest and for their time; to Dustin Hilliard for his sacrifices in order to make this novel possible; to both sets of parents for giving us each the badge of Native Texan and teaching us how to wear it proudly; to Vincent Esposito for his intellectual gifts and for being the closest thing to magic in this world; to Hooshang Zangoei for being Candace's twin soul, her biggest supporter and partner in all things; to Jake Verbeck for being Kimberly's; and to Fox Hilliard and Zander and Nora Zangoei, the most beautiful son and grandchildren in the world, and all of our future grandchildren, for whom the entire concept of this novel was conceived.

ABOUT THE AUTHORS

Kimberly Carver teaches AP English and works as an adjunct professor for Texas Woman's University. She's an accomplished singer-songwriter and guitarist, a mother, and a native Texan, albeit a xenophile. This is her first novel.

Candace Zangoei is a retired English teacher who lives with her husband half-time in the DFW Metroplex and half-time in La Jolla, CA when not traveling. She once served as Kimberly's mentor teacher. She is a proud mother and grandmother, and she is also a native Texan. This is also her first novel.

40893967R00150

Made in the USA
Lexington, KY
21 April 2015